Off Kilter

by

Laura Strickland

A Buffalo Steampunk Adventure

Off Kilter

Cover Art by *Diana Carlile*

The Wild Rose Press, Inc.
PO Box 708
Adams Basin, NY 14410-0708
Visit us at www.thewildrosepress.com

Publishing History
First Fantasy Rose Edition, 2015
Print ISBN 978-1-5092-0182-2
Digital ISBN 978-1-5092-0183-9

A Buffalo Steampunk Adventure
Published in the United States of America

James switched his gaze to the three people who had just disembarked, two men and a woman, and promptly lost all the breath in his body.

They made an unlikely enough trio—one of the men willowy and slender, clad in a splendid suit that screamed wealth, the other broad and squat if also well-dressed. James dismissed both of them almost immediately, for the third of the group gathered all his attention and focused it the way a mirror gathers light.

"That his doxy?" Latham persisted.

She wore one of the new tailored gowns of some thin fabric that fluttered around her slender body in the breeze off the water. Strawberry-blonde hair clustered round her head in a woven crown of curls, and even from fifty paces away James could see the delicate perfection of her features. She stood between the two men like a doe hedged by wolves, and something about her demeanor bespoke the fact that she longed to flee. Suddenly James wanted to tear the two men apart with his bare hands, rescue her, change her world. He knew he could do it, too; at that moment he could best anyone.

"Nice piece," Latham muttered. "Wouldn't mind the job of guarding that."

And just as abruptly, James wanted to tear Latham apart also, a visceral reaction that flowed from the core of his being outward to his fists.

"Button it," Tate snapped before James could. "That's our client, Mr. Sebastian Boyd—one of the wealthiest men you'll ever meet."

And with him, James amended in his head, the most beautiful woman he ever hoped to behold.

Praise for Laura Strickland

"The world building is phenomenal."

~*Daysie W. at My Book Addiction and More*
~*~

"Laura Strickland creates a world that not only draws you in, but she incorporates it…seamlessly. …the kind of book that keeps you awake well into the wee hours, and sighing with satisfaction when you've finished the very last page."

~*Nicole McCaffrey, author*
~*~

"As I read I became so involved with the story, I found it difficult to put down the book. …Definitely …an author to watch."

~*Dandelion at Long & Short Reviews*

**Other Books by Laura Strickland
available from The Wild Rose Press, Inc.**

Dead Handsome: A Buffalo Steampunk Adventure
~*~
Devil Black
His Wicked Highland Ways
~*~
Daughter of Sherwood
Champion of Sherwood
Lord of Sherwood
~*~
Christmas Stories:
Mrs. Claus and the Viking Ship
The Tenth Suitor

Chapter One

The Niagara Frontier, May, 1882

"Hey, Ugly! Yeah, you, there—I'm talking to you!" The taunt reached the ears of James Kilter from clear across the busy Buffalo waterfront, and he turned his head involuntarily to search out the source. "Look, lads," he heard, "it's the ugliest man in the city, out for a stroll."

A crowd of ruffians occupied the far side of the street—none above twenty, all thieves and pickpockets—led by that rogue Charlie Crowter. Crowter, dressed in ragged pants, shabby vest, and with a disreputable cap pushed to the back of his head, stood at the forefront, grinning his enjoyment.

"What do you think, boys?" Crowter chortled even as James paused, his hands curling into fists. "Should something that hid-ee-yous be let out into daylight where innocent kiddies might see it and take fright?"

"Hell, no!" shouted one of his dutiful henchmen from the back of the group.

"Hell, no," Crowter repeated. "Any hound that ugly should be shut in a dark kennel and beat regular with a big stick."

At those words, anger, hot and raw, coursed through James. A man of few illusions—those having been stripped away from him at a young age—he knew what he was: ugly, just as Crowter said, a monster barely fit for human sight. He could handle such insults but not the cruelty. Everyone in this city knew him for his defense of the abused and downtrodden—dogs in particular. And they knew him for his righteous temper as well as his ruined face.

"Ooh, Charlie, watch out," quipped another of Crowter's crew. "He might come across the street."

"I ain't scared of him," said Crowter with more than a touch of bravado. Over the busy pavement, his gaze met James' and clashed.

You should be scared, James thought but didn't say it aloud. He'd had past run-ins with Crowter while doing his job, working security. Crowter invariably got the worst of it, which was no doubt why his pride spurred him to challenge James now.

Good thing I'm too busy to go over there and smash his face in, James thought. On his way to meet his boss, Tate Murphy, and pick up their next assignment, he dared not linger. But he felt the impulse—his clenched fists ached with the desire to strike.

"Kilt his own mother, did that mad dog," Crowter continued to goad. "Why do you think they call him 'Kilt-her'?"

"She should have kilt him when he came out of her, ugly as he is," another of his cronies opined.

But he hadn't been born like this, James thought angrily, the damn fools. And that wasn't how the story went. Not that he needed to waste any breath or explanations on this bunch of louts.

As Tate always said, he might need that breath someday.

Yet people on the street, sensing a confrontation or maybe hoping for one, had begun to stare; workers going about their business, steamcab drivers, servants hurrying on errands.

Much as James might like to provide them a diversion, he dismissed Charlie Crowter with a glare, squared his shoulders, and tucked his head well down before resuming his walk.

"Curdled any milk lately?" drifted after him as he ate up the sidewalk with his long stride. Crowter should know better than to tangle with him. James might be ugly, but he made two of that little runt in both height and muscle.

Later, he promised both himself and Crowter silently. *When I'm not bound on business.*

The harbor came in sight then, sparkling in the afternoon sunlight like a carpet of jewels. The scents of the waterfront assailed James' nostrils at the same moment: river water, tar, and steam. James expanded his chest in a deep breath. Other smells lay beneath those predominant, mainly piss and garbage. But James, born in this city, loved every bit of it.

Something in him responded to the color and bustle of the scene before his eyes. Men unloaded cargo from two ships; boys carried out tasks or lingered hoping to lift what they could. Horse-drawn drays and steam wagons competed for space, ready to pick up orders. Clatter and the clamor of voices filled the air in at least five languages.

James' quick eyes searched the scene seeking Tate and miraculously located him standing with other members of the crew as well as a Buffalo police officer.

Tate saw him at almost the same moment and lifted

an arm. "Here, lad."

Hands still crammed in his pockets, James made his way to the small knot of men. When he got close enough he recognized the copper as Brendan Fagan, a friend of Tate Murphy's. Fagan headed Buffalo's hybrid unit—half man and half machine—even though Fagan was all human. James spotted none of the hybrids nearby, and he relaxed slightly; the darned things made his skin crawl.

Fagan glanced at him and gave a nod but kept talking to Tate. Two big micks, James thought, though he didn't say it aloud. In this city birds of a feather really did flock together, which resulted in a lot of interesting neighborhoods: Irish, German, Hungarian, some English, and a community of former slaves who'd moved north after the war two decades ago. Both Tate and Brendan Fagan had been born in Ireland, and it showed: Fagan's brown hair caught a gleam of red in the sun; his broad, strapping frame nearly matched that of James' employer. Tate—short for Tater, or Tattie in Irish—had a head of flaming red curls and enough freckles to mark him well as a man of the old sod.

James exchanged looks with his fellow employees, all of whom he knew well. Bucky LaPlatte, who hailed from French Canada, Stan Illiov, and Phil Latham stood stolidly like men who knew how to take care of themselves.

James joined their ranks silently while Brendan Fagan took his leave.

"We're on it, but keep your eyes peeled, lad," he told Tate. "The problem seems to be worsening."

"Will do," Tate told him and turned to his men as the Irish copper walked off. "Hear that, lads? The

4

bastards struck again."

"Where?" asked Stan emotionlessly. The Russian rarely betrayed his feelings, his voice colored only by his thick accent.

"Three girls went missing from that dance last night at the grand hotel. Nobody saw a thing."

James grimaced. Since the beginning of spring, young women had been disappearing without a trace, mostly lasses employed in the houses of the wealthy. James didn't even want to think about what might have happened to them.

"Just the same as the others," Bucky observed. The hulking man from Montreal had been a crewman on the St. Lawrence before an injury made him throw in his lot with Tate.

To be sure, James thought now, Tate had a habit of employing the maimed and disenfranchised.

Tate nodded grimly. Each of the missing girls, according to their friends, had been there one moment and gone the next, as if whisked away by magic. "Whoever's after doing this, he's fecking efficient. And that brings me to our assignment. Big man wants his bit o' fluff guarded while he's in our lovely city."

"Round the clock?" Phil asked.

"No, only when he's not with her."

"And that takes four of us?" Latham persisted.

"We'll see, shall we? Ah, will you look at that." Tate's ever-present brogue deepened with enthusiasm. "Have you ever seen a ship so grand?"

An airship approached across Lake Erie, heading for the landing strip at the foot of Perry Street. James caught his breath in wonder. Airships made a common enough sight in the city; the wealthy owned and

5

flaunted them. Their use had currently come under scrutiny for suspicion of shifting illegal cargo, and rumor had it the military was developing its own fleet.

James had to admit a fascination with them. On his day off he often came down here to watch the landings. He had never seen one of this size or brilliance. Half the length of a city block, it boasted an envelope of bright blue, and the gondola caught the sun in a blaze of gold.

"What the hell?" Latham barked. The ornery Englishman abhorred ostentation. So, ordinarily, did James. Yet now he narrowed his eyes in admiration.

"That'll be our client," Tate said. "Come on, lads. Let's see what the man wants with us."

The landing strip lay some three blocks over, and they went at a jog, breaking sweat in the warm sun. By the time they got there the party had begun to disembark from the gondola—and what a party it was.

The servants came first, a virtual bevy of them, all hurrying importantly. James rocked on his heels and watched them roll out a carpet—an actual frigging red carpet—from the door of the gondola across the bricks on the street. The gondola continued to spew a crowd of people, sycophants no doubt, and James became distracted by the airship itself. Tate had promised to buy him a ride someday from a man who booked excursions out over the lake, but for now he could only imagine the pleasure. He wondered what it would be like to own such a glorious toy and acknowledged he'd never know. He couldn't even conceive of the required riches.

"That him?" Latham asked.

"Aye."

James switched his gaze to the three people who

had just disembarked, two men and a woman, and promptly lost all the breath in his body.

They made an unlikely enough trio—one of the men willowy and slender, clad in a splendid suit that screamed wealth, the other broad and squat if also well-dressed. James dismissed both of them almost immediately, for the third of the group gathered all his attention and focused it the way a mirror gathers light.

"That his doxy?" Latham persisted.

She wore one of the new tailored gowns of some thin fabric that fluttered around her slender body in the breeze off the water. Strawberry-blonde hair clustered round her head in a woven crown of curls, and even from fifty paces away James could see the delicate perfection of her features. She stood between the two men like a doe hedged by wolves, and something about her demeanor bespoke the fact that she longed to flee. Suddenly James wanted to tear the two men apart with his bare hands, rescue her, change her world. He knew he could do it, too; at that moment he could best anyone.

"Nice piece," Latham muttered. "Wouldn't mind the job of guarding that."

And just as abruptly, James wanted to tear Latham apart also, a visceral reaction that flowed from the core of his being outward to his fists.

"Button it," Tate snapped before James could. "That's our client, Mr. Sebastian Boyd—one of the wealthiest men you'll ever meet."

And with him, James amended in his head, the most beautiful woman he ever hoped to behold.

Chapter Two

Catherine Delaney fought down her nausea and gazed around the place where she stood, a seething morass of movement and confusion. Noise and humanity surrounded her in equal measures, all poised at the edge of the glittering water. Workers and steamcabs fought for space, and the sun beat down mercilessly. Suddenly she found it hard to breathe.

Coming in on the airship from Canada, she had refused to look down. Flying—a thing she'd never done, before her life came apart—made her ill, the swaying of the gondola, the hiss and pop of the steam engines, and the presence of the man at her side.

He sickened her most of all.

Sebastian Boyd. Should the devil become incarnate and walk the earth, he would do it in the form of this man, deceptively handsome and intrinsically, relentlessly evil, with a genius for harm.

She struggled to draw a breath of the pungent air and fought to command herself. She could not weaken, could not begin screaming now, for once she began she wouldn't be able to stop.

"I am supposed to meet a man," Boyd said in his nasal whine, "and he had better be here. I sent word ahead."

"Yes, Boss," said Carter. That was what Carter usually said. That toad of a man, a bootlicker of the first water, seemed to exist only to please Boyd: a brown nose on bandy legs.

"Security," Boyd elucidated. "I can't possibly watch my new possession twenty-four hours a day, can I?"

"No, Boss."

Possession, Catherine thought, and bile rose to the back of her throat. The urge to strike out at the man at her side, to batter him and flee, to wend her way through the teeming area that bordered the airstrip and toss herself into the water, became nearly overwhelming.

How far might she get? Five steps or ten before Boyd's hateful hands recaptured her? She hated it when he touched her. Almost anything would be better. *Almost.*

"Mr. Boyd?"

A group of men approached out of the confusion, and the first of them, the tallest, spoke Boyd's name. A huge strapping fellow, he wore a workman's suit, and his orange head lay bare to the afternoon sun. Broad features marked a face so plain it looked oddly attractive. He might be a pugilist, and not above thirty.

"Ah, Murphy?" Boyd said in satisfaction. "Good."

"Pleased to meet you, sir." Murphy put out a beefy hand, which even after only two weeks Catherine could have told him was a tactical error. Boyd did not touch people often, which, so far, had been the only thing saving Catherine's sanity.

Boyd nodded, and Murphy withdrew his hand. The four men at his back said nothing, and Cat turned her gaze from Murphy's pleasant face to examine them.

Big men all, though not as hulking as Murphy. The

first had black hair and olive skin, a thin nose, sensual lips, and a scar on his chin. The second wore a disagreeable expression and a bowler hat that, scuffed and battered, looked like it had been through the wars. The third—

Cat looked at him and her thoughts stuttered; her mind recoiled, not quite able to take in what she saw. A monster, she thought first, and then, correcting that initial impression, no—a man. But by heaven, what had happened to him? And how could anyone go through life so?

Distracted for the first time in days from her own misery, she stared. He too had reddish hair, very dark. Her mind sought for the word: auburn. But it grew from only one side of his head. The other, a mass of scar tissue, sported no hair at all, just mottled, thickened skin. The affliction spread down the right side of his face as well, a ghastly half-mask that dominated his appearance. Whatever catastrophe had befallen him—a fire, Cat would guess—had left but half an eyebrow on that side. His right ear had been reduced to an overgrown mushroom, his jaw a sweep of shiny pink.

Ugly, Catherine's reason told her. Yet his eyes, deep blue in that terrible countenance, met hers without prevarication.

"Your message said you're looking for some security," Murphy stated. He indicated the four men at his back. "You want round-the-clock service?"

"I require only one man." Boyd wore the emotionless mien Catherine had, in so short a time, learned meant he would not negotiate. "But I wish to choose him. I don't like narrow options."

"All right." Murphy seemed taken aback but

recovered well. "How many hours a day do you need?"

"That will vary. I need a guardian for Miss Delaney at the times I'm not with her." He gestured at Catherine. "She will not be out of your man's sight, and I'll hold you responsible, Murphy, for any breach."

"Perhaps two men—" Murphy began.

"I want one." Boyd cast his gaze over the men at Murphy's back, considering each in turn. With a flicker of his eyes he made his choice. "Him."

Catherine stifled a gasp. Boyd had gestured at the man with the half face.

Murphy turned and directed a long look at the man in question. "Good choice. Kilter is one of my best."

"I would not expect you to bring me a man who can't do the job, Murphy," Boyd snapped. "I want him to start immediately."

"Very well, sir." Murphy pronounced it "sor," but the Irish lilt did not disguise his distaste. "How long will you be in the city?"

"That has not been determined. I'll have him as long as I need him."

"Fine. The fee is—"

"The cost doesn't matter, and I don't deal with such things. Present your bill to my business manager."

Murphy turned to the chosen man. "You all right with this assignment, Kilter?"

The man nodded. So far he had not taken his gaze from Catherine save to glance once at Boyd, his expression unreadable. For some reason, a frisson traveled down Catherine's spine, half dread and half anticipation.

"A vehicle is supposed to meet me," Boyd said, promptly dismissing Murphy and his remaining men.

"Come along."

They moved off, Catherine still trapped between her two hateful captors but now with another behind. She thought back to the moment, two weeks ago—just fourteen short days—when she had learned her fate. She wondered how she had survived so long. Sheer stubbornness, no doubt.

"Locate our ride," Boyd told Carter, and they paused while Carter went ahead, the sun pounding on the top of Catherine's head like a fist.

Boyd swung round and looked at the man at their back—Kilter, Murphy had called him.

"Do you understand your duties? You will watch over Miss Delaney at all times, not only to keep her from harm but to prevent her straying when she is not in my company. She has an unfortunate tendency to stray. I will hold both you and your employer responsible if that occurs on your watch. Think of yourself as her guard dog. No one is to get near her but me."

Humiliation flooded over Catherine like a drench of hot water. Boyd treated her as if he had just purchased her, which in truth he had. Somehow she kept her head high, but her gaze strayed to Kilter's face, seeking his reaction. He remained expressionless, save for his eyes. Those narrowed for an instant before he gave a nod.

"You can rely on me to do the job for which I'm hired, Mr. Boyd."

"So I should expect." Boyd gave one of his thin, merciless smiles. "Ah—that must be our vehicle now."

The largest steamcab Catherine had ever seen drew up; Carter flagged it down and began speaking with the driver.

Under cover of the noise, Boyd bent his head toward Catherine to say, "At least, my dear, I need not worry about you cheating on me with your guard—he is far too ugly and repellent, is he not?"

****

Ugly, James thought, even as he slid into the rear seat of the steamcab. That made twice in less than ten minutes. And how many times had he heard that word over the past ten years? So many it didn't matter what a piece of filth like Boyd said of him now.

That Sebastian Boyd truly was a piece of filth James had no doubt. Arrogant and with a cruel streak a mile wide, he immediately put James' back up.

James told himself a job was a job; he need not like the man to work for him. Yet something here smelt wrong. And he had not missed the fact that Boyd wanted him to overhear that last comment.

Had it been aimed at Miss Delaney or at him? As if such a creature as she would ever spare him so much as a glance...

Which was the whole point, wasn't it? Boyd wanted a fierce watchdog whom he need not worry about poaching on his territory.

But Miss Delaney made an unlikely sort of doxy, if such she was. James had seen plenty of those in his time, even high-class ones such as Boyd might hire for a thousand dollars a night. They usually carried an aura, even the best of them.

The steamcab had four rows of seats and a gleaming black exterior at least fifteen feet long. The driver disappeared up front, and James found himself relegated to the back row with the squat, thick-set man

Boyd kept as a go-fer. Boyd and Miss Delaney sat in the row ahead so James could see only the backs of their heads.

Better get used to it, he told himself. This would likely be the view from now on. And he had no complaint with viewing even the back of Miss Delaney's head, exquisite as the rest of her.

Curious thing, though: most doxies—or hired escorts, as the upper class tended to call them—exerted themselves to entertain their clients. Miss Delaney did not speak a word to Boyd and in fact drew herself up so as to be sure not to touch him.

James thought of Rosie, a lass of the waterfront who—were the price right—might sometimes be persuaded to accept him when his need proved great. Even Rosie touched him, if only in the dark, with more eagerness than Miss Delaney displayed.

Yes, even despite his unquestionable and enduring ugliness.

Chapter Three

The steamcab stopped at one of Buffalo's grand mansions. Situated on The Avenue near the traffic circle that bisected North Street, it boasted three tall stories and a stone facade. No sooner had the cab drawn up than a small army of steam servants spewed forth from the elegant front doorway.

Boyd climbed from the cab and stood like a minor god while they all bustled around him. The henchman preceded James from the rear door onto the sidewalk.

He saw Miss Delaney step out and stand on the curb in front of him, looking up at the building. She swayed on her feet; for an instant James thought she would fall down.

Instinctively, he stepped forward and caught her by the elbow. A tingle, akin to how he imagined lightning must feel, traveled from the point where his fingers touched her flesh up his arm and straight to his head.

He expected her to flinch—most women did, at contact with him. Instead she turned her head and gazed into his eyes.

Once again James caught his breath. It felt precisely like being punched in the chest. His heart stumbled and then recovered to beat double-time.

"All right there?" he asked.

She parted her lips to respond but didn't—at least not in words, though he saw a wealth of answers in her eyes.

Hazel eyes they were, a hazy, peaty green-brown guarded by brown lashes. Set slightly tilted in her delicate face, they should have been bright with light and enthusiasm. Instead James beheld shadows, defiant strength, and banked misery.

Most certainly she was not all right. Nothing was, about this situation. If Miss Delaney occupied the place of Boyd's doxy, it was against her will.

James experienced a rush of familiar feeling: protectiveness. A crusader at heart, he could not stand to see anyone abused, be it an animal or a fragile woman.

But he let go of her arm, telling himself she would not want him, of all men, playing her white knight. He had a job to do, nothing more.

"Come," Boyd called as he might to a hound, and the whole knot of them moved off up the walk and through the grand doorway, James following at Miss Delaney's heels.

Amazing what money could do, James thought as he gazed around the foyer. He didn't know who had built this place or who owned it now, but the sheer ostentation of the building and fittings boggled his mind. Like the airship back at the waterfront, he found it difficult to reconcile the kind of money that might be spent on foot-high oak moldings and curlicues carved round the ceiling—not when, as a boy, he'd known a potato for supper to be wealth.

But, he reminded himself, his business wasn't to think—no more than the steamies that trundled about organizing the luggage, a veritable army of them.

From around them emerged a human butler, a tall

figure clad all in black who approached Boyd obsequiously.

"Welcome, sir, and I hope you enjoy your stay. My name is Riles, and I will do whatever I can to make you comfortable."

Boyd snorted. "I was told there's an office. I have business to conduct."

"This way, sir."

"And bring me a drink. Then show the rest of my party to their rooms."

"Yes, sir."

Boyd went off with the butler, and James watched the tension drain from Miss Delaney's slender back.

Carter gave him a look from beady eyes. "You know what to do, right? Don't let her out of your sight. If you lose her, there'll be hell to pay."

He went off in Boyd's wake, leaving an awful silence behind. The steamies, all carrying luggage, moved off also, and very soon James and his charge stood in the sumptuous foyer virtually alone.

I'm not hired to talk to her, James told himself. It's more a matter of my big body between her and the door. For quite obviously she didn't want to be here, and presumably she would leave if she could.

But she didn't move, save to tangle her trembling fingers together. And then the butler reappeared, gave James a carefully guarded look, and focused on Miss Delaney.

"Madame, I will show you to your quarters. This way, please."

Quarters, was it? James followed the butler, or more accurately the fluttering hem of Miss Delaney's dress, up a broad sweep of staircase to a sumptuously carpeted hallway and thence to a door at the end of it. Riles said nothing as he opened the door with a flourish and showed Miss Delaney in.

Not a room but a suite of them, all decorated in rose pink and soft gray. High windows dominated the chamber they entered, along with a fireplace flanked by two rose-colored wing chairs and faced by a sofa. Through an interior doorway James could glimpse what looked like a bower of roses—pink flowers splashed across the wallpaper and on the coverlet of the huge bed.

For an instant his mind rebelled. He could not imagine Miss Delaney in that bed alone. He reminded himself he barely knew her and, anyway, he had no reason to believe she would be alone. Presumably, Boyd meant to join her there.

"Sitting room." Riles stated the obvious. "Bedroom." He swept them into the rose bower. "And wash room. Also"—he indicated a second room off the bower, a small place that housed a narrow cot, obviously intended for a maid—"for your bodyguard, as requested."

Bodyguard, was it? James stole a look at Miss Delaney's face, which had frozen into an expressionless mask, all but her eyes, which were those of a chained dog.

"If there is anything you need, madame, please don't hesitate to ring the bell beside the bed. Would you like a steam servant assigned to you?"

Violently, Miss Delaney shook her head.

Riles took himself out, leaving the two of them in the bower alone.

Do not look at her, James told himself. Afford her

what privacy you can, which from the look of this is to be precious little. He knew for a fact his ruined face did not betray much of what he felt and doubted she would see any of what surged through him—sympathy and dismay. She wouldn't look at him anyway. Why should she? He must seem even more an abomination in this beautiful place.

He heard her draw a breath and ached to turn his gaze on her, but instead stared away into the air at nothing.

But then she spoke, her voice low and unsteady. "This is nothing more than a prison."

True. James' eyes moved to her face without his volition. No longer expressionless, it had contorted with emotion: anger, rebellion, and panic. His heart sank within him. While in Tate's employ he had supplied no end of security in difficult situations, but nothing approaching this.

Hastily, he debated his options, which appeared few, fought his instincts, and lost.

"Are you here against your will, Miss Delaney? Because if you are—"

Her gaze flew to his again, tangled and held. "Then what, Mr. Kilter? He did say your name's Kilter, didn't he? He owns me. Nothing can be done."

"Owns you? Nobody owns anybody in this country, not anymore."

"Is that what you think? If so, you have no idea what money can do."

He did, though, or at least the lack of it. The lack of money could cause a man to lose his pride, could make a woman rise before daylight and work till dark to see her children fed. It could send a boy to a job far too dangerous for him, one that scarred him for life.

"I, Mr. Kilter," she said bitterly, "have been bought and sold. And there's nothing you, I, or even God can do to change it."

James had his own ideas about God, that villain who allowed terrible things to happen in His world. But he would not voice them or any of the other things that crowded his mind.

"You are not my bodyguard," she added, "but my jailer."

He'd already figured that out, as well as why Boyd had chosen him: far too ugly to tempt the prisoner to indiscretions.

"Listen," he said very softly indeed, "if you are in need of help, I will go to my boss. Murphy has a good heart."

"If you are fond of your employer, Mr. Kilter, you will keep him out of it, unless you want to see him ruined."

James thought furiously.

She tilted up her chin. "Oh, I know what you must think of me: that I'm his fancy woman, a glorified prostitute."

James shook his head, even though he had.

"He hasn't touched me—not yet. He is saving that pleasure for when he thinks it will hurt me most."

Rage rose in a bubble to James' head. "That doesn't have to be—"

"Yes, it does. Please, I appreciate your kindness, Mr. Kilter, but you know nothing of the situation. Just do your job and let me endure my fate."

No, James thought in utter denial. But out of respect for her he nodded, went back to the outer room, and took up a post by the door, where he composed himself in the required stance, feet wide, hands folded one atop the other.

And he pretended he couldn't hear the sound that soon floated to him out of the bower—that of Miss Delaney sobbing.

Chapter Four

Morning dawned with a seep of sickly gray light that let Cat know it rained outside, the world in mourning. She woke in the big, rose-colored bed and lay for a moment as she had each morning since her life was sold away, trying to convince herself none of it had really happened.

As always, she failed. A heaving knot of sickness gathered in her stomach as memory rushed in.

She thought back to the night last month when her life fell apart, three days after her birthday. Since then she'd known nothing but terror, grim determination, and sacrifice.

She shivered even though she lay beneath luxurious blankets and a duvet. Her limbs felt cold all the way through. She could barely catch the beat of her own heart.

Better for her if that heart stopped in her breast, if she slipped away in the night rather than face the future. For she could see no other way out of her misery.

She had tried escape and failed. She had attempted to bargain with the monster who held her. The threats and consequences had been swift and terrible.

He wanted her to live with this humiliation and dread, to contemplate the inevitability of the moment he would come to her door and take the prize he'd won. He wanted to break her first. For all her courage, she knew herself very nearly broken.

Would it happen here in this lovely room? Could nothing save her?

She tried to reason through it as she had already a hundred times. It did not matter so much what happened to her, Cat, so long as Becky remained safe and out of Boyd's clutches. And Cat's sacrifice had assured that, hadn't it?

Her mind worried the question, chewed round it the way a rat might gnaw cheese. It was a good thing that they had left Toronto and come here instead. Distance provided Becky with more protection. So long as Boyd's attention remained on Cat, he wouldn't turn his eye back toward her little sister.

She stirred in the bed slowly like an old woman and stretched her ears, listening to the house. Somewhere, steam servants must be stirring. They always did around Boyd, like wasps around a proverbial honey pot. But in this sumptuous place she could hear nothing. And she supposed her guard, Kilter, must be out there beyond her closed door, in this suite of rooms that had become her prison.

Kilter. Her mind fastened on him as it might on a stray beam of light in darkness. When she first saw him at the airstrip, she'd been appalled by his appearance. He made a shocking enough sight with his half-ruined face and patchy head. But she wouldn't call him ugly, no—she must reconsider that initial label. She who had looked into Boyd's face recognized true ugliness.

And Kilter's eyes...how alive they looked in that terrible mask! How much they conveyed. She'd seen sympathy there, yesterday.

But, she reminded herself, he could not become her

ally. No one could help her, not unless he or she wished to invite ruin on a scale barely imagined.

Summoning strength from deep inside, she pushed back the covers and climbed from the great maw of the bed. Thick carpeting met her bare feet. She tiptoed first to the window and pushed aside the flowered draperies.

The house faced east, the river some blocks to its back, and ordinarily the morning sun must flood this room, but not today. Rain wept down on a scene as gray and bleak as Cat's heart. Trees, newly leafed, bent before drops hard as stones, and the street shone wet.

Even so, people moved about below. A milkman made his rounds, using an old-fashioned horse-drawn dray. The horse stood with its head bowed before the onslaught of wet, as much a slave as Cat.

Her heart stirred with sympathy for the beast; how she wished she could free all the enslaved of the world, or at least of this city.

Others hurried by—mostly men on their way to work, so it appeared. Steamcabs jostled past, emitting black trails of coal smoke, and one or two ragamuffins splashed through puddles, their feet bare as Cat's own.

Where was Boyd at this early hour—where the monster she feared? Still in his bed, curse him? Why could he not die in his sleep?

Perhaps, rather than escape, she should plot for that—Boyd's death. For if she managed it, if she found a way to stab or smother him in the dark, she would help so many besides herself.

"In payment I will have a woman—one of your household." She heard him say the words to her stepfather once again. *"It is my customary price. I want the young girl."*

24

Becky, barely thirteen years old. Cat remembered the sharp horror she'd felt, the rush of wild, protective determination. In the end, in the face of her mother's tears and her stepfather's spinelessness, she'd persuaded Boyd to take her instead.

That didn't answer the question: How many other times had Boyd done this, taken women in payment and then destroyed them? And would he follow through on the threat he had whispered to her when first she passed into his hands?

What had happened to her courage, that which flared so bright when she made her choice for her little sister's sake? Over the ensuing days, it seemed to have bled away in droplets and left her hollow. She needed to gather it up again, if only to find a way she might kill Boyd, or herself.

An image of Kilter flashed through her mind again. He had the strength to accomplish either deed: wide shoulders, big hands, strength in his movements. She wondered where he was now—still out there beyond the closed door of this flower-choked room, no doubt, though she heard no sound from him.

Perhaps he slept. Did such men, always on guard, sleep? If so, did he dream? Were his dreams half so terrible as hers?

Curiosity, an emotion lately leached out of her, got her to the door. The sitting room lay in gloom; she could see no one. Was he in the narrow chamber designated as his own?

She stepped out into the parlor, and beside the outer door a shadow stirred. Surely he had not been standing there all night? Perhaps, like a horse, he slept on his feet.

"Miss Delaney, are you unwell?"

Yes, she was unwell—sick to her very heart. But she didn't say so, just stood there listening. What an attractive voice he had, deep and mellow and so very male. She wondered again what had happened to him, how he came to be, physically, nearly as ruined as she.

Help me.

She ached to speak the words but couldn't. Instead she swayed on her feet and, as he had yesterday on the curb, he stepped forward quickly and grasped her elbow. As she had then, Cat felt the impact of his touch, the warm fingers on her skin, strong yet gentle.

"Here, sit." He guided her to the nearest chair and eased her down. She could barely see him in the dim room, but she could feel the concern emanating from him.

"There, now," he said softly, meaningless words yet comforting, for all that. "You are chilled to the bone. Wait there."

He let go of her arm, and Cat's heart protested. *Don't leave me*, she begged silently, yet he disappeared from her vision. In his absence, she shivered violently.

But he soon returned with the duvet from the bed, like a bundle of roses gathered in his arms. He wrapped it around her as he might around a child, lifting her bare feet onto the seat of the chair and tucking the warmth close. Then he crouched beside the chair, his eyes level with hers.

"Better?" he asked.

Yes, it was. She turned her gaze on him, tried to see him among the shadows. Details blurred; she could see the fall of dark, reddish hair on the left side of his face and little else. Yet a calm, steady strength continued to flow from him.

She reached out from the nest he had made for her till her fingers touched the flesh of his forearm. He started as if the intensity of the contact shocked him.

"Miss Delaney," he began.

"Catherine," she whispered. "Call me Cat."

He didn't repeat the name. She supposed he would consider doing so unprofessional, but she didn't care. She wanted him to see her as something more than what Boyd declared her to be.

"Do you need a physician?"

Swiftly she contemplated the question. Could a physician provide a way out? Perhaps some medicine, if prescribed, could be taken all in one dose and so end her life.

But any physician sent for now would be selected by Boyd, in his pay and under his thumb.

"No. Just stay with me for a moment, Mr. Kilter." Her fingers clenched on his arm. She felt better, stronger with him near. "That's an unusual name...Kilter."

"I'm an unusual fellow—as you can see." How was it she could so easily sense his emotions, virtually hear what lay in his mind? The slight edge of irony in his voice said he mocked his appearance. She wondered what it must be like to walk through the world presenting such an aspect, and she shivered again.

"Talk to me, please," she beseeched him. She wanted his voice in her ears, to beat back the darkness.

And, bless him, he stayed where he was with her hand on his arm. "The way the story goes, an ancestor of mine came to this country years ago and landed here when this city was little more than a rough place hewed out from the trees. He was running away, not to; he'd fled his home in Scotland under threat of deportation. Ironic, isn't it? He avoided being sent away by sending himself away."

"We do as we must," Cat said.

"So we do. Anyway, running as he was, he dared not give anyone his true name. But he turned up in a kilt, you see, so they called him 'the kilter' and it stuck. He became what he appeared—as we so often do."

"And sometimes don't. Sebastian Boyd looks like a human being."

"Ah." He hesitated an instant. "Whereas I do not."

Her heart protested it; she could feel the humanness streaming from him, the very best of humanness, but she couldn't argue against the reactions he must encounter every day.

Instead she said, "So you—and all your kind—became the Kilters?"

"There's another theory. My enemies say the name describes the action. They believe my mother died at my hands, that I 'kilt her,' in common speech."

"But you didn't." Cat couldn't say why she felt so certain, save for what she sensed emanating from him, steady and sane.

"I didn't. But you have to admit it makes a good tale." He drew a breath. "They also declare that from time to time I go 'off kilter'—when I lose my temper, that would be."

"Do you often lose your temper?"

"Only when I encounter injustice."

"Then you were clearly the wrong choice for this post."

"Perhaps I was." He made as if to rise to his feet

and step away. Cat's fingers tightened on his arm, keeping him where he was.

Persistently, she sought his eyes in the gloom. "Or maybe, Mr. Kilter, you are the right choice." The only choice, a glimmer of light in her darkness.

"Miss Delaney, I doubt that very much."

Chapter Five

"I will not need your services this evening. I am holding a dinner party, and Miss Delaney will be in my company until late. You can take yourself off. Just be sure and return by morning."

Morning? James twitched at Boyd's words and hoped his expression remained impassive. Dinner parties, as he well knew, did not as a rule last all night. What about the hours between? What would happen to Miss Delaney—Catherine—after the guests went home?

Ah, but he had no say in that, much as his heart might wish for one. But since their exchange early this morning, he'd felt protective toward her, far too protective.

He could only accept his orders. He stood in the entry hall where Boyd had delivered them and watched the tradesmen and women bustling in. One of them, obviously a seamstress, came leading two steamies laden with fabrics, ribbons, and other finery.

He needed to go back to headquarters for a conversation with Tate. But he didn't have to like abandoning Catherine to whatever fate Boyd had in mind.

He nodded, threaded his way out through those arriving and into the rain. It still pissed down as it had most the night. He'd had little to do but listen to it while he stood at his post throughout the dark hours. After Miss Delaney stopped weeping, and he assumed she slept, he'd heard little else.

Despite the rain it felt good to be out of that place. He paused on the sidewalk, looked up at the grand facade, and found Miss Delaney's window. How must she feel knowing she couldn't leave? For if he wanted to, he could quit.

She could not.

He wouldn't quit, though, he silently promised himself and her. It would feel far too much akin to deserting her. He wasn't quite sure what had taken place between them in the sitting room early this morning when she'd reached out and anchored herself to him—or him to her. Some intimacy beyond describing.

James never shared intimacies with women, other than prostitutes. He'd grown into male adulthood looking like a monster, which repelled ladies rather than attracted them.

Miss Delaney might well be a prostitute, he reminded himself. At least, she admitted to being bought—the very definition of prostitution. He would dearly love to know her story, for she bore no resemblance to any doxy he'd ever seen.

She'll be busy all the day and evening, he reminded himself now, with fittings and then a great, fancy dinner party.

But what after? The devil whispered to him: What then?

He cursed softly, tucked his head well down, and slogged off through the rain. He had his orders, damn it.

Headquarters lay on Niagara Street in an old,

crumbling building that had escaped the fires back in '12. Tate always said the place might well benefit from burning, but Tate pumped a lot of his profits back into the community and had little to spare for beautification projects.

Once the shipping offices of a lumber baron, the place now crouched in a moldering pile, all weathered gray wood and dull windows. It looked and felt better inside. Tate had his office on the ground floor along with supply and weapons rooms. Upstairs slept the men in his employ who had nowhere else to stay. Out back lay what Tate called "Kilter's kennels."

The kennels had grown slowly, one abandoned dog and then two. Tate—his heart as big as his Irish fists—could not bring himself to deny them refuge. James built the wire enclosures with his own hands, bought the rugs, bowls, and feed out of his own pocket. Now there were ten cages and a larger enclosure where rough doctoring took place.

At first James looked after his rescues alone. Gradually, others in Tate's employ began to take part. Now someone was always on hand to let the animals out, and to feed or clean up after them.

"I'm running a fecking dog nursery here," Tate complained, but he hadn't put his foot down about it, not once.

James' fellow members of security had even accompanied him on raids a few times, either to rescue animals in need or mete out retribution. Of course there were always those, like Drappot, who called him soft for what he did.

"They're hounds, Kilter—animals," Drappot had jeered more than once. "Put here for mankind to use any way we will."

James didn't believe that. No one had been put in the world to be ill-used. Thinking on it, he pictured Miss Delaney again, her eyes wide and filled with dread.

And of all the men he didn't want to meet, who should he encounter now on his way to the kennels?

Drappot, built like a fireplug, was probably as wide as he stood tall, and all of it muscle. He had a sharp, ferrety face, dark eyes, and a shock of blond hair rumored to be bleached. Off the streets like most of Tate's crew, he had a tendency to fight dirty, and Tate had spoken to him several times about throwing his weight around in bars when off duty. He had a mean streak, too, that loved to ridicule others. He particularly enjoyed mocking James.

Someday he'll push me too far, James had once warned Tate. *And I'll take him apart piece by piece.* But it hadn't happened yet.

Now Drappot greeted him with a glower and the words, "Damn dog of yours barked half the night, Kilter. I thought about coming down and strangling it."

The dogs barked but rarely; many of them were too sick or had been cowed to the point where they didn't dare make a sound. James didn't have to ask which dog. He'd brought her in a week ago after catching her master beating her with a chain. James, in a fury—or off kilter, as Drappot would probably deem it—had used the chain on the man before carrying the dog home.

His hearing in court was scheduled for next week.

Now he eyed Drappot and thought, I'd like to see him try and strangle Greta. She had barely even let

James near her, since she recovered.

"Sorry about that," he said with absolutely no regret. "Wouldn't want you losing any sleep. God knows your disposition shouldn't get any worse."

"You ever think that bitch's master might have beat her for a reason?"

"You ever think about jumping into the river with a sack of bricks tied to your feet?"

"You mean like your ma should have done to you when you were born so ugly?"

It was just a taunt, James reminded himself: Drappot knew very well James hadn't been born like this.

Drappot smirked. "That why you kilt her? Because she let you live?"

"What's going on here?"

James knew that voice with its rich Irish brogue. He twitched in response but didn't break eye contact with Drappot even when Tate strolled up to join them where they stood.

Drappot answered the boss, "That new bitch of his yapped all night, Tate. Never tell me you didn't hear it."

"A deaf man could have heard it," Tate replied.

James did look at him then. "Sorry, Tate. I'm sure she'll calm down in a day or so."

"Calm down or get shot," Drappot said.

"Now, Samuel," Tate soothed, "sure the beast is hurtin', scared and alone. She'll settle soon."

"Not soon enough, Tate. I don't know why you tolerate it. Not fair to the rest of us."

"I'm sorry to hear you think so, Samuel, but you know if you're not happy staying here you have only to go. Plenty of rooms in this city. I'm that sure you could find somewhere."

"I'll give it some thought," Drappot retorted, clearly annoyed, "and think about taking my services elsewhere also."

Tate crooned, "You just do that, if you feel you must. I'd be sorry to see you go—you're a valuable member of staff—but you do what you will." A glint came into Tate's eye. "Just as I do."

Drappot snorted and stalked off.

"'Valuable member of staff'?" James echoed then.

"So he is, think what you will. The man's a badger on certain jobs and relentless on hunting people down." Tate eyed James. "And the dog did bark most the night. I think one of the lads came down and tried to calm her—Relsky, probably."

It would be Relsky, James reflected; the big Russian had a soft heart.

"She doesn't like the dark," James said helplessly. "And she's little more than a pup."

"I know." Tate's hand came down on James' shoulder. "Best perhaps to farm her out, if anyone will take her."

James always tried to place his dogs once they recovered. He didn't think Greta ready for that but didn't say so. Instead he asked his boss, "Come and see her with me now?"

"All right," Tate assented. "I have a few minutes. New client coming in, though, after."

The yard looked depressing in the driving rain. Six of James' wire kennels were occupied, with Greta in the largest of them. A big dog with a grizzled brindle coat, she stood nearly chest high on James if she got up on

35

her feet. She rarely did, but preferred to crouch and growl.

The other dogs all ran to the doors of their enclosures when James and Tate approached, some wagging their tails, if they had them. One or two were ready to leave; James had an ongoing active search for likely homes.

He now went about distributing a pat here, a gentle caress there, where welcome, along with soft words. As always, his heart filled in this company. These creatures didn't care what he looked like. His mutilated face meant nothing to them.

Lastly he approached Greta's cage. She hunkered low, lifted her lips, and growled at him. When he moved closer, the growl heightened to a snarl.

"You may have a problem there," Tate opined.

"She's still healing. Give her some time, eh, Tate?"

"I may have a mass exodus of employees soon."

James went down on his heels at the door of Greta's kennel and gazed at her unhappily. "Is there hope for you, girl?" he asked softly. "If so, you're going to have to let me in."

Greta flattened her ears and rolled her eyes.

"Speak to her again," Tate urged. "I'm after thinking she likes the sound of your voice."

"Sweet girl, pretty girl. I'll not let anything bad happen to you again, so I promise."

Tate clucked his tongue. "Careful, laddie, not to make promises you can't keep."

"I'll keep it," James vowed. "Just you wait and see."

Chapter Six

Cat shuddered slightly as she gazed around the room. Boyd's dinner party consisted of ten businessmen, all, from their appearance, high rollers. Cat knew the look of such company; her stepfather fancied himself one, but he was small-time compared with Boyd, and no mistake.

Many but not all of these men had arrived with women on their arms. Cat could not tell the women for wives or prostitutes, but all came clothed in great splendor and the latest fashion.

Which explained Cat's attire. She looked down at herself again in wonder. The dressmaker had brought an unfinished gown which she had fitted to Cat in one afternoon.

Cat had never worn or imagined wearing such a dress. A creation of amber silk and gold lace, it fit as if molded to her body and revealed more cleavage than Cat actually possessed. This had been achieved via a contraption of whalebone and wire that thrust what bosom she did have upward into what she considered indecent view.

Not only most of her breasts but her shoulders lay revealed, her sleeves mere puffs of lace half way down her arms. Of course, she had to acknowledge as she looked around the parlor where she and the rest of the ladies had withdrawn, leaving the men to their brandy and cigars, the other women were similarly attired.

"You're new," said the woman in red, eyeing Cat frankly. Cat had no hope of remembering her name; the introductions had taken place *en masse*, and Cat, prey to nerves, had not been in a good position to keep anything straight in her mind.

The woman in red seemed bold and confident. She'd lit up a small cigar as soon as they reached the parlor and now sprawled in an armchair, her eyes gleaming.

"I recall the one Boyd had before her," said the woman in aqua. "We met them in Montreal. You were there, Rose. Do you remember?"

Rose, appropriately, wore a shocking gown of rose-colored satin so lowcut it made Cat's garment seem modest. She shook her head. "Must have been before my time. I've been with Jefferson only a year last November. Look at what he bought me." She indicated a pendant displayed prominently on her generous bosom. "One-carat diamonds." She smiled in satisfaction. "Only took five kisses *down below* to get that out of him."

Cat's eyes widened, though none of the other women so much as batted a lash.

"You have to give them what they want," said the woman in purple, "no matter how bent their desires. I don't suppose you'd know anything about that, Noreen—you being married."

A woman in glittering black replied, "My dear, a wife in my position is nothing more than a whore with permanent status. Roger likes it doggie style—and often. How about you, sweetie?" She switched her gaze to Cat. "What's Boyd's pleasure? We heard he's into bondage."

Cat's stomach roiled and a blush swept from her engineered cleavage upward.

"I heard," said a woman in silver, again not affording Cat a chance to reply, "he doesn't like it at all. That last girl—what was her name?—claimed he seldom came near her."

Rose leaned forward eagerly. "But when he did—whips and chains all the way." She cast Cat a look of mock sympathy. "But no whip marks where it shows, of course."

They're just trying to frighten you, Cat told herself. The bunch of nasty-minded crones. They want a reaction; don't give it to them.

But what if it were true? What if he came to her room tonight? If he did, she supposed she would have to follow through on the commitment she'd made. Better her than Becky.

"I heard," said a woman in blue, "Boyd can only get it up for young girls." She ran interested eyes over Cat. "How old are you, dear?"

"Nineteen."

"Yes, but," Rose spoke up again, "she doesn't look it. You look about sixteen, with that slim build," she informed Cat.

"Even sixteen's too old for him, from what I hear." The lady in blue lowered her voice. "I was told he likes them under fourteen."

Becky was just thirteen, Cat thought, her heart sinking. What if Cat didn't succeed in pleasing him, for all her sacrifice? Becky was the one he'd originally wanted; what if he went back to that well again?

She turned her gaze on the woman in blue. "How

do you know this?"

"Word gets around," the woman in blue replied without spite. "They all have their little quirks. And men as powerful as Sebastian Boyd tend to get what they want."

He's a perverted monster, Cat thought, and suddenly feared she might vomit, losing the small portion of dinner she'd forced herself to consume.

The ladies began speaking then of another woman of their acquaintance, who'd had the poor judgment to get pregnant by the man who kept her, and all too soon they were joined by the gentlemen, who brought the brandy with them.

The conversation turned to business, dry and seemingly interminable. Balanced between boredom and repugnance, Cat feared the evening would never end.

Yet when it did—when the guests at last began making their departures—her fear flared brighter. She could not get past the conviction that this would be the night Boyd made the first of his demands.

By the time the last of the couples left, seen to the door by Boyd himself, she felt sick with apprehension. When he returned to the parlor and closed the door carefully behind him, she swayed on her feet.

"Well, Catherine, I have to say you make a damn poor hostess."

Cat looked back at the evening just past and supposed it true. She lacked the confidence and sophistication of the other women and felt utterly unequal to the position wherein she had been placed.

Carefully she said, "I apologize."

He approached her the way a cat might a mouse,

his eyes glittering. "When your father sold you to me to cover his debts, I was assured you would be accommodating."

"He is not my father." Cat spoke through suddenly dry lips. Everett Kraus had married Cat's mother when Cat was the age Becky was now and Becky only seven. Cat felt proud to say she didn't carry that craven fool's name.

"Ah, yes, stepfather." Boyd's eyes, pale gray in color, examined Cat slowly from head to toe and back again. "I hope you mean to perform better in the bedroom than you have in my dining room."

Cat's knees promptly threatened to fail her. She reached out and caught the back of the nearest chair, and Boyd's mouth quirked in what, for him, might pass as a smile.

"How long have we been together, Catherine?"

"Two weeks."

"Two weeks, more or less," he confirmed. "During that time, I have asked little of you."

He took another step closer. Cat's heart began to pound like a piston in a steam engine.

"But I have provided for you," he went on in that emotionless voice. "Food, drink, shelter, that fine room upstairs, and a splendid wardrobe on order. I hope you are grateful."

Of all the feelings teeming in Cat's breast, she could find no gratitude, save for the enduring fact that she and not her beloved little sister stood here.

She blinked at Boyd as he took still another step, near enough now to touch her if he wished. He reeked of cigar smoke and liquor. How much had he taken to drink? Dare she hope, if he accompanied her upstairs, he might succumb to sleep instead of lust?

"You truly are a lovely thing," he said. "Quite tempting. Take your hair down for me."

"What?" Cat faltered.

"You heard me. I will expect you, Catherine, to be completely obedient when we are together. Whatever I ask, you will do without question."

Cat raised unsteady hands to the arrangement of her hair. A woman she'd never seen before had been sent in well before the guests arrived to dress it for her in a grand pile of upswept curls.

Now her fingers moved clumsily as she felt for the pins and let the curls fall beneath Boyd's gaze. What did she see in his eyes? Something at once curiously detached, cold yet avid. Did he want her or just her humiliation?

Perhaps both.

"Ah," he said, once her hair hung about her shoulders. "You look like a child."

A chill chased its way up Cat's spine as the words of her recent companions came rushing back at her.

Boyd raised a hand and brushed her cheek with the backs of his fingers. In contrast with his cool gaze, his skin felt hot. Cat lifted her chin in defiance of her terror, and as if in response he trailed his hand lower to touch her bosom and slide all the way down to the edge of her dress, which rode just above her nipples. For one horrifying moment she thought he would thrust his hand inside her bodice.

He spoke in a low, threatening voice barely above a whisper. "What would you do, lovely Catherine, if I bade you strip off that dress? What if I told you to get down on your knees and service me?" Something dark blossomed in his eyes. "Do you understand of what I speak?"

Cat understood. Had her recent companions not spoken of just this? Diamonds, indeed.

But she felt the heat come to her skin. She couldn't. She simply could not.

"Shall I tell you what you would do?" he went on. "You would obey. Because that is what you promised when I spared your family. Is it not?"

Calling upon all her courage, Cat nodded.

"Good. Good, because I can still go back and remake our deal, you know. Take what I want."

Becky, Cat thought, and her heart clenched in her chest. "I mean to be accommodating," she told him.

"Pleasing."

"Pleasing. Just so long as you keep to the agreement."

"I will, if you do. That is how I do business, and never forget this is business." His gaze flicked over her again. "Trying you is a delight I will save for another evening. Go to your room now. It is late, and your guard will be back on duty soon."

Cat drew a long, unsteady breath. Did that mean she was safe tonight?

"Go," Boyd told her again, and she fled as if chased by seven devils.

Chapter Seven

"I feel like hitting something or someone," James confessed to Tate ruefully. "Feel like beating him half senseless."

Tate shot him a close look and then quirked an eyebrow. The two men sat in Tate's office, Tate with his heels on his desk. The big Irishman enjoyed a beer. James, knowing he would shortly report back for work, had refused one.

"That's not like you," Tate said. "Sure, I've seen you pummel fellows a time or two, even seen you go off your head—"

"Off kilter?" James asked wryly.

"Aye, but there has to be a damn fine reason, and usually you don't think about it beforehand."

"Maybe there is a reason."

"Well now, perhaps you should begin with telling me who you'd like to hit."

James smiled darkly. "I wouldn't mind beginning with Drappot, spending a while on that pisspot Charlie Crowter, and working my way up to my new employer."

"Ah." Tate contemplated that. James knew a razor-sharp mind dwelt behind that broad, seemingly innocuous countenance. "Crowter and Drappot aren't worth your time. You should be used to Drappot by now."

"I should." Usually James would be able to shrug off Drappot's words. He feared his current inability to do so signaled some other underlying disturbance.

"'Tis that last target troubles me, lad," Tate went on. "Do I need to pull you off this job and put somebody else on?"

James thought about it. It might be a very good idea. Yet he remembered the way Miss Delaney's fingers had anchored him to her in the dim room. It had nearly killed him to leave her today on Boyd's orders. Was she all right? Did she need him?

"Kilter?" Tate prompted. "Should I be worried about this? You're hired to serve the client, remember—not Miss Delaney. And if you lose your wick, it'll reflect on me. A man like Boyd, sure, he could ruin me."

James knew that, and he bore deep affection for this man who sat across from him. Tate had been one of the few to look past his appearance, the only one to give him a chance in spite of it.

Rather than answer Tate's question, he said, "You know why he picked me."

"I know." Tate's feet twitched on the desk. He didn't like talking about James' appearance.

But James stated it. "He wanted a big, ugly guard dog."

"Aye. But, lad, the guard dog isn't meant to turn on the one who feeds it."

"You're the one who feeds me, Tate."

"And men like Boyd feed me in turn." Tate contemplated the matter for a moment before he offered, "She's a bonny wee thing."

She was.

"You've never been prey to the many-fold perils of attraction by the opposite sex, have you?"

"I think she's there against her will. He has some sort of hold on her."

"No doubt. Men like Boyd go through their lives with holds on other people."

"I haven't figured out why, Tate, but she's terrified."

"Lad, you can't change the world. Much as you might want to, you can't rescue every stray. It happens."

"It shouldn't."

"Agreed. But people do as they must in this life. Is that fair? No. Can you go down to the waterfront and offer a way out to every doxy who earns her living on her back?"

James raised his eyes to Tate. "She's not like that."

"Lad, you don't know what she's like. And we don't want to get on the wrong side of that man. I think I need to pull you off this job."

"No."

"For your own peace of mind. I've seen evidence of your big, soft heart, laddie. Hell, it lies out there in that kennel."

James thought about it. How easy it would be to walk away, let someone else take the post with Boyd, go on to another meaningless job. One thing he had learned: it was always easier to walk away. Something he'd learned about himself: He seldom did.

He rose to his feet. "Time I got back to my post."

Tate tipped his face up and regarded James seriously. "Are you sure about that?"

"Yes."

Tate's boots came down off the desk. "If you find anything illegal going on there, James, if you catch even a whiff of something proving the girl's being forced against her will, bring evidence to me. I'll talk to Fagan."

"And he'll send in his goon squad?" The automaton division of the Buffalo Police force had become the talk of the City these two years past. Nearly twenty strong, they were the creations of a pair of mad geniuses called Mason and Charles, who had fused steam units with the flesh of human cadavers, mostly Irishmen murdered at the city jail. After it all came to light, the ethical question remained of what to do with them. Brendan Fagan, the Buffalo police officer who had helped uncover the plot, had formed an automaton league, virtually unstoppable.

"Perhaps." Tate didn't smile as James expected. "Just, come to me before you do anything daft like busting Boyd's head in."

"Will do, Boss."

****

James went out into the driving rain and drew a deep breath. The waning night smelled of all the things he considered endemic about Buffalo: coal smoke, the river, wet paving stones, and a faint, underlying pong of old garbage. He thought about hailing a steamcab and then decided to walk, letting his long legs eat up the distance.

When he arrived at Boyd's, lights still lit the ground floor rooms despite the hour. The window he knew belonged to Miss Delaney's room, though, was dark.

One of the human footmen let him in. The house

might be illuminated, but the downstairs lay quiet. Where was Boyd? Upstairs in that dark room with Miss Delaney? Or did she lie there alone?

"Returning to my post," James growled at the footman who, a mere lad, barely came to his ear. He could feel all the carefully constructed sense Tate had tried to instill during their conversation draining away. Something about this place raised all his protective instincts.

The footman gave him the kind of look he might afford the boogie man. Dripping water, James went off up the broad stairs and thence to the suite of rooms assigned to Miss Delaney.

A steam servant stood outside her door—a guard?—quiet as if switched off. It jerked to life when James approached, gave him a blank stare, and then trundled off, whirring softly.

Did that mean Boyd wasn't inside? Surely he wouldn't bother to assign a guard if he were there with Miss Delaney. Still, James hesitated with his hand on the knob. What if he went in only to find them together, engaged in some lewd act? What if Boyd crawled all over her, touching that delicate body and violating her perfect skin?

Better surely, he told himself sternly, than an abomination such as himself thinking about touching her. And he had been, ever since she laid her fingers on the back of his arm.

Did he forget what he was?

With an abrupt movement, he turned the knob on the door and entered the suite. It lay dark and silent, as if under a blanket made of night. Indeed, the only light came from the streetlamps outside the windows, trickling through the raindrops that coated the glass.

Did she sleep? Was she alone?

Tiptoeing even though the thick, rose-colored carpet cushioned his steps, he moved through the sitting room and paused at the door of the bower, which stood open. Silently he stood, almost afraid to see.

At first it looked as if the big bed lay empty. He blinked and made out Miss Delaney's head on one of the pillows. She lay there alone, her body barely making a mound beneath the duvet.

He breathed a sudden gasp that might have contained relief. Alone and safe, for now.

And he'd best remove himself from the doorway before she awakened and saw him standing there like something from a bad dream.

He moved hastily and, as if in answer to his thoughts, promptly encountered the mirror that hung over the fireplace on the sitting room wall. Like a man in a trance, he approached the shining silver expanse and regarded himself.

Usually he avoided mirrors. And usually dim light such as this proved kind to him. Not so much now. This mirror contained a dose of honesty and, as if he'd never seen it before, he eyed his image.

Ugly, they called him on the street, and yes, it was true. When with Tate, he sometimes forgot the factual evidence of his appearance, but he faced it now. Children had been known to cry at the sight of him. Ladies turned their eyes away, but he would not. He needed to look in full.

A big man, he stood a strapping two inches over six feet, with broad shoulders and a narrow waist. Nothing wrong with his body, then, save the mottled skin that spilled down his right side, as if a bucket of scars had upturned over him. His face had taken the worst of it when the valve failed and the boiler exploded at him that day. He'd barely had time to turn his head so that only one side took the steam and boiling water rather than both. It had geysered out at him when the metal fitting blew, coated him like liquid fire, and trickled down from the top of his head, burning through layers of skin all the way to the bone.

A miracle he hadn't lost his right eye, said the old doctor who eventually came to tend him. What a monster he would have been then. As it was…well, he had few illusions about himself.

His employer at the time of the accident hadn't liked spending money on his workers, most of whom were children. He had refused to take James to a doctor and had left him lying in agony on a cot, freezing and burning at the same time in the unheated dormitory up under the eaves, where the man called Gorman let his workers sleep. The pain had almost stolen his senses. By the time one of his fellow workers brought the doctor, who would come for a penny, little could be done for him, and he was fit only for the charity hospital on Franklin Street. He'd lain there for weeks, alone and unvisited, before being thrown out onto the streets, a horror of scabs and healing scars.

The hair had never grown back on the right side of his head. He couldn't grow beard on that side either, so later, when beard grew in on the other side, patchy, he'd formed the habit of shaving scrupulously.

Not that it helped.

He stared now into his own eyes, dark blue pools in the dim light.

Gargoyle, he taunted himself. *Monster*. Better say it before the bonny wee lass sleeping in that bedroom did.

As if he had conjured it, a shadow stirred behind him. A white blur appeared in the mirror at his shoulder, and his heart sank in dismay. The last thing he wanted was to be caught mooning at himself like some mesmerized outcast from the circus.

"So you've returned." The words made barely a whisper that floated in the dark. James bent his head, avoiding her image in the glass. What if a steam explosion hadn't been his fate? Would he be able to turn to her now, a man to a woman, as he wished?

Wished with all his being.

"I heard you"—her voice caught—"and I feared you were someone else."

He spun to face her. She stood on her bare feet, clad in a nightgown of purest white. He knew he should turn his eyes from her, look anywhere else, but to save his life he couldn't.

"Sorry if I startled you."

"No, I'm glad you're back."

"Are you all right?" He inspected her as best he could in the gloom.

She didn't appear harmed, but, as he knew, not all wounds showed.

"Yes. No. I don't know." She shivered. "I don't want to be alone." Her gaze reached for his, beseeching. "I understand it's not part of your job, Mr. Kilter, but might we sit together a while? I do not think I can bear to go back in there by myself."

James fought a war, swift and fierce, inside his heart. It was not his place to sit with her. But he could no sooner send her back into her solitary confinement as order an abused dog back into the hell from which it had come.

He drew a great breath and expelled it again before he said, "Come and sit then, but leave the lamp unlit, if you please."

Chapter Eight

Cat knew very well why Kilter wanted to leave the lamps unlit. But what had he been about, staring into the mirror when she came up behind him? Surely he must have been forced long ago to accept the way he looked.

She tried again to imagine how it might feel to go through life with such a countenance, one that looked half melted away. Her heart clenched in sympathy.

Yet here in the soft gloom of the sitting room, he didn't look so different from other men. The faint light from the windows threw half his face into shadow— only the lopsided haircut looked terribly strange.

She wondered why he didn't shave the left side of his head. Some act of defiance, perhaps. He had very nice hair, thick and glossy.

"Talk to me," she begged, not caring for the unfairness of the request. She had no right to ask him to amuse her. But desperation made her reach out to him in helpless appeal. "Tell me about yourself. How did you come to this position, guarding other men's prisoners?"

"Are you his prisoner, then?"

"Please, I don't want to talk about me. I need a distraction." Because if her mind kept chasing itself like a rat in a maze, she feared she would self-destruct.

"So that's what I am. A distraction." Irony colored

his voice.

"I'm sorry. I don't mean to be patronizing."

"You're not. I guess it's easy to be curious about someone like me."

"Do you mind?" A foolish question, but it was out before she could catch it back. Of course he minded. Who wouldn't?

He took a moment before replying. The dim light trickled over him when he tipped his head. "No point in minding, is there? Where would it get me?"

The same might be said about Cat's position here in Boyd's hands. What good would it do to rail and weep? She would still have to obey him, and answer his sexual demands when the moment came.

She said softly, "I admire your ability to be so philosophical about it."

"It didn't come easy. Sometimes there are no choices."

"You're right," she agreed. Who would have thought they could be so much alike, this man from the streets of a strange city and she, cast out into the world?

"You'll be wondering how I got like this. It's the first thing anyone wants to know."

"Is it?"

"Some people just come right out and ask. Some don't, but you can see the question in their eyes. Some scream it, taunt me with it."

"How many look past it to the man within?"

He gave a sudden laugh as if startled. "Very few."

Yet as Cat could sense sitting there with him in the dark, much lay within this man: strength, intelligence, and kindness. Pain too, and perhaps sensitivity he sought to hide. She didn't know how or why she could tell so much about him; she just could.

"Do you mind talking about what happened to you, how you…"

"Got like this?" Again he hesitated, so long this time she didn't believe him when he at last said, "No, I don't mind. It was an accident. After my mother died"—his voice faltered once more—"I went to work. That's not to say I didn't work at various jobs before that. What child in this city doesn't work? But Ma was earning up till then, so I didn't have to support myself alone. After, I learned what it is to work, to labor till you can't put one foot in front of the other and you ache to the bone."

"What sort of work did you do?"

"I got a place installing boiler units for a man called Gorman. I was skinny enough back then to fit into small places, which was an advantage to him. We are not talking grand jobs, here. Gorman was small time, did work in the homes of people who could barely afford heat. Everything was low grade and low dollar, including the fitting that blew out at me when we were running a test on a new install one day in January. Not an uncommon story; it happens every day. But since I was crammed in a closet with the unit at the time, checking the seams, I had no place much to go when it blew. No time, either. When one of those things goes at full boil, it's instantaneous."

"I see."

"Gorman didn't get me out of the space right away, either. He had a big belly on him and couldn't squeeze in to fetch me. I wound up crawling out myself, but I don't remember that, or a whole lot that came right after."

"You must have been taken to hospital."

"Not then. Children who work for the likes of Gorman heal on their own or not at all. He dragged me back to the dorm where he kept those of us without proper homes, and I lay for days till another of the boys, Benny, brought a doc. By then it was too late to do much for me. Likely not much could have been done anyway."

"How old were you?"

"Fourteen."

Nearly the same age she, Cat, had been when Everett Kraus came into her life.

"What happened after you healed?"

He laughed again, a harsh sound. "After? Well, Gorman didn't have any more use for me, and he tossed me out on what remained of my ear as soon as I could stand. I hung around the waterfront, freezing and hoping for handouts or odd jobs, but handouts were few. I finally got taken on by a man named Cox, to look after his dogs."

Kilter faltered for the first time, and Cat sensed darkness arising in him. At last he took up the tale once more. "He kept his dogs shut away, see, and me with them, so it didn't matter how ugly I was. I found out real quick the dogs never saw daylight unless they went into the pit."

"Pit?"

"Fighting." Kilter drew a breath that expanded his chest. "Of all the terrible things I'd seen by then, I'd never imagined anything as awful as that. I was meant to feed them, clean up after them, and doctor their wounds. I knew how it felt to carry such ugly wounds. And they were vicious creatures, but they accepted me as one of them."

He paused again and resumed on a seemingly different subject. "Do you know they're talking of banning dog fighting in this city? Wealthy men are building steam-powered metal dogs they put up against one another for vast amounts of money, so I've heard. But it still happens in back alleys, just what Cox did."

"It seems a lot of creatures and people are still slaves."

"You said that before."

"It's how I feel," Cat admitted.

"Then why stay with him?"

"I have reasons. There are always reasons. How long did you stay with Cox?"

"Too long. At first I had nowhere else to go. Then it became so I didn't want to leave unless I could take at least some of the dogs with me. The first time I tried, Cox caught me and beat me within an inch of my life. I realized then I couldn't do it on my own but needed help. But who'll help a kid who's nothing but a monster?"

Not a monster at all, Cat thought. She sensed a bedrock of beauty and decency inside this man. And sitting with him in the dim light she truly could almost forget his appearance.

"So what did you do?"

"Well, a short time after that, I met Tate Murphy."

"Your boss?"

"The same. He and some of his pals came across me cornered by a crowd of thugs one evening down on the waterfront. It happened a lot back then, before I got big enough to defend myself properly. My life turned that night, right enough. He chased the thugs away, gave me his hand and a meal, the first proper meal I'd had in weeks. I told him about Cox and what he was doing, putting his dogs in the pit. He told me he'd look into it. I didn't believe it, of course. How could a boy not so much older than me take on somebody like Cox? But only a week or so later Cox's place got raided by the police, the dogs were seized, and I was out of a job."

"Just as well," Cat murmured. "The man was a brute, and that was no place for you."

"Still, a belly with some food in it beats starvation. For you see, though the dogs got taken into care, I didn't."

Cat clutched at the arms of her chair. Her heart went out to the mutilated lad with nowhere to turn. "What did you do?"

"I slept in doorways for a few nights and got hungry, and thought about the choice I'd just made. But, Miss Delaney, there was a lesson to be learned in it: sometimes a person has to weigh in on the side of right even if it costs everything. You might want to keep that in mind."

Cat's heart leaped in her breast. Had he told that whole terrible story only to her benefit? Slowly, she said, "Point taken, Mr. Kilter. But what if the cost of making such a choice for right falls not upon you but on someone you love? What if you knew the man's dogs would be killed as a result of your defiance?"

"Well, I suppose that would be a different kettle of fish. But I've also learned things like that tend to work out if you just keep on believing."

"Believing is very hard, in darkness." How strange it felt to be sitting here at the tail end of the night discussing such things with a virtual stranger.

"That it is. But the actual act of believing brings good things."

He could say that with his ruined face and bleak past? "That hasn't been my experience."

"Nor mine, much of the time. But you have to keep your heart high anyway, despite the taunts and the anger and the urge to strike out and treat people as they deserve. Sometimes," his tone became rueful, "you do strike out, nonetheless."

"So, Mr. Kilter," she challenged softly, "what good came to you out of your selfless act on the behalf of those dogs?"

"Tate found me, came looking for me, no less, got me a place to live, and offered me work when I was able."

"What sort of work?"

"At first, just tasks about his place. Then, when I thought I could face people, I ran errands. Later I took up the job I have now."

It must be difficult for him to face people, even now. Gently she said, "And you grew?"

He answered with a rueful laugh in his deep voice, "Grew and grew. I do not think Tate expected that, but he never left off feeding me, for all that. It is something you will do well to remember, Miss Delaney: there are folks in this world who won't fail you, no matter what."

Chapter Nine

The door of Miss Delaney's suite, at James' back, opened and roused him from the fringes of a light sleep. Long ago he had learned to doze on his feet; he always came out of it in an instant, with all senses alert.

Now he turned his head and saw Sebastian Boyd enter the room. Early as it was, the man was clad to the nines in a white silk shirt and black trousers, with diamond studs at wrists and collar. Behind him came a maid, her arms laden with finery of all colors piled so high James could barely see her face.

Boyd walked past James as if he didn't exist, and without invitation went straight into the bedroom where Miss Delaney still lay abed. The maid, with one horrified glance at James, followed.

Alarm moved up James' spine like a kiss of lightning. Talking to Miss Delaney last night in the semi-dark, he had woven for himself the illusion that he could protect her. He didn't know quite why the instinct to do so felt so strong, but now Boyd's arrival put it to the test. For the man walked in as if he owned the world and everything in it.

"Good morning, my dear." The words might be inoffensive, but the tone made an insult of them.

Smarmy bastard, James thought. He could only imagine Miss Delaney waking—had she been asleep?—to such intrusion.

"Your clothing has arrived, and we are to attend an important event today. Get up and try these things on so I might select what you're to wear."

A murmur of response, indistinguishable by James, came from Miss Delaney. From where he stood he could see into the bedroom and behold Boyd's well-clad back with the little maid at his elbow. He couldn't see Miss Delaney at all.

Surely Boyd didn't intend her to get up and strip off before his eyes? James thought again how she'd looked when she sat speaking to him last night, her hair all tumbled down onto her shoulders, clad in that white nightgown that spewed lace at wrists and bosom: a fragile thing deserving careful handling. Yet now this cretin walked in as if he owned her.

She insisted he did.

Hot rage gathered in the region of James' stomach and moved upward to his head.

"Up, I tell you." Boyd's voice, indifferent to the point of insult, struck like an adder. "Or do I have to remind you what you and your father promised me?"

"Stepfather." The word possessed a modicum of defiance. James heard Miss Delaney move from the bed, though from where he stood he still couldn't see her. "Mr. Boyd, I will try those things on if you wish. But please allow me to do so in private."

Boyd gave a harsh laugh. "Do you think you have anything beneath that gown I haven't seen on other women?"

"You have not seen what I have beneath this gown, sir. You cannot expect me to—"

"I can and do. You will walk out on my arm this day as a valuable asset. You will wear what I say, smile

61

when I bid, and go where I tell you. Now try on these dresses, the lavender first."

Silence fell in the bedroom. It was broken when Boyd reached out, swift as a snake, as if he seized Miss Delaney by her arm. "Must I strip you down myself?"

James started forward, made it three full steps before he thought of the ramifications should he intervene. The bastard wanted to humiliate her, true, but he could not actually hurt her if he meant to show her off. But oh, James' heart went out to the girl as he heard a hiccoughing sob.

"Do not snivel. What woman cries over beautiful clothes? And what did you expect when your father sold you to me?"

"Stepfather." The word was barely a whisper. The maid, whom James could see, moved forward, and James lost sight of her. But he could still see Boyd from behind, arms crossed as Miss Delaney presumably removed her nightgown in the morning light.

"The lavender gown," Boyd snapped at the maid. "Help her with it. No—no undergarments."

Why not? James broke out in a sweat all over his body. What did the man intend to do with her, and why insist on such indecency?

He stood like a rock, aching, while rustling sounds ensued. Then Boyd said, "Now try the green."

The procedure continued. Boyd stepped forward, presumably to inspect his prize, and James lost sight of him in turn. He debated what to do. Should he make a scene? He had no right. And many people would insist there was no real hurt in this, beyond the humiliation.

He, James, had suffered great humiliation in his life. Bruising as it might be, he knew a person could survive it.

"Adjust that neckline," Boyd snapped at the maid. "Lower. Hmm. Now the blue gown."

Catherine's voice came, quavering. "Where are you taking me?"

"Boat races on the river, but not just for enjoyment. I expect to conduct a great deal of business today. And I expect you to assist me in that, do you understand? You will be accommodating to the men you meet. None of your sullen pouting. Smile at them, and if they touch you, act like you enjoy it."

"Touch me!"

"Don't worry, nothing will get out of hand. The green, I think," Boyd went on, presumably to the maid. "Do something with her hair; I want it to look elegant. And give her a bath first. I want her at her most tantalizing."

He turned away then, and his arm came into James' view, but the man hesitated and said, "Oh, and Catherine—you can prepare to make yourself welcoming to me later tonight."

He stalked from the bedroom then, moving with disdainful confidence. Puffed with his own importance the man might be, but James knew it wouldn't take much for him to break Boyd in his hands. He needed, though, to school that impulse just as he must school the emotions inside.

Boyd never looked at him as he swept by to the door. "I won't need you today after all," he told James as he passed. "Be back tomorrow morning, instead."

Tomorrow morning, James thought even as he nodded. And what might befall his charge before then? He didn't want to leave her; it felt wrong. But he knew orders when he heard them. He longed to walk to the door of the bedroom, not to see his charge stripped bare but to lend her some shred of reassurance. Yet he had none to lend and, like an enraged shadow, he slipped out the door.

What to do? James' every instinct bade him protect Catherine, and as he left the grand house, passing steam servants and human ones alike, he thrashed out ways and means in his mind. He could attend these boat races on the river, let Catherine see him and know someone who supported her was near at hand. But would she want him to witness her further humiliation?

Yet if Boyd meant her some actual harm, if he traded her off, say, to one of his cronies as part of a business deal…

Yes, and what could James do then? Even if Boyd didn't trade her like any other asset, if he brought her back home, there was still what might happen later tonight. He, James, had no hope of preventing that.

He should have asked her just how she had come into this predicament, why she hadn't run but had let her stepfather trade her away. For, beneath it all, she carried the resolution of a martyr. He'd been too busy banging on about himself, trying to give her a lesson in endurance.

Fat lot of good that would do her now.

Moving like a thundercloud, he stalked off into the beautiful morning. May in Buffalo usually claimed his heart with its blooming trees and soft breezes following the harsh winter, but now he wondered why it didn't rain, to cancel the boat races and whatever devilment Boyd had planned.

He caught himself and his thoughts only when he

nearly stepped off a curb into the path of a steamcab. The driver shrilled the whistle at him and cursed loudly before blowing by in a cloud of hot vapor.

Careful, lad, James told himself. *You'll do Catherine no good dead*.

Ah, but he could do her no good anyway.

Like a homing pigeon, he made for Tate's place. On the way he passed people starting their day: workmen on their way to jobs, housemaids shaking out rugs, crowds of children. Most looked away hastily as soon as they saw him, his countenance revealed mercilessly in the clear morning light. Some of the children followed him for a block or two, hurling insults like stones, until he turned and glared at them and they fled.

Two blocks from Tate's, he happened upon two older lads, their faces twisted in ugly glee, tying a can to the tail of a small mongrel dog.

James knew the drill. The cur would flee for some distance, trying to outpace the clattering racket that pursued it, until it fell in exhaustion, all for the amusement of these oafs.

The anger that simmered in him, already nearly at boiling point, seethed up and ran over. In truth, he lost control of his emotions but rarely; when he did, darkness possessed his mind. He recalled little of what took place during the intervening span of time.

That darkness now rose and gripped him, unstoppable as the blood in his veins. He seized one of the young ruffians and thrust him against the nearest wall. The thin drip squeaked at him while his fellow called, "Monster, monster!"

James knew little more until he came to himself in

the center of a circle of police officers, two of whom hauled on his arms while a third informed him he was under arrest.

Shit, he thought. *How will I get back to Catherine?*

He looked down at the two lads who now lay at his feet like bundles of broken sticks. His fists hurt as they always did after he went off kilter.

"Did I kill anyone?" he asked.

The policeman he addressed didn't bother to answer, merely saying to his fellows who pinned James' arms, "Bring him in, lads, and have a care—this one's an ugly brute."

Chapter Ten

"Well, then, you're a sorry sight, and no mistake." Brendan Fagan, one of the lights of the Buffalo police force, stopped in front of James' cell and glared at him. "Tate's not going to be happy about this, is he? Don't you already have a court date next week for the last assault?"

James shook his head. Truth be told, he wasn't happy with himself either. Losing control only felt good while it lasted, never afterwards.

He looked up and engaged Fagan's gaze. Fagan and Tate had a close friendship, as he knew very well. But Fagan, a tough cookie, couldn't always be gauged. He'd attained a measure of fame two years ago in the automaton affair and now had the reputation of a hard nose in the force.

Seriously, James asked again, "Did I kill anyone?"

"No, but it's a wonder, with those big fists of yours. What's a man your size thinking, taking on two puny lads?"

James tried to remember. "There was a dog. What happened to it?"

"Our men saw no dog."

"Those two boys were tormenting it. I wanted to make them stop."

"Then you tell them to stop, threaten them if you have to. You don't put your hands on them."

"I know." James felt sick to his heart. How could he explain to Fagan that everything else had built up and contributed to him going off his head? How could James admit to Tate, when he came—and he would come—he'd got so personally involved he'd let himself become unprofessional?

He couldn't. Tate would pull him off the job and he'd never see Catherine again.

"Those lads going to press charges?" he asked Fagan.

"Don't know. One's still unconscious and the other has a broken jaw and can't say much. Can't write, either, the ignoramus. So we'll have to wait on that."

"They in hospital?"

"Charity ward for now. But I don't see how it's fair for the good people of this city to pay for the effects of your temper. Do you?"

"I'll pay," James said miserably.

"Damn right you will." Fagan hesitated a moment and then asked in a slightly different tone, "You all right?"

James looked down at his hands. They showed spatters of blood and all the knuckles were split. "Fine."

"Is it true you don't know what you're after doing when one of these fits comes over you?"

"It is."

Fagan shook his head. "You're lucky you didn't kill one or both of them, then. Tate better take care—you do something like that in his employ, he could be held responsible."

"The dog…" James began.

Fagan's blue eyes flashed. "Let me tell you something, Kilter. It's a damn shame what happens to

68

dogs in this city—also cats, children, women…anybody too weak to stand up for him or herself. That's part of the reason I'm on the force. And I guess I can see why you'd want to step in, in the face of cruelty. You're a thoughtful man. But it's time to give some thought to the fellow who took you in when you needed it and did so much for you. You want to ruin Tate Murphy?"

"No."

"Then for God's sake smarten up."

"What's all this, then?" James knew that voice without looking up, but he did anyway and saw Tate join Fagan outside the bars. "You reading my lad the riot act, Brendan?"

"He's a riot all on his own when he goes off his head, Tate. You straighten him out, or he's going to be in here permanently."

Fagan stalked off, and Tate stood gazing at James, his hands deep in the pockets of his rough, brown wool suit. "Well now," he said after a moment, "I don't doubt my friend Brendan is right."

James nodded numbly, tried to get a read on Tate's expression, and failed. "You mean to bail me out?"

"I should let you sit there and stew."

James swallowed a sudden great lump of distress. What would happen to Catherine then? "I need to get back to my assignment, Tate."

"Funny time for you to think of it."

"I know. Fagan's right; I already owe you so much."

"Och, do not get maudlin on me, lad. You'll make me weep. I've paid your fine, but it's to be the last time, do you hear me? Next time you'll be on your own."

An officer came and unlocked the cell, and James

followed Tate from the place in silence. Outside he saw evening had fallen. Where was Catherine now? Back from her day at the river? In her rose bower—alone? Or was Boyd with her?

He shuddered, and Tate gave him a close look. "When you due back on the job?"

"Not till morning."

"Ah. Boyd must be having his way with the little piece, then." Tate's gaze sharpened. "You going to be all right with that? Only you said she's in a spot, and I know how protective you can get. That have anything to do with you beating the snot out of those two lads?"

Too perceptive by half, James thought ruefully. But he said, "I came upon them tormenting a little dog. You know how I feel about that. I snapped. I don't remember much of it."

"You never do. But what if you kill somebody someday, Jamie lad, when you're in that place of not-remembering? What then?"

James had no answer for that, so he said, "I'll pay you back, Tate, for the bail and whatever those boys' care costs, as well."

And Tate replied, "Feckin' right you will."

****

"Well my dear, I hope you had a pleasant day and evening," Boyd said in a smooth, oily voice as the extended steamcab drew up in front of the house.

Cat did not bother to reply. He knew she had not, for he'd set out to deliberately make sure of it. This day, supposedly an opportunity for him to hobnob with his cronies and do deals on the side, had in truth been an exercise in her abasement and humiliation.

He had showed her off like a new toy, bragged

covertly about attaining her, and implied her favors might be available as an enhancement to any deals he made. The implications had been veiled, but not even Cat could claim enough naiveté to misunderstand.

"A pretty little thing, isn't she? A side benefit of a deal in which I did manage to get the upper hand. We all enjoy gaining side benefits, don't we, gentlemen?"

And, "You see there are many ways to sweeten a deal. Miss Delaney comprehends that, don't you, my dear? And she's very obedient."

His associates, not mistaking his point, had looked at her the way they might any other tidbit on offer, with bold, calculating stares that measured the span of her waist, the length of her legs, and the size of her breasts, almost totally exposed by the green gown. They eyed her as they would no decent woman, and Cat realized she had left any claim to decency behind and become a woman who now warranted neither decent respect nor consideration.

Only one man had dared touch her—an aging businessman with a stogie in his mouth, who leaned so close Cat feared the hot ash would fall onto her bosom. Instead, his fingers had found their way there, and had given a hard squeeze before he backed off with a lascivious grin.

Boyd, who observed it all, made no objection, and Cat wondered then if she stared into her fate. After Boyd tired of her, would she pass into the hands of one or all of these men?

Her embarrassment translated to anger as the day went along, and then into an intense hatred for Boyd. Though she had long detested her stepfather and despised her mother for failing to stand up to him, hate made a new emotion for her. It lent the strength needed to keep her chin high even as her cheeks flamed with mortification and even though, as the only woman in the party, there could be no question she was on display.

Now Boyd climbed out of the cab, expecting her to follow as she had all day long. She did, sick to her stomach and with knees that felt wobbly. She feared the worst part of this intolerable day still lay ahead. Did Boyd mean to stay with her tonight as he'd threatened, strip the revealing gown from her, and stake his personal claim before passing her on?

She couldn't bear it, not when she hated him so.

Yet he tossed his jacket aside to one of the steamies and gestured for Cat to ascend the stairs ahead of him. When she reached her suite she looked for Kilter, even though she knew Boyd had dismissed him till morning.

"Inside," Boyd told her brusquely.

In the sitting room, he shot his cuffs and removed his tie, eyeing Cat all the while. *Think of Becky,* she bade herself fiercely, *who might be here instead of you, a mere child.* But it didn't help much when Boyd eyed her and ordered as he had once before, "Take your hair down."

Cat didn't move, and he approached her the way a tomcat might a wounded bird. "Do as I tell you, God damn it, or do I need to get rough?" A smile twisted his narrow face. "I warn you, I might enjoy that."

With fingers that shook violently, Cat took her hair down.

"You make a valuable asset," Boyd said then. "That's plain from today's reactions among my colleagues. You are beautiful, no question of that, and it matters more than what I can see in your eyes. Clearly you'll need to be broken, and clearly you'll need some training before you can provide the kind of pleasure my associates expect."

Cat's knees now shook so hard she feared she might fall down. She no longer wanted to defy him— she wanted to run and hide somewhere, sobbing.

He unbuttoned his shirt, and bile rose into the back of her throat.

"Tell me, Miss Delaney, are you a virgin? Your father assured me you were."

"Stepfather." Cat's lips barely moved.

"Quite frankly, had I been him, I would have had you. But he's a stupid man, at best."

He stepped toward her; she wondered wildly if she could fight him off. She would use everything at her disposal—nails, feet, elbows. Not a muscular man, he would nevertheless have no mercy.

"Are you a virgin?" he persisted.

"Yes."

"Well then, I won't want to spoil that. You'll be worth so much more intact. Take off your gown."

"Please, no."

"You wish to beg, do you? Oh, I assure you, Miss Delaney, you'll beg before we're done. You wish to leave your gown on? That, too, can be titillating. On your knees."

"No. I do beg."

He reached out and tugged down her bodice—it didn't need to move far to expose her breasts. He now spilled from the front of his trousers, engorged inside white silk underdrawers.

"You will accommodate me," he told her, "and you will accommodate my associates when I tell you—at dinners, at business meetings. Do you understand? So you'd best get used to it."

She couldn't. She'd bite him first, fly at him and rave. No one who knew him, no one in this house, would be surprised at screams coming from this chamber.

"On your knees. Move, I tell you! Or do I need to call a couple steamies to hold you down?"

Hate and revulsion filled Cat in equal measures. She moved, but not as bidden. Instead she flew at him, all teeth and claws, like her namesake. He would learn they didn't call her "Cat" for nothing.

Chapter Eleven

"Not here? What do you mean, she's not here?" James stared at Carter, Boyd's little toady of a henchman, who had met him at the door of Boyd's house with the news. The place looked all sixes and sevens, with servants and steamies hurrying in and out in the gray morning light. "What's happened?"

"You're not wanted," Carter told him. "That's all you need to know."

James' heart began to beat hard and high in his throat. All night he'd been uneasy about Catherine. Now his worst fears seemed justified. What had Boyd done to her? Raped her? Injured and sent her to the hospital?

Carter added succinctly, "You will not be needed henceforth."

"But where's Miss Delaney?" James looked past Carter and through the open door as if he might see her. Surely that was a physician there inside, with a black bag. His heart plummeted sickeningly. Did "not here" from Carter translate to "dead"?

But Carter buttoned his lip, went inside, and shut the door firmly. James backed down the stairs, reluctant to leave. Turning, he met the gaze of a fellow standing beside what James now recognized as a steam ambulance.

"What happened in there, do you know?" James

asked.

"Confidential," the fellow replied, looking askance at James and his ruined countenance.

"Oh, come on—I work there, but I've been turned away. I have a right to know why."

"Well, you didn't hear it from me. Rich fella who lives in there? His doxy attacked him, did a right job on him, too."

"She kill him?"

"No, he ain't dead, but hurt bad enough. We're on standby, but no hospital in this city's good enough for him. They've already called in four doctors."

James' mind reeled. "Where's the woman gone?" he asked.

The ambulance attendant shrugged. "Nobody knows. Ran off, she did, after."

A great breath escaped James. Ran off where? She knew no one in the city, and he was all too aware of the dangers that might befall her.

"Thanks," he told the attendant.

"Remember, you didn't hear it from me. Hey, buddy, what happened to your face?"

James started and gave the fellow a glare.

"Just professional curiosity," the man said. "Steam burns, right? Those are some of the worst I've ever seen, and I've worked with burn patients."

"The contents of a whole boiler erupted on me before I could move away."

"Figured it must have been something like that. You ever hear of Dr. Roesch?"

"Who?"

"He's the man who got involved with that crew of steamie hybrids that came to light a couple years back."

"The ones in the police force?"

"That's them. We in the medical profession heard Roesch is studying the methods those two madmen used to graft skin over metal. They say he's made some great advances. Might be able to help you."

"You think so?"

"Could be worth your while to talk to him. He's pricey, though." The man raked James with a comprehensive glance. "Probably more than you can afford, come to think of it."

James just nodded, since there seemed nothing to say. He tucked the name "Roesch" into his memory and took himself off up the street.

How could he figure out where Catherine had fled? He tried to imagine what must have taken place yesterday, or last night, to cause her to strike out at Boyd. She seemed so delicate, yet there was nothing helpless about a young woman who would knock a man down.

Would she run to the waterfront? Try to make it back to Canada? Go to the police? He dared not hope she would think to come looking for him, yet she had virtually no other contacts in the city.

He walked back to Tate's slowly, his eyes everywhere, hoping for a glimpse of a strawberry-blonde head and a graceful, narrow back. By this hour the streets were busy, and he caught glimpses of many women, but not the one he sought.

When he reached Tate's, he found the man himself leaning on the jamb of the front doorway, arms crossed and a curious look on his broad face.

"You're back early, old son," Tate observed without moving.

"Job's fallen through. Boyd's in the hands of the quacks, and the bird has flown."

"Has she?" Tate raised his brows. "Any idea where?"

"I wish I did."

"Then go into my office. Somebody here to see you."

James' heart began to slam in his chest. He hurried past Tate, only half aware the man followed him. The door of Tate's office stood closed. He opened it and looked in.

The sight for which he'd been searching the streets met his eyes. She wore a rumpled, tattered gown of green, the bodice of which barely covered her bosom. Her hair tumbled in disarray around a face so pale he wondered how she kept on her feet. Her pretty lips formed a tight line of distress, and her eyes looked haunted.

"Catherine," he said, relief washing through him. "What happened?"

Her only answer came in a rush of steps that carried her across the office and into his arms. His heart pounded harder as she burrowed against him, hands clutching the rough material of his coat, face pressed hard into his shoulder, a woman taking refuge without hesitation.

Protectiveness—never far from the surface in him—swelled. Without thinking of right or wrong he wrapped his arms about her and held her tight.

"Hush now, hush," he murmured, though so far she had not said a word. "Are you hurt?"

She moved her head in denial, and her hair, soft as silk, brushed his chin. So small was she that she came no higher than that; so thin did her body feel he might have broken her in his hands. Not that he would harm one bone of her, one hair, not under pain of death.

"How did you come here?" he asked, but she just burrowed harder. The miracle of it—the true wonder—was that she would touch him this way, voluntarily. Women rarely did, without being paid.

"Well, is this not a touching scene?" The drawl came from behind them. Tate stepped into the office and shut the door firmly.

James spun to face his boss, but Catherine remained in his arms and moved with him.

"Miss Delaney," Tate said softly, "is this the fellow you wanted? Will you tell us now what's been after happening?"

"How did you find me?" Very gently, James eased his hold on her and looked into her eyes. He almost hated to do so; once she got a good look at his face she would surely rethink her position, realize just where she was, and move away.

"I killed him. I think I killed him," she said.

"No, he's not dead."

"He is. He fell. There was blood."

"No, Catherine, listen to me. I just came from there. They've called in doctors, and the ambulance men are standing by, but he's alive."

"Oh, God!" Tears came then, filled her moss-colored eyes, and spilled over. "I thought…"

"Listen to me, listen." James rubbed her mostly bare shoulders in a gesture meant to convey comfort. "What did he do to you?"

"I—" She shot an agonized look at Tate. "I can't speak of it."

"Give us five minutes, Tate, please," James appealed.

"Look here, old son. I can't be having this. You're in my employ and I'm hired by Boyd, which makes me involved. I'll not be crosswise of a man like that if I can help it."

"Five minutes."

Tate went out, the door snicked shut, and James began, "Now take a deep breath, sit down there, and tell me all—"

"No! No, don't leave go of me. Please hold me, Kilter, please."

James' heart promptly melted. Warmth spread through him from the direction of his groin and straight to his head. Softly, as he might to an injured animal, he crooned, "I'll not let go, not if you don't want me to."

"Never let go," she implored.

Chapter Twelve

One anchor existed in Cat's world. It wore a rough coat, had gentle hands, and possessed a deep voice that rumbled through her ear when she pressed in tight. It—he—felt warm to her touch and emitted comfort, a balm to her panic and terror.

But could she speak even to him of her humiliation? Could she describe what yesterday, what last night, had been like?

If she did, would the man, Murphy, send her away? Where would she go then? Just thinking of it made her clutch at Kilter still more tightly.

"Come now." His voice vibrated through her again. "What did he do to you?"

She gulped a deep breath and fought to gather herself, but the last threads of her composure had broken the moment Boyd ordered her to her knees.

She tipped her head back and sought Kilter's eyes; an expanse of ruined skin met her gaze, patchy and uneven from his chin upward. Funny, she had forgotten while burrowing into him, while feeling him, how he looked. Now the impact of his appearance rushed over her, another unwelcome wave of shock. Yet the deep blue eyes looked kind, and trust overwhelmed her reaction.

"It's so filthy and demoralizing, I hate to say."

His lips, so close above hers, twisted in what might

be an ironic smile. "More demoralizing than walking around with half a head of hair?"

"Yes. Not that I pretend to understand how you feel." She caught her breath again. "At least, Mr. Kilter, you still own yourself and are not available to sweeten a business deal or…" For the life of her, she couldn't tell him what Boyd had said: *You will accommodate me, you will accommodate my associates when I tell you—at dinners, at parties, at business meetings…*

Kilter's big hands moved comfortingly over her shoulders again. Did he realize he touched her naked flesh? She stood before him in very little, just this dress with its scrap of bodice and nothing underneath.

"He threatened to pass you to his cronies, is that it?"

"That's what the day at the river was all about. He was showing me off like a prize mare, a carrot dangled before a herd of asses. That's all I was. Then when we got home he brought me to my room." Her cheeks flamed with heat, and she dropped her gaze from Kilter's for the first time. "He asked if I were…if I were—"

"Untried?" Kilter supplied the word.

"Yes, and when I said I was, he told me he wouldn't spoil that because it made me more valuable. He meant to use me as part of some deal, you see, even as he took me in a deal from my stepfather. Like a thing and not a person at all. He implied there were other ways he could…could…"

"You needn't say it; I understand." Again his hands moved across her back, a gesture of protection. If only Cat might stay here with him forever, where she felt safe. But his boss, Murphy, would never allow such a thing, for surely she brought ruin in her wake.

"I reacted; I didn't think. I flew at him, scratched and clawed." Ruefully she added, "They call me 'Cat' for a reason, you know. I knocked him down, and he struck his head on that little table, you know the one with the marble top. Oh, Kilter, I can't go back there. What am I to do?"

"You wait it out."

"But what's going to happen? He's still alive, you say?"

"He was, when I left there."

"Then I can't stay here, can't bring him down on you. For I fear he'll come after me."

"He might."

She expected him to thrust her from him then; instead the big hands stroked her hair. She wished she could press her head into his chest and stay there, but instead she drew away. He released her immediately.

Once more she sought his eyes, hauling up her determination. "I must leave. If he comes after me and finds you—"

"He won't come so soon. He's in no condition at the moment. Anyway, why would he expect you to run here?"

Did a second question lie beneath that one? Did he wonder why she had run to him? All that lay between them was conversation shared in the dark, a certain feeling of intimacy. Instinct had brought her; she didn't think she could explain that.

"I don't know." Wildly, she shook her head. "He has the means to send out a small army through the city." Again she told him, "You'd be mad to help me. I never should have come."

At that moment the office door whispered open and Murphy walked in. "Well? Have you come to some understanding?"

"I can't send her back," Kilter told him. "The man's abusive, Tate."

Murphy swept Cat with a comprehensive glance. "She does not look harmed."

"Not so you can see, maybe."

"Laddie," Murphy began, "I know your heart's in the right place, but this is a right nest of hornets."

Kilter shifted on his feet. He stood beside Cat now, both of them facing Murphy, but his hand still held hers tightly.

"He's right." Cat cast Kilter a look. "I'll leave."

"Where will you go?"

"I don't know." Tears flooded Cat's eyes; she fought the emotions down.

"Can you go back to your family in Toronto?"

"First place he'll look." Surprisingly, Murphy spoke the words.

"He's right." Panic rose through Cat again. "It's my family who'll suffer for this. How could I have forgotten?" She turned to Kilter. "What if he takes my sister in my place? She's the only reason I agreed to go with him in the first place." Her lips trembled. "He likes young girls. I must go back. I won't have Becky at risk because of me."

Kilter and Murphy exchanged glances.

With deceptive mildness Murphy said, "Disgusting, that. Man has no business with a girl under the age of consent."

"My stepfather will give consent on her behalf," Cat told him. "In order to save himself, he will. That's why I said I'd come."

"Craven fecker," Murphy murmured. "Well, lass, I do not see how we can help your family."

"If we could just get the sister away somewhere safe," Kilter suggested.

Cat's heart leaped, but Murphy shook his head. "From Toronto? And, laddie, do you really want to get in the middle of this?"

"No. But I won't abandon someone in need."

"Aw, shite, lad—excusing my language, miss, but the situation does warrant. Perhaps we can get her out of the city, if we act quickly."

"Where?"

"Damned if I know. But if she stays here it spells ruin for all of us."

"I'll go," Cat said again helplessly. "I don't want to bring trouble down on either of you."

"Hush," Kilter told her once more, and his fingers tightened on hers.

Murphy gave Kilter a speaking look, but he said to Cat, "Lass, have you relatives elsewhere to whom we might send you? Another city in Canada, perhaps? I'd be willing to pay your fare."

"That's kind of you." Emotion threatened to block Cat's throat. "I do have a grandmother in Halifax, but she's old and sick."

"Cousins there, or anywhere in this country? Friends? Must be someone you can turn to."

"Nobody in a position to help."

"I've old friends in Boston, but I can't send you there before I contact them." Murphy seemed to reach a decision. "Jamie, lad, you'll have to take her to Roselyn for now. Roselyn's me sister," he added for Cat's benefit. "Runs a boarding house over on Prospect. You can stay there till we figure what's to be done. But"—this time Murphy's gaze raked Cat—"you can't go anywhere looking like that. Attract too much attention."

Futilely, Cat tugged at her bodice, using the hand not held fast in Kilter's.

"Wait here," Murphy bade them and went out again.

"He's very kind," Cat whispered, and her throat grew tight again.

"Tate? Heart of gold, and solid gold at that."

"I've caused nothing but trouble." Cat's fingers twitched in Kilter's, but he didn't let go. "I'm a pariah."

He turned his head to look at her, his eyes intensely blue in his patchwork face. "You can say that? You've no idea what being a 'pariah' means."

"I'm sorry." Again her eyes filled with tears; this time they spilled over.

"Don't cry," he bade her. "You'll like Roselyn. And no one will think to look for you there for a day or two."

Murphy reentered the office, this time with a bundle of clothing in his hands. "Put these on, lass. We'll burn the dress out back once you've gone. Bundle all that hair into the cap, mind. We can't have you recognized out on the street. James and I will wait outside."

Cat accepted the clothing and nodded. Reluctantly, she released Kilter's hand. Both men went out, and sudden cold rushed at her, along with reaction.

For an instant she thought her legs would collapse beneath her. All her strength seemed to have gone out the door with Kilter. No, James. Mr. Murphy called him

James, or Jamie. She liked "Jamie." It suited him somehow, despite his size and appearance.

Shivering, she stripped off the detested green dress and as quickly as possible donned the clothing Murphy had provided. It proved to be a boy's trousers, linen shirt, and cap. Good thing she was so thin, she thought ruefully as she buttoned the shirt. Without the built-in wire and whalebone that reinforced the scanty bodice of the gown, her bosom virtually disappeared.

Just like that of a child. No wonder Boyd was interested. *Murphy had it right—he's a craven fecker.*

With the cap crammed on her head, Cat opened the office door. Both men stood outside with their backs turned as if to provide her an extra measure of privacy.

Gentlemen, she thought, despite their rough appearances.

"Here, Mr. Murphy." She held out the green dress. "I never want to see it again."

"And you won't." Murphy jerked his head at Kilter. "Off you go, lad. You'll have to walk. 'Twould look suspicious, hailing a steamcab at this hour."

Kilter turned his eyes on Cat. "Can you manage?"

Wordlessly, she nodded. She wished he'd take her hand again, but a man and a lad wouldn't walk so through the city.

"Then come along."

"Thank you, Mr. Murphy." Impulsively, Cat turned to the big Irishman. "I know you don't have to help me and I'm a complication you don't need."

"Not sure how much I can help you, lass. Boyd's a powerful man. But for now we'll try and keep you safe. Go along with Jamie, now."

Gratefully, Cat went.

Chapter Thirteen

"Jamie," Cat said a bit breathlessly as they hurried along. At least she hurried; Kilter appeared to walk at an easy enough pace, but his stride made two of hers. "That's what Mr. Murphy called you."

Kilter slanted a look at her. The light of the clear morning proved merciless to his scarred face, exposing each shiny patch of skin, but she didn't see that so much as the tentative expression in his eyes.

"James," he said carefully. "Nobody but Tate calls me Jamie."

"Tate?" she repeated in inquiry.

"Short for Tater." He smiled. "You know, because he's an Irishman."

Must be nice to belong to a world where folks shared affectionate nicknames, Cat reflected. Of course, Kilter got called a lot of less affectionate names, as well.

As if suddenly realizing he forced her pace, Kilter shortened his step. "Don't let Tate's bluster fool you. He's a good man."

"I can see that. He has no reason to help me. Neither have you."

He shrugged and thrust his hands deep into his pockets. "As I say, you'll like his sister, Roselyn. She's kind as Tate and twice as fierce."

"Is that a good thing?"

"You have to be fierce if you want to survive in this city."

Cat nodded gravely. "Perhaps I can change my identity, take a new name, and find work somewhere. I could go into service. These big houses must need staff."

"Most of them are employing steamies now, or a combination of steamies and human servants." He grimaced. "A steamie can work round the clock rather than just twenty hours of every twenty-four. But we'll see, Miss Delaney. One thing at a time."

"Please do call me Catherine," she insisted. "Or Cat—those close to me call me Cat."

He nodded soberly. "And you can call me—"

"Ugly! Hey lads, there's Mr. Ugly! Out ruining this beautiful morning again are you, Mr. Ugly? Hey, boys—grab a rock. We'd better kill it before it spreads."

Kilter's head jerked up and a change came over him, visible anger pouring through his frame. Cat peered past him and saw a crowd of ruffians on the far side of the street, gathered on the corner like so many raggedy crows. Their leader wore a patched coat and filthy cloth cap, not unlike her own, and had a thin face, sharp as a hatchet.

"Who's your friend, Ugly?" he called. "Surprised the boy would be seen in your hid-ee-yous company."

"Who's that?" Cat asked, her eyes narrowing.

"Charlie Crowter—local self-appointed bad boy," Kilter growled. "Just ignore him."

"He has a mouth on him, hasn't he?" Indignation flooded Cat, bringing strength. "What does he have against you?"

"This." Kilter gestured roughly to his face. "In case you haven't noticed, I'm too hideous to be seen in daylight."

Cat glared at Crowter. "Talk about ugly," she called just loud enough to be heard.

"Keep your voice down," Kilter told her. "You sound like a girl."

Cat never broke the glare she directed at Crowter, but she lowered her voice to a roughened pitch when she called across the street, "Have you looked in the mirror lately, cur? Who are you to go throwing stones—or names—at anyone?"

"For God's sake," Kilter muttered.

"Ooh," the ruffians all hooted together.

"Big insult!" Crowter brayed. "Is that your friend, Mr. Ugly? Looks like he escaped from the bottom of a coal bin."

"Must be blind," one of Crowter's cronies chortled, "to walk alongside you!"

Crowter preened himself. "I might not be the handsomest fellow in Buffalo, but I'm damn well better to look at than ol' Melty Face!"

"Why, you little piece of filthy—!" Cat forgot at that moment who she was, as well as who she pretended to be. She sprang off the curb, every bit as full of ire as she used to be in the face of her stepfather, and launched herself across the street. Only Kilter's grip on her arm held her back.

"Ignore them, I tell you!" he insisted under his breath. "Not worth showing who you are."

"The pipsqueak wants a fight, boys!" Crowter and his fellows formed up into a squad. Several of them produced crude weapons from their pockets, billy clubs and metal objects through which they threaded their fingers. "Let's give it to him."

Kilter lifted Cat off her feet and back onto the curb. "Come on. You don't want any of that."

Cat did. She wanted in the worst way to bash Crowter in the mouth, bust all his teeth, and make it so he could never taunt Kilter again. But even in the face of her indignation she realized if she started a brawl here and now Kilter would be forced to wade in, and she'd endanger both of them.

"Not worth my time," she declared loud enough for the gang to hear. "Let's not soil our hands with them."

"It's a regular rooster, boys," Crowter cried. "A fighting cock! But will you look at the size of it? We'll have to call it 'Bantam.' "

"Ugly's got a Bantam!" they all called as Kilter dragged Cat off down the street.

Still angry and indignant even as the cries died away behind, Cat wrestled with her emotions. She glanced into Kilter's face but failed to discern what he felt. He caught her eye and one corner of his mouth twitched.

"Meant to take them all on, did you?"

"They deserve battering."

"No question. Why is it you say folks call you 'Cat'? Because you're all claws and teeth, is it?"

"I don't like bullies. And whatever you say about—about your appearance, they have no right to treat you that way."

"It's just words," he said stonily.

"But they hurt." She challenged, "You mean to tell me that doesn't bother you?"

"I've learned to deal with it, haven't I?"

Liar, Cat thought, though she didn't say it. She could feel distress streaming from him as clearly as if he expressed it. But she'd stepped into his world now, and if he wanted to play the stoic, she would respect that.

She frowned. "Well, they need taking down a few pegs."

"Much as I appreciate you leaping to my defense," he said dryly, "that could only have ended badly when your hat fell off."

"I know. I'm sorry. Forgive me?"

The look he shot her this time was startled. "Nothing to forgive, Miss Catherine."

"Cat," she stipulated. "After that, you had better call me Cat."

****

The boarding house proved to be a tall, narrow building in a busy neighborhood that pulsed with the life of the city. A group of children played hopscotch out front. Given what had just happened, Cat half expected them to scatter at Kilter's approach, but these must be used to his appearance, for they gave Cat curious looks and kept playing.

At the curb stood a horse-drawn dray loaded with an assortment of items from brooms to clothing. And when they climbed the steps to the front door, Cat saw a man just inside wearing a cloth cap, speaking to a woman who could only be Tate Murphy's sister.

Big and rawboned, she wore a brown dress and pinafore, both crisp and clean, and towered over the tradesman. The broad, plain countenance that looked so ordinary on Murphy lent her little beauty, but the look she shot Cat and Kilter over the visitor's head seemed kind.

Kilter caught Cat's arm, and they paused just outside the door.

"You bring me a copper pot and three yards of linen next Tuesday," the woman told the tradesman, her voice a rich roll of Irish. "And the jars next week, mind."

"Yes, ma'am." The tradesman tipped his cap, turned about, and caught sight of them behind him. He gave Kilter a startled look before he scuttled out the door and down the stairs to the dray.

Cat flinched again on Kilter's behalf. He met with the same reaction everywhere he turned.

Yet the woman's plain face lit when she turned to him. "Morning, James. What brings you down this way?"

"Morning, Roselyn. Tate sent me to ask you a favor."

"And what's my big lug of a brother after wanting from me now?" Roselyn turned lively eyes on Cat. "Who's this...lad?"

"This is the favor, actually," Kilter told her ruefully. "Mind if we come in?"

"I'd be hurt if you didn't. The kettle's on, and you'll take a cup of tea. I've been up since dawn, and I've earned a break."

Swiftly, she turned and led them down a long hallway, past a dining room, and into a large kitchen. A kettle sang on a coal-fired stove, and a young girl bustled about putting plates into a cavernous sink. The back door stood open, admitting air and the sounds of activity from the next street. Beside the door, in a box, Cat saw a dog with a number of puppies.

"How's the litter?" Kilter asked, going immediately to hunker down beside the animals. The mother dog, a brown mutt of obviously mixed ancestry, abandoned her offspring to press forward eagerly and greet him.

"Fine, now," Roselyn replied, "though they'll be underfoot in a few days, and that will never do. You're going to have to find another place for them, James, lad."

"I know." Kilter's big hands caressed the bitch's head with careful gentleness. Already Cat knew that touch and didn't blame the bitch for wagging her tail and pressing against his knee.

Roselyn cast Cat a look. "James has a way of gathering strays, hasn't he? And foisting them on anyone who'll help him look after them. Found this little dog floating in the river, he did, more dead than alive and ready to whelp. Asked if he could leave her here just till her pups came into the world."

"Looks like she's grateful," Cat murmured around the sudden lump in her throat. The bitch, her tail a blur of motion, now licked Kilter's wrist, and her pups tumbled toward him.

Roselyn shot her another look. "And I suppose you'd be yet another stray?"

Kilter got to his feet. "We're in a bit of a pickle, Roselyn. Tate thought you might offer some shelter for a while."

Roselyn heaved a sigh. "Best sit down and tell me all about it."

Chapter Fourteen

"So Tate thought you might be willing to have Miss Delaney stay here just till we can decide what's to be done," James concluded his explanation to Roselyn, who had listened quietly throughout, her careworn hands folded. A spunky, quirky woman, he nevertheless knew her heart to be every bit as big as her brother's.

He shot a look at Catherine, who'd kept far from quiet during his recitation. She'd squirmed in her seat, interrupted several times, and virtually steamed emotion throughout. Funny how he could sense so very clearly what she felt. Funny too how her true nature had begun to come out, proving her far different from the gentle maid he'd first taken her to be. A firebrand she was. He couldn't imagine how Boyd had kept her in check so long.

But why did she stare at him so? She'd scarcely taken her big, hazel eyes off him since he started talking. Such scrutiny made him uncomfortable, to say the least. The last thing he wanted was to appear hideous to her.

"Well, well," said Roselyn, who had sent the little maid off about some errand while they spoke together. Her generous lips tightened. "That is a fix, and no mistake." She asked Catherine, "Where's your family, then?"

"In Toronto. It's only my mother and sister about

whom I'm concerned."

"Aye, sure, I get that picture. You've already consigned the stepfather to hell, haven't you?"

"Where he belongs." Catherine leaned across the wide wooden table impulsively. "I had to protect my sister; you see that."

"I do, and her but a lass. 'Tis to your credit. But what makes you think the stepfather won't do the same again if Boyd returns to him?"

"That's my worst fear." Catherine chewed on her lip. "I need to get a message to my mother and warn them."

"Sure, a message can be sent," Roselyn said. "Toronto's not so far. Question is, will your mother heed your warning and leave the scoundrel?"

"She hasn't yet, and I've begged, beseeched, and threatened."

"I'll ask you this, woman to woman," Roselyn said. "Why won't she leave him? Do you know?"

Catherine bit her lip harder. "He's a good-looking devil." Her gaze flicked to James, and he wondered if she made a hasty comparison. "But weak to the bone. Besides, she's the kind of woman who thinks she needs a man to provide for her."

"And you're not?" Roselyn's homely face split in a wide smile. "You and I are going to get along just fine, then. Me, I've been looking after myself a long while— more hindered by that troublesome brother of mine than otherwise."

"I can see that," Catherine said admiringly.

James sat quietly and chucked the brown mutt behind her ear. She'd climbed out of the box and into his lap as soon as he sat down. One by one her pups had followed, tumbling over the floor to his feet, where they cuddled in.

"Well, my opinion is"—Roselyn usually did have an opinion—"you need to get your sister away even if the mother will not come."

"Do you think I can?" Catherine leaned forward still more intently.

"You can do anything at all, lass, if you set your mind to it. Meanwhile…" Roselyn reached a swift decision. "You'll stay here with me, just till that bastard, Boyd, figures out whether or not he means to die."

"Oh, Miss Murphy, that's so good of you! I'm willing to earn my keep, of course, working round the place." Catherine considered. "You'll need to train me, though."

Roselyn laughed. "Fine lady, is it, trained up as a housemaid?"

"Not so fine." Catherine spread her pretty little hands. "Only look at me."

"When it comes to that," Roselyn murmured, "I think it best that you remain disguised as a lad a while. I've a set of boarders coming and going in this house, and we wouldn't want anyone flapping his gums and leading the hounds here. That means you might have to cut your hair."

James made an involuntary sound of protest, and Roselyn eyed him. "Well, she can't be wearing that cap all the time, can she? And we'd better come up with a likely name."

"Albert," Catherine said promptly. "Will you call me Albert, after the queen's consort?"

"The queen of England, you mean? Saints preserve

us, lass, you're not in the Commonwealth now. But Albert it is." She slanted another look at James. "A bit pretty for a boy, isn't she? Think she can pass?"

He returned Roselyn's look steadily. "If you keep her close. I wouldn't like her out on the streets anyway. If Boyd survives his injuries, I expect he'll stop at nothing to find her."

"Oh, I'll keep her close. Problem's going to be housing you, lass. I can't put you in with any of the men, for obvious reasons. And 'twould be scandalous to put you in with Dottie when she thinks you're a boy. There's a room at the top of the house, but I doubt you'll like it much. Hot and musty, and the window's stuck shut."

"I don't mind." Catherine touched Roselyn's chapped hand. "I'm ever so grateful to you. I only hope I won't bring trouble down on your head."

Roselyn looked amused. "I hope so too. James, lad, why don't you take her up and see can you persuade that window to open? I'll scrounge up some clothing and tell Dottie a new lad's come to stay. I'll be up shortly with the shears for that hair."

Very gently, James lifted the brown mutt from his knee and placed her back among her brood. He got to his feet. "Come along then," he told Catherine.

Immediately she reached for his hand. Roselyn slapped it away. "None of that! How would it look, a big drink of a man holding hands with a lad?"

"Sorry." Catherine looked remorseful. "I forgot."

"Well, don't forget." Roselyn directed a fierce look at both of them. "Your safety might depend on it."

James struggled for something to say while they climbed the three flights of stairs at the back of the house, and failed. Things changed far too quickly for his liking. Though he appreciated Roselyn offering Catherine refuge, he felt uncertain about continuing the ruse and certainly didn't like the idea of Catherine's glorious hair, which she'd now stuffed back into her cap, being shorn.

The room in question occupied the back corner of the tall attic and had recently been used for little but storage. Boarders' rooms occupied the floor below; Dottie and Ben, the lad who ran errands for Roselyn, had rooms on this floor as well, but surveying this closet with misgiving, James acknowledged it to be the least desirable location in the house.

"Are you going to be all right here?" he asked dubiously, finding his voice at last.

"It's fine." Catherine indicated the cot in the corner. "I doubt I'll be up here much. Our house staff in Toronto always kept busy working and seldom had time to rest." Her lips quirked. "Funny, isn't it, how things turn about?"

"And not for the better," James muttered.

"Don't say that. My life as a lady of supposed means was no happier than this may prove. I only worry for Becky now."

"Give me her address before I leave, and Tate can send a message."

She turned and stepped up to him. "I wish you didn't have to leave."

Suddenly, James couldn't catch his breath. He told himself he could blame that on the close air of the room, but he knew he lied. She'd pulled off her cap when they entered the place, and her red-gold hair once more tumbled about her face. Her eyes clung to his, unwavering.

What would she do if he reached out and caressed that matchless hair? Before he could let himself answer the question, he raised his fingers and brushed it lightly. Soft it was, so soft, like the white fluff of a dandelion.

She smiled. "You needn't look so scandalized. It will grow back, you know."

"Not scandalized. I—" He longed to tell her just how beautiful he thought her, but she must have heard that a thousand times and didn't need it from him. He blinked and caught a sudden glimpse of his right hand, scarred and mottled, in juxtaposition with her glowing curls. He jerked the offending member away as if stung.

"What is it?" Catherine whispered. "What's wrong?"

Helpless, he shook his head. For the first time in many years, his heart truly protested his appearance. Why couldn't he look the way a man should, if only for her eyes?

Her gaze grew serious. "You will come back and see me?" she beseeched. "Soon?"

"I will, or Tate will send someone else as soon as there's any word."

"You. I know I've no right to ask anything more, but please—you come."

His heart quivered within his chest. "I'll try."

"You got that window open yet?" So distracted had James been by what he saw in Catherine's eyes, he hadn't even heard Roselyn puffing her way up the stairs. She appeared now with a set of kitchen shears in her hand and looked round the place. "Worse than I remembered, it is. We'll get it cleaned out, lass, and clean sheets for the cot, as well."

"Lad," Catherine reminded. "And this room will be fine."

"Sit down there, then, and let's get you shorn."

James turned away to the window as Catherine perched on the edge of a wooden packing box. The window in question looked down over the tiny yard, with a glimpse of the next street to the left. Swollen shut by heat, it resisted his efforts, and he wrestled with it even as he listened to what happened behind him.

"No need to worry now, Albert—I cut all the lads' hair. Scads of experience."

Snip, snip.

"I'm not worried at all."

"Mind, now, you're going to have to try and think like a male. Won't be easy, like, to turn off half your brain, but necessary for the duration. Right, James, lad?"

"Ha, ha," James said, and felt the window move slightly beneath his hands.

"Of course"—*snip, snip, snip*—"you'll only be able to do one thing at a time—men are notorious for that."

James longed to glance behind at the bright tresses that must now litter the floor, see if Catherine still looked beautiful. He fought a brief battle with himself and then stole a look. One side of her head had been successfully cropped; the other still sprouted a bright fall of hair.

Like him. No, not like him, because she was still beautiful, so very beautiful.

She smiled at him, and his poor heart spasmed once more.

"How bad does it look?" she asked.

And he answered, "Not bad at all." The window lifted beneath his hands, and fresh air streamed in.

"Ah, now, that's grand. If you squint your eyes, you should be able to catch a glimpse of the river from that window," Roselyn told Catherine. "Canada and home, for you."

"This is my home now." Catherine didn't take her eyes from James.

Snip, snip, snip. He stood and watched openly as the bright tresses fell, each one a wound. When it was done, that criminal act, she still didn't look like a boy, not to James, but a bit less like a fine lady.

"There, now." Roselyn ruffled her hand through the cropped hair, and James' fingers twitched. "Albert, lad, I forgot to bring up the broom and dustpan. Your legs are much younger than mine; run down the three flights, will you, and fetch them? You'll find them just behind the kitchen door."

Catherine arose, flashed James a cheeky grin, and went.

Roselyn gave James a thoughtful look, bent down, and deliberately chose a lock of hair from the pile at her feet. This she passed covertly to James' hand.

"Here, lad. You just take that, and tuck it close to your heart."

Chapter Fifteen

"Albert, lad, fill up that bucket again—nice clean water, mind."

Cat groaned inwardly and straightened her aching back. Three days had passed at Roselyn's boarding house, and it had been nothing but work, work, work from sunup to sundown. Astonishing, the sheer amount of labor it took to run such a place, at least the way Roselyn Murphy wanted it run. Tasks seemed endless, and the scrubbing never quite got finished.

Moreover, Roselyn proved to be an equal-opportunity slave driver. She didn't so much assign lads' and lasses' duties as share the pain around. So far Cat had polished furniture, scrubbed every floor in the place, and begun learning to cook.

Ruefully, she cast a glance at her hands, which had once been white and well-kept. Now red and almost as rough as Roselyn's, they stung when she immersed them in water.

How many buckets had she hauled since she came here? Far too many. But she could fairly say Roselyn worked herself twice as hard as she worked anyone else.

And Cat sincerely did like the woman. She liked Dottie, too, who seemed to possess limitless energy and loved to chatter while she worked, very much like a bird. Cat had already heard all about Dottie's past, far more horrific than Cat's; at the age of four, Dottie had been sold by her father as a runner for a man who owned a weaving factory—shuttling bobbins from place to place on the floor. After enduring two years of that life, she'd been injured when a bolt of fabric fell on her, and tossed out on her ear. Taken in by a charity run by the wives of German immigrants on the east side, she'd gone out to work again at the age of eight, laboring for a grocer. When the man became abusive, she eventually saw a doctor, who directed her to Roselyn's door.

Now, at only fourteen, she worked tirelessly all day and confided to Cat early on, "I'd stay here and work for Miss Murphy for free if I had to. She's kind enough, though, to pay me a little bit of wage in addition to my keep. I was able to save up and buy these boots, see?"

She pointed a little toe from beneath the edge of her worn but clean dress. Cat thought of the many pairs of shoes and slippers she'd gone through in her life, tossed aside casually, and marveled that this girl could be excited over a pair of plain brown boots. But she nodded respectfully.

"So, Albert," Dottie concluded sweetly, "you just keep working hard, and maybe you can earn yourself some decent clothes."

Cat had followed that advice and continued working hard. Her arms protested hauling the heavy buckets and—because it seemed like a task for a lad—she learned to wield an axe and split kindling in the tiny kitchen yard. She carried endless bowls and platters to the table—the men who lodged with Roselyn had seemingly bottomless stomachs—and helped with mountains of dishes. At night she slept like the dead, too weary to dream.

But now, now... She paused beside the kitchen window and looked out, wishing James—or Jamie, as she called him in her own mind—would come. Not only did she crave news of Boyd's condition—surely the villain must be dead by now if he meant to die—but she missed the big, gentle man.

As if her wishing had conjured him, she saw someone enter the kitchen yard—wide shoulders, long legs, auburn hair tumbling across one side of his face. She caught her breath in delight.

"It's Jamie!"

Roselyn shot Dottie a quick look. "Mr. Kilter to you, lad. Didn't he bring you here to safety?"

Roselyn had told Dottie that Kilter had rescued Albert from an abusive master, an excuse to keep her close to the boarding house.

Now Roselyn nudged Dottie. "Be an angel, lass, and run upstairs. Make sure all the beds are made tidy. Then you take a break; out with you into that sunshine."

Happily, Dottie went, but not before Roselyn dug in her pocket and gave her a penny. "Buy some of that candy you like so well."

"Oh, thanks, Miss Murphy!" Dottie's smile lit her face.

Cat knew how she felt. She couldn't keep a smile from her face as she opened the kitchen door to Kilter.

"Well, hello!"

"Hello, there." He paused in the doorway and examined her carefully. She tried not to mind that she stood clad in boys' shabby clothing, or that dirt smudged her hands and face. A smile quirked the good side of his mouth. "Working hard, are we?"

"You have no idea." Cat widened her eyes at him. "Do you have news about…about—"

"Hush," Roselyn said quickly, and hurried to shut the door behind Kilter after shooing him in. "Don't speak any names here."

Cat bit her lip, then went and closed the wooden door that led to the long, narrow dining room. When she turned back, she caught Roselyn and Kilter exchanging glances.

"Do you have word?" Roselyn asked.

"Yes. Tate sent me."

"Then sit down, lad. I'll put the kettle on. Albert, you sit too." Roselyn moved as she spoke, her hands already busy with the kettle. "How dire are things?"

Kilter sat, and Cat took the place opposite, where she could look into his face. His gaze touched hers before he said, "There's some good news and some bad. Tate wanted me to let you know he's sent a messenger up to Toronto and your family."

Roselyn leaned against the table. "That's the good news, I'm thinking."

"Yes. We haven't had word back yet, but he's told the man to offer your mother and sister sanctuary if they're willing to come away with him."

"That's very kind," Cat said. Tate Murphy barely knew her, yet he went to such lengths on her behalf.

"That's my big, soft-headed brother for you," Roselyn half joked.

"Please thank him for me." Cat searched Kilter's face again. "And the rest of it?"

"We've had word Boyd's likely to recover. He's in a nursing facility on Elmwood Avenue and said to be angry. Very, very angry."

Cat flinched inwardly. "How do you know?"

"A friend of Tate's is walking out with one of the nurses there. She says he's vowed to find Miss Delaney no matter what it takes. He's already authorized a squad of men to move through the city and hired a small airship to search from above."

Roselyn grunted. "Criminal waste of brass, that is. Only imagine having such money to toss around."

Cat fought the feelings of panic and terror rising inside. "I haven't a chance, then. I'll have to leave here, Miss Murphy."

Roselyn and Kilter both looked alarmed. "Are you mad?" Roselyn asked.

"I'll not bring trouble to your door," Cat vowed, "not when you've been so good to me." Perhaps she'd be better off just turning herself over to Boyd now, before she brought harm down on the heads of her friends.

What would Boyd do to Roselyn if he discovered she'd been sheltering Cat? To Kilter? Cat shivered at the thought of disaster befalling him because of her.

Kilter's blue eyes, so bright in his half-ruined face, became worried. "I don't think there's any need for that. I've come only to warn you about staying close and keeping to your disguise, nothing more. As many resources as Boyd may have, Tate and I know hiding places in this city." He made room on his knee for the little brown dog, whose name Cat had learned was Blossom, and the mutt cuddled into him trustingly.

Lucky mutt, Cat thought ruefully. How she'd like to shelter in his arms. Instead, she said, "You have no reason to place yourselves in jeopardy by helping me. Boyd could ruin Mr. Murphy's business, all he's worked to build. I hate to think what he could do to you."

Kilter shrugged. "So far, he has no reason to suspect we're helping you or that you're hidden here. The instant he does, we'll move you." He gave Cat an intent look. "Neither of us is the man to abandon someone in need."

Cat drew a deep breath that tasted of reassurance. "Thank you, that's very good to know. Please thank Mr. Murphy also, for all the trouble he's taking."

Kilter nodded, and the auburn hair tumbled over the good side of his face. Cat wondered how he might have looked had he never been burned; she suspected he would have been devastatingly attractive, with those high cheekbones and long lashes.

Her heart clenched at the very thought. How terrible it must be for him. Yet right now he represented the largest part of her security, and she watched his big, scarred hand move over Blossom's brown head with increased envy.

The kettle began to sing, and Roselyn reached down two cups and saucers. It had been so long since Cat had been waited on, she nearly leaped up. But Roselyn forestalled her by putting a plate of shortbread on the table.

"There, James, lad, your favorite." She shot a look at Cat. "You can take the Scotsman out of Scotland, but can't take the Scotland out of him—or the love of shortbread. First time I met him, he cleaned a plate."

"Nobody makes shortbread like you, Roselyn," Kilter said appreciatively.

"And here's your tea. The two of you sit and talk; I've tasks elsewhere in the house."

What tasks? Cat wondered. It seemed they'd already taken care of everything. But she craved a few minutes alone with Kilter, even if they spoke only of frightening possibilities.

Roselyn went out, quietly shutting the door to the dining room behind herself. Cat considered all the things she wanted to say and chose one.

"Too bad Boyd didn't die and do the world a favor."

Kilter looked startled. For an instant his fingers paused on Blossom's fur before resuming their gentle motion. "True. Of course you'd be in worse trouble than you are."

"Is there worse trouble? Not only has Boyd sworn vengeance against me—for that's what he's done—but I've dragged people into it with me. I mean it. I'd be better off giving myself up now."

"You wouldn't," he said quickly. "We haven't begun to exhaust our resources. Trust me."

"I do trust you." Completely, implicitly. "I just don't want to bring trouble down upon you."

He shrugged awkwardly. "Not as if I haven't been in deep trouble before. Just look at me." The corner of his mouth quirked again. "Or, rather, spare yourself and don't."

It took Cat an instant to grasp his meaning. When she did, she flushed with annoyance. "I think, James," she used his given name deliberately, "you over exaggerate the effect your appearance has on me."

That made his gaze leap to hers once more, startled. She could see the emotions race through his eyes: denial, embarrassment, disbelief. Ah, then, he didn't think she could look at him and see anything but a monster. She would have to convince him.

"Oh, I know people like that awful Charlie Crowter sneer and beat you over the head with it," she said quickly before he could speak, "and I can't imagine going on so. But please, at least accept that it doesn't matter to me."

"Doesn't matter?" he repeated, a man stunned. "How could it not matter?"

"Because that's not what I see when I look at you."

"By God, what do you see?"

"A kind man, a gentle man. A good man. My friend, I hope. Are we friends?"

Slowly, he nodded.

"Then," she said with a flash of fire, "don't you dare try and tell me how I should or should not feel about you!"

He shook his head, and his gaze momentarily fell to rest on the dog's head. Cat could see—could feel—he still didn't believe. But when his eyes lifted to hers again they held fervor equal to hers.

"And I will do everything I can, Catherine, to keep you safe. That I do promise."

Impulsively, she reached across the table, her hand a silent demand for his. In response, he lifted his scarred fingers from the dog's head and placed them in hers.

"Friends, then," she said devoutly.

"Friends," he agreed, and she squeezed his fingers as if she'd never let go.

Chapter Sixteen

"Tate, have you ever heard of a doctor in this city called Roesch?"

Tate paused in the act of sweeping the yard and shot James a look. The two men had spent the last hour cleaning out the kennels behind the building this warm, sunny afternoon.

"Might have," Tate said cautiously. "Why do you ask?"

"A man mentioned him to me," James said with false nonchalance. "One of the medics back at Boyd's. Said he might be able to do something about this face of mine."

"Some kind of operation, you mean, on them scars?"

"To make me look human." James thought again of Catherine, so beautiful despite her lad's clothing and cropped hair, sitting across the table from him at Roselyn's. *You over exaggerate the effect your appearance has on me.* A nice sentiment, a sweet lie, but one he just couldn't bring himself to believe. How could it possibly fail to matter to her, even if she had declared herself his friend?

Tate's gaze softened, and he clamped a hand on James' shoulder. "You already are human, lad—far more so than half the feckers in this city."

"I said I want to *look* human." Bitterness filled

James' voice. "What do you know about this doctor?"

"Only what I've heard through Brendan Fagan. Roesch is the doctor, see, the police called in to study on those hybrid steamies after the warden, Maynard, got tossed out and things were cleaned up at the jail. He examined the methods those two mad geniuses used to keep skin growing over metal."

James said nothing, and Tate asked, "What's in that head of yours, lad?"

"I'm thinking I should go and see him."

"What's brought this on?"

James sat back on his heels in front of one of the cages and frowned. The dog inside pressed itself into James' hands through the now-open door and wiggled in delight.

"After all"—Tate nodded at the animal—"those of us who love you don't care."

"Maybe I care. Have you thought of that? Maybe I'm fed up with looking at myself in the mirror while I shave half my face, and with seeing how I look reflected in strangers' eyes."

"Ah, well." Momentarily taken aback, Tate stood staring away at nothing. "I can't imagine the services of such a man would come cheap."

"Then I'll need to earn more. Give me a second job. Or if you don't want to, I'll look elsewhere."

"Peace, lad." Again Tate's hand came down on James' shoulder. "I didn't say I won't help you. You know you're like a brother to me, more than anything."

James refused to look at Tate again, but tears blurred his vision. It had been years since he'd cried over anything—he'd learned too well, back before his face healed, how tears stung. Stoicism, that was the only way.

He blinked fiercely. "You're not a wealthy man, with money to toss around. You work hard as anyone."

Tate mused, "But this wouldn't be tossing money around, would it, lad? Tossing money around would be going on a bender or spending it on the ponies. Go see the doctor if you want to. See what's what, and then talk to me again. If he's after saying he can help you, we'll find a way."

James' heart wobbled between hope and despair. *If he can help you.* A big question.

The dog crawled into his lap and licked his chin. Why couldn't the rest of the world see him the way these animals did?

"You know I'll pay you back, Tate," he said, still not looking at his friend.

"Damn right you will." A laugh filled Tate's voice. "Now back to work with you, and look sharp."

****

It didn't take long for James to ferret out the doctor's location—not one of the big houses on Elmwood or Delaware, as he might have expected, but a modest building down on Franklin Street. He even walked by it later that week, but he didn't go in. Honesty forced him to admit he feared to, not because of any potential pain or even embarrassment but because if Roesch said he couldn't help him, James' last hope would die. And right now he needed to hold on to that hope.

Catherine remained on his mind and in his heart all the time. She danced through his inner vision and he saw again the way she'd looked at him, the smile in her eyes. He felt the way her little fingers clutched his across Roselyn's kitchen table, fiercely tight.

He saw once more how she'd appeared the first time he beheld her disembarking from Boyd's airship, her hair a blaze of red-gold in the afternoon light. Unquestionably the loveliest woman he'd ever seen.

And that made good reason why he couldn't give her his heart—poor battered and blackened member that it was. Even if his wildest dreams came true and Roesch agreed to operate on him, if he underwent a surgery or a set of them, he could not imagine he'd look perfect or anything close to it.

Catherine, beautiful Catherine, deserved perfection.

Put these feelings away from you, idiot, he lectured himself. You knew you'd never have a woman in your life other than those who take money to bed you. You knew all the while love was for other men.

Still, his anguish affected his mind. He was so surly during his court appearance, he nearly won himself jail time instead of just a fine. Tate complained about him being cranky around the place, and he got into an argument that very nearly came to blows with that wretch, Drappot.

"Shut that dog of yours up nights," Drappot warned him, "or I'll do it for you."

"Touch one hair on her body and you'll not move again," James returned, aching—just aching—for an excuse to pummel the smaller man.

Then, three days after James' discussion with Tate, the boss came to him, looking grim.

"Jamie, lad, I've just had word that fecker Boyd's out of the hospital and back in the grand house on The Avenue. Brendan Fagan, it was, sent me the news. Apparently Boyd's had the authorities in, asking what can be done to track down his 'assailant'."

"Catherine, you mean."

"Aye. He was told the police would make what inquiries they could. Brendan, now, Brendan may have his suspicions that we're involved. I've been asking him to keep me informed, after all. But he'll not rat on me. There's a brotherhood even beyond that of the Buffalo police force."

"Of Irishmen."

Gravely, Tate nodded. "Brendan says that Boyd, not satisfied with the official response, has vowed to increase his efforts to find wee Catherine. Here's where it gets dangerous."

"Yes." Boyd would employ all his resources, which were undoubtedly considerable. "Why can't he just let her go?"

"Men like him don't. 'Tis a matter of pride with him, isn't it? He's not about to relinquish what he considers a possession. Anyway, you'd best get over to Roselyn's and warn them. I know they've been keeping the lass close, but they'll need to be twice as careful now."

James just nodded, but his heart leaped. An excuse to see her again, his *friend*. A mixture of eagerness and frustration gripped him, not half of the flesh.

"And stay away from Drappot," Tate said. "I don't need any more complications."

The afternoon brooded around James as he went: close, gray, and threatening rain, the kind of weather than often placed him on edge—as if he wasn't already on edge enough. The streets seemed even more crowded than usual, choked with steamcabs, cart grocers and pedestrians, forcing him to shorten his stride, detour around immobile groups, and grow still more aggravated.

On the corner of Prospect and Carolina Street, very nearly in front of Roselyn's boarding house, traffic had come to a complete stop. At first glance, James thought there had been an accident. He could see two steamcabs halted at the intersection, both exhaling trails of vapor like impatience, and foot traffic seemed to be diverting around them. Not until he reached the corner itself did he see the problem.

A delivery wagon had halted in the intersection, half blocking it, leaving room for pedestrians but not cabs to get by. One of the horse-drawn wagons it was, well-loaded with coal, and its driver had disembarked to deal with his recalcitrant horse.

James' stomach soured; he detested steamcabs on general principle and because of their noise and dirt. But he knew very well a delivery or carriage horse's existence could be grim and terrible. They worked long hours, often without adequate food or care, and his heart bled for their plight.

He eyed the horse in question, now: a well-aged beast, it stood as if carved of rock, all four hooves set, looking like it might never move again. Its driver, obviously furious, shouted at it and gestured, to no avail.

Keep out of it, James told himself. There's nothing you can do for the poor beast. It happens all over the city and, as Tate always says, you can't save everyone.

But the ugly frustration that had gathered inside him for days stirred, and when he saw the driver go back to the wagon and take up a crop, it threatened to burst like water from a dam.

"Move, you misbegotten pile of bones! Move or I'll teach you better!" The driver began to rain blows upon the unfortunate animal. Pedestrians looked away, the steamcab drivers turned their heads. Only a couple of steam servants out on errands—slaves just like the horse—stood and stared, they and James. But he didn't stand; he hurried forward as fast as his feet would carry him.

Before he reached the wagon he saw the horse's legs begin to tremble. It went down slowly, front legs first and then the back, with the red-faced driver still whaling on it.

"What in hell do you think you're doing?" James didn't recognize his own voice. Surprise arrested the driver's arm, and he gazed into James' face, startled. His eyes widened with alarm.

Had James been thinking clearly at this point, he might have divined the man's thoughts: *monster*. James knew his face, never pretty, became truly frightening when rage overcame him. And rage now had the upper hand.

The driver raised his crop again. The next blow never descended because James gripped the arm with a force just short of that needed to break the bone.

"Leave go of me!"

"Stop beating your animal."

"Not mine, the ugly, scrawny nag. Belongs to my boss, and I'm sick of him giving me the oldest horse in his stable. Let go, I tell you! This is none of your business. And I have to get the friggin' thing to move, don't I?"

"No."

"I can't leave it here blocking the road." The man

drew his arm from James' grip and struck the horse once more—one last time. Light that also, somehow, contained a great deal of darkness exploded behind James' eyes.

He snatched the crop from the fellow's grasp, snapped it between his hands, and tossed it away, telling himself he needed nothing but his two fists. With rampant satisfaction, he smiled into the bully's eyes and waded in.

Chapter Seventeen

Cat had nearly finished peeling her way through a mountain of potatoes when Dottie burst into the kitchen, dust cloth still in hand, and cried, "Come quick, Miss Murphy! There's a man gone mad in the street, beating someone to death."

Roselyn, kneading bread dough at the other end of the big table, swore under her breath—words Cat imagined no respectable woman should know—and drew her fists from the dough.

Breathless, Dottie continued, "Ben says he thinks it's your friend, Mr. Kilter."

"What?" Cat leaped up and her paring knife clattered onto the table. As she moved to the door Roselyn cried, "Albert—don't you be going out without your cap on your head!"

But Cat paid no heed. She trod on Dottie's heels, and they burst out the front door together, joining a crowd that already contained many onlookers. Cat blinked in disbelief, and then blinked again.

A large cart horse, still in its traces, had gone down in the street. Cat couldn't tell if it lived or had expired on the spot. Two figures beside it had become the center of all attention. One of them she recognized as James Kilter, though had he not been so constantly on her mind these past days she might not have known him. His damaged face, now further disfigured by a terrible grimace, looked barely human, and his eyes blazed.

The other man—the cart driver?—lay beneath him, back on the bricks of the street and doubtless unconscious. That didn't keep James from striking him again and again with fists like hammers, without so much as a hint of the mercy she usually saw in him.

"Christ!" she breathed. And then, racing forward without a thought she cried, "Jamie! Jamie!"

By the time she worked her way through the intervening onlookers and reached the confrontation, two Buffalo police officers had arrived. One of them threw out an arm and barred Cat's way when she would have rushed in.

"Here, lad, keep back."

"But I know him. I know him!"

"Which of them?" asked the officer. Surely close to the age of retirement, he sweated in his too-tight uniform, looking unhappy with the situation. But his partner was a big, strapping fellow who looked all too capable of taking James on.

"Him!" She supposed she made no sense; she didn't care. "Jamie, Jamie!"

Kilter did not respond. Blood spattered his fists and seeped from half a dozen places on his opponent's face.

"Get him up out of there, Kelly," the first officer told the second. The big fellow went in, seized James, and pinned his arms behind him, hauling him up.

But so great was Kilter's rage he threw the fellow off and turned on him, blue eyes blazing. His gaze slid over Cat without recognition. Some sort of wild madness did indeed possess him, and the strength of a thousand.

The crowd gasped and murmured. Would James be so reckless as to engage in fisticuffs with a police officer? The two big men squared off, and Cat's heart sank violently.

The big officer closed and grappled with James, who again threw him off with apparent ease. Roselyn chose that moment to hurry up, puffing.

"Do something!" Cat entreated her. "What's come over him?"

"Gone off kilter, he has," Roselyn declared. "It's happened before. Sweet saints and the holy mother, this can't end well."

Indeed, it couldn't. The senior officer loudly began to inform James he was under arrest, while the young one circled with obvious intent to seize him yet again.

James threw one more punch that crashed into the big officer's jaw, rocked him back on his heels, but didn't fell him. Then James turned and went to his knees beside the stricken cart horse.

The crowd exclaimed as he put his arms about the beast and tried to lift it up, and Cat's heart constricted in her chest. He'd moved from mindless violence to total compassion.

Yet no man, however strong, could hope to lift a ton of cart horse. The animal stayed down, its head nodding, with James Kilter entreating it beneath the gray sky.

An emotion Cat couldn't name took her forward. She dodged the big police officer, who stood looking on, and went to her knees at James' side.

"Jamie, let me help."

He disregarded her as if she weren't there. His big hands, smeared with blood, caressed the horse's neck and withers, and he crooned like a gentle song, "Come on, my beauty. Get up for me. It's safe now—I've served the brute as he deserves. Come on, I'll call the anti-cruelty league and get you clean away from him, so I will."

The horse's ear twitched, and it blew out a breath. James' arms closed about it again, and he lifted. Cat added her puny strength to his, but still the poor beast failed to rise.

Cat bleated over her shoulder, at the crowd, "Help us!"

A few souls came forward—a man carrying packages which he set aside, a maid from one of the nearby houses, even a steam servant, its metal surface gleaming in the dim afternoon. With gentle care, they urged the animal up. It struggled to rise, and Cat felt someone take the place at her side. From the corner of her eye she caught a glimpse of blue and, to her shock, realized she stood shoulder to shoulder with the big police officer.

The cart horse heaved and came to its feet.

Some members of the crowd cheered. Even Cat knew that a horse down in distress rarely got up again. She looked into James' face, hoping for some sign of satisfaction, but saw bewilderment and hard anger yet.

"Very heroic, my lad." The elder of the two officers stepped up to James. "But you're still under arrest for assault and battery."

James looked not at him but at Kelly, the officer who'd helped lift the horse. "Will you make sure the anti-cruelty league is called? I'll not have this animal go back to that bastard."

Kelly nodded. Cat, who stood between the two

men, looked into his face. Incredibly, only then did she realize Kelly wasn't entirely human. Shock raced through her: he must be one of the automatons covered with human skin; she'd heard about them.

"What about your victim?" asked the first officer, the human one.

Roselyn fought her way to their side. "Officer, I know this man. He works for my brother, Michael Murphy. You can see he was provoked. The cart driver clearly abused this helpless animal."

"That, ma'am, doesn't justify beating the man half to death."

"It does," Cat murmured, and shot another concerned look at James, who stood like a man coming slowly out of a nightmare. His gaze swept over Cat, still without recognition, and moved to the face of the hybrid automaton.

"Sir," it—he—said, "you must come with me."

"All right."

"Jamie. Jamie!" Cat seized both his forearms; her touch seemed to steady and rouse him. The confused, blue eyes focused on her for the first time.

"Sir." Roselyn stepped in and spoke to the elder officer, not the hybrid. "Surely there's no need to take him to the station. It's plain what happened here. That lout was abusing his animal."

"I sympathize, ma'am, really I do. I hate bullies, myself. But he laid that fellow out." The officer nodded to the steam ambulance, now just arriving. "The man will have to go to the hospital."

Roselyn gnawed her lip and eyed James. "I'll send word to Tate," she told him. "Don't worry; he'll be down to the station directly."

Laura Strickland

James' gaze never wavered from Cat's, and his forearms, beneath her fingers, had gone rigid.

The elder police officer lowered his voice and whispered to Roselyn, "What's the matter with him? Is he mad?"

"A crusader, is our James Kilter," Roselyn replied. "Carried away by his fervor sometimes."

"Fervor, is it?"

James bent his head toward Cat's. His mottled face, which had been flushed with rage, was now pale beneath its scarring. "I was supposed to warn you," he said.

"Warn me?"

"Boyd. Looking for you. You must stay close." His eyes caressed her. "Safe."

"Come along then, son. You're going to the station."

The first police officer gestured to the automaton, who drew James' hands from Cat's grasp.

"No," she said, "let me go with him."

"Now, sonny, the jail's no place for you, not if you're smart. You wait here while we take care of this."

"Please," Cat beseeched, and tears came to her eyes. And, as he was hauled away, inexorably, she cried, "Jamie!"

James' broad back twitched, but he never looked back at her, not once.

Chapter Eighteen

"Jamie!"

Catherine's cry still echoed in James' ears as the police marched him to where the paddy wagon waited nearby. His senses—and his sense—returned to him slowly, the darkness clearing away like rainclouds after a storm. But there was a great black span of time during which he could not remember what he'd done.

There had been a horse and a man abusing it. He looked down at his hands and saw them spattered with blood, likely none of his. He heaved a great sigh.

Not again. What had he done? And Catherine—Catherine had been there, had witnessed all.

That was it, then. Any hope he'd ever had of winning her—of having her—had just died on the bricks of the street. Not that he'd had any real hope anyway. Oh, she said she was his friend, and that was generous of her, but for all his wanting it could go no further. Only look at him. Look at her. Even with Roesch's help he would be a freak, at best, and he'd no assurance of Roesch's help.

He jerked a look at the police officer beside him— a damned automaton, a hybrid at that. If rumors proved true, Dr. Roesch would have studied him. He would know the man.

James might ask…but no. The hybrids made his skin crawl, and anyway, he was under arrest. Besides, there was no point; he'd just destroyed any chance he ever had with Catherine.

Fool that he was! He'd been supposed to protect her. Fine lot of good he could do her now. Yet the man had been beating the horse, an animal clearly too exhausted to pull its load. He couldn't just stand by, could he? No matter what it cost him.

The human police officer opened the back of the paddy wagon and pushed James in. The interior smelled of other men's sweat, puke, and despair. James sat on the bench and put his head in his hands.

Catherine. As the dark mist cleared, he saw the look in her eyes when she clutched at him. Oh, what had he done?

When they reached the station the big automaton, whom the other officer called Kelly, hustled James out with brusque efficiency and stood by while he was booked, motionless as a steamie on shut down. What did they expect him to do? Go off kilter again? Wreck the place? No, for all the fight had gone out of him, leaving him sick and cold.

Every officer on duty must have filed past while the sergeant processed him, to stare. Kelly met each of them with an implacable gaze that, though intent, moved them on. And after, it was he who accompanied James to a cell, putting him into the last empty unit alone even though the other two had multiple occupants.

Kelly stood for a moment and regarded James through the bars, and James wondered what he thought. Did hybrids think? The broad, good-looking face seemed curiously hard to read. Yet surely he, James, should be the last to question what went on behind a mask.

"You want me to contact someone for you?" Kelly's voice must come from a mechanical voice box, yet it sounded like that of no steamie James had ever heard, clear and very high-quality. James had to remind himself these units burned coal, like any other mechanical. Only their appearance—and some ineffable essence—made them seem human.

The opposite of me. It's my appearance makes me less than human.

He shook his head. Sick to the heart, he couldn't imagine lumbering Tate with this. Struggling to think, he realized Roselyn would no doubt send a message to Tate anyway. But he, James, deserved to be left here to rot.

Kelly stepped closer to the bars. His eyes, a curious shade of green, rested impassively on James' face. "The way cart horses are treated in this city is abominable. They are no better than slaves. I will make sure the animal in question is rescued from its owner's hands."

James heart leaped. "Thank you."

Kelly nodded. He turned on his heel and marched out, leaving James feeling marginally better. Maybe he'd done some good after all.

****

"Well, and sure this is getting to be an unfortunate habit. Did I not just buy your way out of this place a few days ago?"

James looked up when he heard the familiar voice, and the despair that hovered around him like a cloud deepened. He felt sick to his heart, and the sight of Tate, his broad face creased in a frown, did nothing to help.

"Just leave me," he said. "I deserve to be here. Go home and forget I exist."

He wished he could forget he existed. Ugly, foolish, and prone to rages—what good could he do in the world? As the hours in the cell dragged by, he'd convinced himself he had absolutely no value and had ended up where he belonged.

"Ah, so it's that way, is it?" Tate returned. "Sitting there drowning in self-pity, are you?"

James glared at his friend. "Any better suggestions?"

"Aye. Pull yourself up by your socks and resolve to live a better life."

"Better?" James laughed bitterly. "How is anything better for me being in the world?"

"Those dogs back in the kennel might claim to be, plus that poor cart horse back there. I heard what happened from Albert and Roselyn."

Albert. James groaned. "Albert saw what I did."

"Not setting a perfect example for a young lad, are you? Unless you want to teach him to stand up for what he believes in."

"Go away, dammit, and leave me alone."

"Is that what you really want? To stew in here?"

"Yes."

"Because you will. They've hauled the coal driver away to hospital, but I can't imagine he'll fail to press charges, can you?"

"No."

"That means jail time, unless I can talk to Brendan."

"Don't bother, Tate. You've done enough for me."

"Ah, well, I'll just abandon you to your misery,

shall I?"

James lifted anguished eyes to Tate's face. "You'll look after the dogs, will you? And—Albert?"

"I thought you'd rather be on that task. But since you're willing to renounce the world and all your responsibilities with it…"

"I didn't say that."

"Aye, laddie, I think you did. If you change your mind and want my help, send word to Brendan or tell Officer Kelly. He seems to have taken an interest in you—don't ask me why."

Perhaps because a freak knows a freak when he sees one, James thought. He lowered his head back into his hands and never looked up as Tate walked away.

****

"Is he all right? Jamie—is he all right?" Cat virtually threw herself at Tate when he entered the boarding house, stopping just short of seizing hold of the big Irishman.

Tate gave her a kind look tinged with sympathetic impatience. "Depends on your definition of 'all right,' Albert. At the moment, he's fallen into a well of self-pity and decided the world is better without him."

"But that's not true." Aghast, Cat stared into Tate's face. "You must convince him otherwise."

"You think I didn't try? Ah, Albert, you don't know what our James is like when he goes off kilter. He is never too happy with himself, after."

"I don't care." Cat drew herself up to her full height. "Take me to see him, then. I'll convince him."

Tate exchanged looks with Roselyn, who stood drying her hands on her apron. "At the station? I think not."

"Wherever I have to go, I will." Cat drew a determined breath. "You don't know me very well, Mr. Murphy. But I'll do anything—anything—to help those for whom I care."

"Care, is it?" The corners of Tate's eyes crinkled. "Right now he doesn't think anybody should care for him—thinks he doesn't deserve it."

"All the more reason for me to tell him differently." Cat would pour out what lay in her heart if she had to. But she couldn't be all that sure what did lie in her heart. The past hours, since Jamie was hauled away, had proved agonizing. Her emotions made such a tangled knot in her chest she didn't know how to unravel them.

"Please," she beseeched Murphy.

"Best you stay here for the time being. Despite what he says, I'm working on getting the lad out of there, with the help of some friends on the force. He'll have to report back before a judge, of course, and it's his third infraction in a couple weeks. Doesn't look good."

Cat thought, wildly, about chances and opportunities. What if she and James ran away together, started somewhere fresh? But she couldn't do that either. She had her sister to consider.

"Mr. Murphy, have you had any word from Toronto?"

"No. But James was on his way here to warn you when all hell broke loose. Boyd's out of the hospital and on the warpath. That's why I say you should stay close. Roselyn, keep Albert in, will you?"

Dryly, Roselyn reminded him, "Albert has just been out in the street, and without his cap, for all to see."

"I know better now. But please, Mr. Murphy, will you bring Jamie by here when he gets released, so I can assure myself he's come to no harm?"

"I'll do my best, so long as you'll have a care meanwhile. Stay in your room or the kitchen, where the boarders can't see you. Boyd has deep pockets and you never know who'll rise to the bait."

"Aye, run off to your room now, Albert," Roselyn bade. "Leave me to have a word with my brother."

Cat climbed the battered wooden stairs, her heart like a stone. Would Roselyn decide Cat's presence here made too much of a complication and ask her to leave? If so, Cat could scarcely blame her.

Her room, when she reached it, felt close and stuffy, but she shut the door anyway, then went to the crooked window and forced it open. The furor in the street had cleared as if nothing had ever happened. Both the horse and the coal wagon were gone. Rain pelted down in big, angry drops from a sky as gray as granite. Folks hurried about their business with determined strides and hunched shoulders.

Cat thought again of Jamie as she'd last seen him. She knew him to be a champion of animals—especially those downtrodden—and to possess a generous heart, but what could cause him to leave go of his senses that way?

Off kilter, Murphy called it.

Upon that thought she saw Tate emerge from the door three stories below and leaned out to call down. "Mr. Murphy—a word with you, please."

Murphy glared up at her. "Get inside, for God's sake. I'll come up."

She heard his large boots clattering on every flight and awaited him at her door.

"Holy Mary, 'tis a hot box up here, and no mistake," he observed. He shot her a close look. "Quite the comedown for you, isn't it, Miss Delaney?"

"I'm not complaining. Please, Mr. Murphy, if you can spare me a minute…"

"Little more than that, lass. I need to see a man about releasing a fool from a jail cell."

"That's what I wanted to discuss."

"Somehow I thought it might be. Interested in Jamie, are you, lass?"

"Interested?"

He arched his brows in a manner that made his meaning clear. "Interested. You being a young woman and him a young man—despite what he claims."

Cat's cheeks flamed, but she tipped up her chin. "It wouldn't do me much good, would it? It isn't as if he's attracted to me."

"If you think that, you're more an idjit than you look."

"He's an extraordinary man."

"That he is, and one with a load of trouble on his shoulders."

"That's what I wanted to ask: this 'off kilter' thing, as you call it. Why does it happen?"

Murphy shrugged heavily. "He has triggers. The main one is abuse."

"Tell me, please."

"I'm not sure he'd be wanting me to do that."

"But I need to understand. If I—if he…" Abruptly Cat's words failed her.

"Are you after saying you'd like a future with

him?"

"I don't know, do I? I like and respect him immensely. At least, I did."

"Before you saw him half beat the life out of someone?" Murphy sighed. "Well then, lass, James had a complicated sort of love-hate relationship with his ma. His pa died early, when he was no more than a wee sprog. There was a younger child also, a sister."

"Oh."

"James' mother had to go out and work long hours to keep her bairns fed. It's a common story in this city and many others, and especially hard for women with no man. James both adored his ma for the terrible sacrifices she made, and abhorred how she took out her weariness and inability to cope."

Aghast, Cat wondered, "She never beat her children?"

"Do not look so shocked. As a child, were you never whacked?"

Dumbly, Cat shook her head.

"Ah well, a swat here or there, or the slap of a wee hand, may be called for—who am I to say? James and his sister got more than that. Eventually he stood up to his ma to protect little Janet.

"I'll tell you now, Miss Delaney, so you do not hear it elsewhere: the rumor mill in this city says James killed his mother one night—'kilt her' is what they say when they taunt him. Not true. I made it a point to find out when I decided to help the lad, plus I heard the story from James' own lips.

"He came upon his mother hitting wee Janet one night, and got between them. His ma had knocked the lass down, and she continued with hitting Jamie, as

Laura Strickland

well. He shouted at her, 'Keep it up, Ma, and you'll kill both of us!' The woman came to herself, so he said, went pale as a sheet, and fell down dead before help could come." Murphy grimaced. "James always blamed himself."

"For God's sake, why?"

"He asserts his mother worked herself to death—the doc said it was her heart—for his and Janet's keep. Ironic that, for wee Janet perished soon after her ma, from the battery her head had taken."

"He lost them both?"

"He did. And since then any kind of cruelty—especially toward those weaker than him—has been a trigger, his only one, so far as I can tell."

"Thank you for telling me, Mr. Murphy."

"You've no need to fear him, lass."

"No, I know that."

"And please don't harden your heart against him."

Cat didn't think she could.

Chapter Nineteen

"I don't want to stop at Roselyn's," James said stubbornly, and not for the first time. Morning had come, but the rain still pissed down, and the smell of the river hung heavy in the air. Glad as he might be to get sprung from the small cell at the jailhouse, he felt like finding some other hole into which he might crawl.

"I told Miss Delaney I'd bring you by."

James shot Tate a resentful look from the corner of his eye. And there it was, the reason he didn't want to stop at Roselyn's. He didn't think he could bear to see Catherine. At the same time, he longed to see her. It was enough to drive a man mad.

"Why did you tell her that?"

"She's worried about you, lad. The last time she saw you—"

James drew himself up against the rain. "I am perfectly aware how I must have looked the last time she saw me." As if he weren't already repulsive enough. "Tate, I can't."

"Thought you'd set yourself up as her protector. How are you going to protect her from a distance, lad?"

"All that's over and done."

He'd thrown it away in the street, while pummeling the cart driver. The man's name, as he'd since learned, was Schmidt. Tate said he was in hospital and expected to make a full recovery. "Lucky for you," Tate had added. "If you're truly fortunate, you'll get off with another fine."

A whopping big one, no doubt. Where was James expected to come up with the money? There went any hope of begging or borrowing funds to pay Dr. Roesch, and any hope of making him less a monster.

"Tate," he said now, "I just want to go home." He'd not slept in that place, with both his mind and heart too full.

"Do I look like I care what you want?" Tate returned.

"No."

"Come do your duty and set the lass's mind to rest."

The clatter of dishes and the smell of home cooking greeted them when they entered the kitchen. To James' surprise, his stomach rumbled. He hadn't wanted to eat inside, either.

Dottie shot them a surprised look and then hurried out to the dining room with a heaping bowl of potatoes.

A lad with a narrow back labored at the stove. Only she wasn't a lad, as James saw when Cat turned around. Her eyes widened at the sight of him, and her face transformed with joy. The ladle she held dropped from her hand.

"Jamie!"

She flew around—or perhaps over—the end of the table and launched herself into his arms.

And oh, how she fit there all warm and ardent, pressed against him. She clenched her arms about his middle and pressed in tight, cheek against his chest above his heart and head tucked beneath his chin. James froze for an instant, the wind knocked from him by

136

more than just the impact, before folding his arms around her.

Dimly he saw Tate move past them and take up a station at the door to the dining room, assuring no one could come in, but most of James' attention centered on the trembling woman in his arms, and the intensity of her embrace.

The agony that had filled him for days seemed to ease for the first time, as warmth took its place.

"Are you all right?" She tipped her face and gazed into his eyes, but her arms never loosened.

He longed to say, *Don't look at me.* Shame made him want to push her away, even as he ached to keep her where she was. He found himself incapable of speaking a word. Instead, he nodded.

"You're sure? You weren't harmed during that fight? Has a doctor seen you?"

"Not me." His voice sounded gruff to his own ears. What was that he saw in her beautiful eyes? It couldn't possibly be meant for him. "I put that other fellow in hospital."

"He was a brute."

"That doesn't make it right, what I did." He forced the words out.

"Of course not. But the way I see it, you had tremendous justification." She reached up and touched the good side of his face, then put her fingers through his hair. A smile further lit her eyes. "You're all wet."

"It's raining pretty hard. But Tate said—he said you wanted to see me." James resisted the impulse to close his eyes and press into her hand, pretend for a minute that he was just a man with a beautiful woman in his arms.

"I did, oh, I did! I've been on pins and needles. What happens now? Are you out for good?"

"No. There'll be a hearing and probably a sentencing."

"Well, never mind. We'll cross that bridge when we get to it."

We? Madness rose in a wild bubble to James' head. But this made a good kind of madness.

Someone tried to come in the kitchen door. Tate hissed to whoever was on the other side and then slipped through, leaving them alone.

"Thank goodness. I thought he'd never go." Catherine gazed up into James' eyes and linked her arms around his neck. He stiffened. The soft skin of her left wrist brushed against the scar tissue that covered his right cheek. She shouldn't…she shouldn't be touching him that way. Abhorrence on her behalf rose inside.

But she seemed to see none of that. The smile in her eyes became daring and wickedly bright.

"I promised myself I would do this as soon as I saw you again."

As simply as that—as if it were not a miracle of the first water—she rose on tiptoe and pressed her mouth to his.

Wonder flooded through him, tangled with a measure of horror and unbearable need. He knew very well that half of his mouth, the lips thickened and twisted, barely resembled a mouth at all. That she would consent—more, choose—to touch it with her perfect lips like rose petals almost felled him where he stood. On the heels of those emotions came desire, roaring like a train. He'd wanted this woman from the moment he saw her, and now, against all likelihood, he had her in his arms.

As simple, and as incredibly complicated, as that.

He groaned like a dying man, and she opened her mouth beneath his. This could not be what it seemed—blatant invitation. She couldn't possibly want his tongue in her mouth. But that organ, acting without his volition just like the one lower down, thrust forth and claimed her sweetness in rampant victory.

Catherine, he wanted to say, but there were no words, only the way she trembled and pressed tight against him so he could feel her breasts beneath her shirt, as surely she must be able to feel the strength of his arousal. Did she know what that meant? Would she realize a monster desired her and back away?

For an instant he felt certain she must, for she broke the kiss and said unsteadily, "I was so worried for you. And Mr. Murphy said you might not want to see me."

"I didn't."

"Why?"

"Because." He unlinked his hands from where they'd settled at the small of her back, just above her delightful bottom, and gestured wildly to the side of his face. "This."

"Fool!" Emotion flared in her eyes, and she pressed herself still closer, parts of her cradling pertinent parts of him. "When I look at you I don't see…" Again she caressed his face, touched his hair. "Jamie, people are part good and part bad, light and darkness. Can't you see that? But inside, you're all light."

He hung his head. "I'm not, Catherine. I beat a man in the street."

"I see—"

"Hush." He raised his hands also to cup her face, silken soft and all perfection. He wanted this moment, wanted to pretend when he looked at her that the impossible might be true.

But Catherine said stubbornly, "I see you as you are, not as you appear."

Impossible. A wonderful, beautiful thing for her to say, but beyond what he could believe. If he couldn't ignore his face, how could she? And he got reminded of how he looked every time he gazed into someone else's eyes.

Except now, gazing into hers.

Emotion exploded through him, lifted his heart. He trembled where he stood.

"So," she spoke softly, with that teasing note back in her voice, "are you going to stand there staring at me, or are you going to kiss me again?"

Kiss her? He wanted to go down on his knees, throw himself at her feet, worship her from her toes to the top of her shorn head slowly and deliberately, taking extra time over certain places between. Yet she raised that challenging gaze to him, lifted that sweet bud of a mouth, and he fell into her, lost like a man overboard at sea with no hope of land.

The door to the dining room snicked open as someone peered in. He heard Roselyn's voice exclaim before the door shut again. He didn't care, he didn't, he didn't. He was far too busy feeling complete.

Chapter Twenty

Morning sun beat insistently on the tiny window of Cat's room and quickly heated the air. She opened her eyes, wondering why she felt so marvelously different, and then remembered what had happened in the kitchen last night.

Jamie.

Ah, Jamie. A smile curled her lips and she stretched in the narrow cot, testing a body that seemed to have awakened aroused. She'd dreamed of him most the night. Curiously, in the dreams she'd seen him as he might have been, should have been, his face unmarked, one side reflecting the handsomeness of the other—the way she saw him in her heart. She'd kissed him in her dreams too, again and again.

No wonder she awoke on fire for him. The taste of him still seemed to fill her, and the elusive, beguiling scent that went straight to her head. The feel of his big, warm hands seemed to have imprinted itself all over her body, wherever he'd touched her last night. She loved the way he touched her with careful gentleness that made her feel priceless. She closed her eyes and remembered how the damp from his clothes had soaked through hers to the skin, how she'd ripened and peaked for him, how the weight of him, pressing against her, made her long to offer him anything and everything. She'd never yet lain with any man, but she'd wanted to beg him to stay the night, had longed to bring him up here with her, fuse her body with his, and own him completely.

But she'd seen the look in his eyes just before passion filled them. She knew he failed to believe she desired him.

Oh Jamie, Jamie.

How to convince him that what she felt, she felt true? How to convey that she'd hungered for the feel of his mouth—misshapen or not—on hers? That ever since he'd held her in comfort, back in her room at the vile Boyd's, she'd craved the feeling of being safe in his arms?

Not half of what she craved now…

She should be shocked by herself, but she wanted James Kilter between her legs where no man had been, wanted him badly. She rarely gave in to desiring anything for herself. Oh, she'd had clothes and hats, even jewelry. But her real desires had been for others— her mother and Becky. She wanted them safe and happy, and still did.

Now, though, she wanted something solely for herself—Jamie Kilter. She would battle for him if she had to, fight the way she had against Boyd's advances, like an angry cat. But she knew she'd be battling first against Jamie's doubt.

How could she convince him that, to her, he was a whole man and wholly desirable? She could think of one or two ways, and her lips curved again in an anticipatory smile.

She rose from the cot and went to peer out the window. Last night's rain had cleared, and the sky looked fresh-washed, the last clouds driven by a breeze from the direction of the river. Where was Jamie now? Mr. Murphy had dragged him away last night, after Roselyn came into the kitchen and declared in a scandalized whisper, "Shameless! What would my guests say if they saw a great lump of a man and a lad kissing?"

A tap sounded on Cat's door, and it opened to admit Dottie's head. The girl, already clad for work, wore a white cap and a look of avid curiosity.

"Albert, can I come in?"

Cat crossed her arms over her chest. She wore only undergarments and feared the girl might see too much, but Dottie grinned.

"Don't bother. You're not really Albert, are you?"

"Come in and shut the door."

Dottie obeyed and perched at the end of the cot, a look of wonder on her sharp face. "Who are you, then?"

Cat gave her a searching look. "Can you keep a secret?"

"I can."

"I'm a woman, as you've guessed, in a lot of trouble and hiding out here for now. Someone's looking for me, a terrible man."

"I thought it must be something like that. Miss Murphy wouldn't say a thing when I asked. To tell you the truth, I had my suspicions even before I tried to come into the kitchen last night and saw the two of you. Who's the terrible man that's looking for you?"

"Probably better if you don't know."

"How does Mr. Kilter come into it?" Dottie's eyes widened. "Why were you kissing him?"

"Why do you suppose?"

"Well, I've been wondering about that all night.

The only person I've ever kissed was the butcher's boy. Did more than kiss him, truth be told."

"Dottie!"

"And the butcher's boy's no beauty—looks a bit like the butcher's bulldog, in fact—but he's not..." Words failed Dottie. She made a gesture of futility with her hands.

"He's not what?" Cat demanded.

"You know."

Cat sincerely liked Dottie, but now protective anger arose in her breast. "Say it. You might as well. Thousands will."

"Half a man."

Rage ignited. "James Kilter is not half a man." She had felt all of him, in the kitchen.

"Half a face, then. And half—"

"Do you suppose that's all I'm looking at?"

"Hard not to look at it, right? I'm only being honest."

Honest, appalled, and disbelieving. If Cat couldn't convince Dottie, who had no dog in the fight, how would she ever convince Jamie?

"He has beautiful eyes."

"Has he? I'll admit," Dottie said, "I find it hard to actually look into his face."

"More loss for you, then." The anger inside Cat flared brighter.

Dottie shrugged. "Each to her own, I guess. But why kiss him?"

"Because I wanted to. I still do. I can't wait to kiss him again. I hope it'll be today."

Dottie's shoulders twitched. She got up from the cot. "You're angry. I'd hoped we could be friends, but—"

"We can, so long as you never say anything cruel about Jamie Kilter."

"You love him."

"Eh?"

Dottie stated it again with the inevitability of fact. "You're in love with the man."

Was she? Cat's eyes widened. Could it be? She desired him, yes, like a rampant fire burning. She meant to have him by hook or by crook, as soon as she could. But for her, love had always been so elusive, difficult to find and impossible to cultivate. Certainly it never exploded into a woman's life in the midst of other complications.

She barely knew Jamie Kilter. A conversation in the dark, a feeling of trust, a couple of kisses. But oh, she could so easily fall for him if she hadn't already...

"Dottie!" The cry came from downstairs, saving Cat the necessity of putting her confused feelings into words.

"Have to go," Dottie said. "The boarders want to eat again." She turned to the door and then hesitated. "You want a word of advice? Keep your cap on. You're much too pretty without it."

****

"Did you get any sleep, lad?" Tate's big body threw a shadow against the bright morning sun. James, who hunkered down in front of Greta's kennel, cast a look over his shoulder and shook his head.

"Never went to bed," he admitted. "Been here all night trying to get Greta to trust me."

Tate scowled; his broad face looked homely in the sharp light, but James would take "homely" any day of the week.

"How's she doing?"

Greta, ears flattened, lay half way up the run, her eyes fixed on James. She whimpered but didn't otherwise protest Tate's presence.

"Better, but if I walk away she starts to bark."

"Means she's beginning to accept you. Trust's a funny thing, isn't it, lad? My old ma used to say it's the foundation of any relationship. Without trust, there can't be anything more."

James stayed where he was and said nothing.

"You want to talk about it?" Tate asked.

"'It'?"

"What I saw going on in Roselyn's kitchen last night."

Talk about it? James barely wanted to think of it, though he seemed incapable of focusing on anything else. The memory of how Catherine felt in his arms, and all the accompanying sensations, had kept him from sleep.

He got to his feet. Greta flattened herself to the ground but didn't move away.

He told Tate, rationalizing Catherine's actions as he had most the night, "She was just worried about me. That's all."

"Didn't look like 'all' to me. Aye, lad, women do get worried, bless them, but the question is why was she so worried about you?"

"We're friends."

"Maybe so. But in my experience friends don't throw themselves into one another's arms the way she threw herself at you."

James grimaced and growled, "Don't, Tate."

"Don't what?"

"Don't build up something that's not there." He couldn't handle false hope, couldn't endure the resultant disappointment.

"She already trusts you, lad."

"Trust's not the same as…" James couldn't say the word, couldn't even let himself think it.

"You suppose so? I don't. As I've just said, 'tis the foundation for far warmer feelings."

"Maybe." For normal men who looked human.

Tate made a rough gesture. "That dog there, now, Greta, she's starting to trust you. You'll win her acceptance, and next will come love."

"That's the way it is with animals." And it was the reason he loved them so, the way he'd admit to loving nothing else.

"No, lad, I think that's the way it is with everyone. Do you suppose Greta cares how you look? It's the kind hand that matters to her, the soft voice."

James had no reply to that, and Tate just stood there a moment as if letting his words soak in. "When's your court date?"

"Three days."

"I was thinking it might be a good idea meanwhile to settle you at Roselyn's, just to keep Miss Delaney safe."

"Send someone else."

"She'll not want someone else."

"Tate, please." James drew a breath that shuddered through him.

"I can't help believing you're the man for the job."

James shut his eyes against the glare of the morning light and a surge of pain. "It's impossible."

"Is it? I would have said 'twas impossible, when you brought Greta here, that she'd ever let you near her. Now she's half way to loving you."

James opened his eyes and regarded the dog, who had her eyes fixed on him with unswerving attention.

Softly, Tate said, "Miracles happen every day, lad. You only have to watch for them."

James hoped so, for he needed a big, whopping miracle, and he needed it soon.

Chapter Twenty-One

"I wondered if I might see Dr. Roesch." James stared into the visage of the steam unit that opened the door. An advanced and no doubt very expensive model, it still didn't match the sophistication of hybrids like Kelly. But it had been fashioned to look like a housemaid or housekeeper, and rather than mere indentations in its metal skin it had glass eyes.

"Sir, do you have an appointment?"

"I'm sorry, I don't."

"Then I am afraid Dr. Roesch cannot see you."

James stood there with the traffic of a busy afternoon on Franklin Street rushing past his back and wondered how to influence the feelings of a creature that had no emotions. Oh, he knew steamies thought after a fashion and developed loyalties. Imagination, however, did not seem their strong suit.

"Please, it's important." Against implacable denial, James persisted, "Is the doctor in?"

"Dr. Roesch is with a patient."

James' heart leaped. "I can wait till he's free. I'll wait as long as it takes."

The steam unit hesitated and seemed to consider him. It asked, "Is this a very urgent matter?"

"Yes." Urgent to him.

"Dr. Roesch does see emergencies. Come in."

The inside of the building sparkled with

cleanliness, the floor so highly polished James might have been able to see himself in it, had he wanted to. He didn't. The steamie led him through an open door on the left into a room empty except for chairs.

"Please wait here, sir."

James did, fidgeting in every limb. The place smelled of disinfectant and floor polish. Ever since his accident the smell of disinfectant turned his stomach, and that did nothing for his current state of mind. The hospital in which he'd recovered had reeked of this; the memories, far from good, included sickness, pain, and terrified loneliness.

He needed to push all that away from him now. He needed to focus on the miracle Tate had promised.

He'd expected an endless wait, but all too soon he heard voices from the foyer—two men speaking, one departing. Roesch and his patient.

Then the mechanical voice of the steam servant reached his ears.

"A man wanting to see you, Dr. Roesch."

"That was my last appointment, Dahlia."

"I think you will want to see this man."

It thought? Was that a judgment call on the part of the sophisticated unit?

A man stepped to the door of the waiting room, as much a caricature as the steamie, in his way. Short and barrel-chested, he wore elegant trousers and a waistcoat. His dark hair had grayed like his beard, which made a wiry nest that flowed onto his breast. Fierce eyes the color of ice considered James for a moment before they narrowed in curiosity.

"I see. Very good, Dahlia. You may leave us."

James expected to be called away into an

examining room. Instead the man entered the reception chamber, shut the door, and extended his hand to James all in one movement.

"I am Dr. Eberon Roesch. You?"

"James Kilter."

The doctor's grip felt firm; his gaze engaged James' fully.

"Mr. Kilter, no need to ask why you are here." Roesch released James' hand and moved around him, inspecting his countenance by the room's clear light. "Interesting scar patterns. Steam burns or boiling water?"

"Both."

"Taken at close contact, I have no doubt. And sustained."

"A boiler exploded in a closet. I wasn't able to get away."

"These are old injuries. How old?"

"Over ten years."

"Ah. If you had come to me at once, I might have been able to do something."

James stomach plummeted sickeningly. "You mean you can't now?"

"Advances in skin surgery progress on a nearly daily basis. No doubt you heard I am a pioneer in my field. It is why you are here, yes?"

"Yes."

"Yet only so much can be done."

"I thought—hoped—that is, I heard you're doing work taking skin from one person and planting it on another like those hybrid steamies in the police force."

"From cadavers, you mean? I am making trials with that method, yes—but only trials at this point. The creators of the hybrids, Charles and Mason, may have been madmen; they were also geniuses. Such surgery has not been perfected, and the risks are manifold."

"What risks?"

Roesch's icy stare considered him. "Mainly failure of the graft to take, severe infection—death."

"I'd be willing to take the chance."

Roesch waved a hand. "Would you be willing to wear the skin of a dead man, Mr. Kilter?"

"I believe I would."

"Even if it meant you no longer looked like you, and instead looked like the donor?"

"I don't look like me now, at least half of me doesn't."

Roesch shook his head. "To even attempt such a surgery I would have to remove all this thickened skin on your face and—where, on your body, do the burns extend? Let me see."

James unbuttoned his shirt, pulled it off. His only hope as he saw it meant engaging this man's professional interest, making him desire the challenge James represented.

"Ah," Roesch said softly. "Ah."

The scarring extended down the right side of James' neck, across one broad shoulder and, in a mottled pattern, down his chest and right arm.

"Your face caught the worst of it."

"A valve let loose. The boiling water caught me here"—James indicated his head—"and here"—his cheekbone—"and splashed down."

"A wonder you didn't lose that eye. An even greater wonder you survived the ensuing pain. It must have been considerable."

James said nothing, merely stood with his shirt in his hands and the worst of himself exposed.

"It's mainly the face I'm concerned about."

"Indeed."

"Can you help me?"

Roesch sighed. "I would like to, Mr. Kilter, I confess I would. You present a fascinating case. But such a surgery would be time consuming and very expensive."

"We could come to terms."

"Ah, Mr. Kilter, I sympathize, truly I do. But I think not."

James swallowed hard. "If it's a matter of the money, I could try and raise funds." He already owed Tate bail, and Tate's pockets were far from bottomless, but he knew Tate would help if he could.

"Mr. Kilter, it is not so much a matter of money. In fact I would be willing to donate my services; your case is such an interesting one."

James' heart leaped once more.

But Roesch went on, "There is still the cost of the medicines and the cadaver. I refuse to deal on the black market, and suitable donors are hard to come by. There would have to be a reasonable resemblance."

"I'd be willing to wait as long as it takes."

Roesch ignored that. "The main question, Mr. Kilter, would be one of endurance. I would have to strip all that damaged tissue away. The pain would be intense."

James thought of Catherine and the look in her eyes. "I could endure it." He could endure anything.

"You say that now. But there would be weeks of agony and no guarantee of success. In my trials, more than half the grafts have been rejected."

"The hybrids—"

"The hybrids, Mr. Kilter, are living skin laid over steel. Steel feels no pain. The skin, as an organ, does possess that sense, but the hybrids have no brain to translate the signals. You, Mr. Kilter, have a brain that would experience it all."

"Please, Dr. Roesch, don't refuse me. You have no idea how I want this."

Roesch's gaze turned kind. "Oh, Mr. Kilter, I think I do."

"Then—"

"With all due respect, Mr. Kilter, desire is not enough. My trials show that when the implant is rejected or if infection rages beneath the bed of the organ, the pain surpasses anything that has come before—in short, anything even you have felt."

"Organ?"

"Never mistake, Mr. Kilter, the skin is an organ, the largest of the body. And I would wish to replace most of the face area in one procedure, in order to reduce the possibility of residual scarring."

"I can take the pain, Dr. Roesch, I assure you." If it gave him the chance to win Catherine, he could withstand anything.

But Roesch shook his head. "It would be irresponsible of me, Mr. Kilter. I've never attempted such a large graft."

"Then this is your chance. I volunteer to be your subject. I'll even sign a paper saying I won't hold it against you if it fails."

"Let me consider on it a while. Where might I reach you?"

"Through my employer, Michael Murphy on Niagara Street. When will I hear from you?"

Dr. Roesch gave him another long look. "Give me a week. But, Mr. Kilter, I wouldn't get my hopes up, if I were you."

Chapter Twenty-Two

"There's a man going door to door asking after you." Dottie put her head in the kitchen where Cat stood at the big sink washing vegetables for dinner. To be sure, she'd never imagined the mere preparation of food required such a great amount of bone-wearing labor. She'd always taken the meals that appeared in front of her for granted.

Now she forgot her aching back and looked up, startled. "What?"

Dottie, her white cap askew on her head, made a face. "Make no mistake, he had a picture of you and everything."

The carrots fell from Cat's suddenly nerveless fingers. A cold chill touched her spine. "A picture?"

"Well, a drawing—of you as a woman." Dottie tipped her head to one side. "You were very pretty, weren't you?"

"How can there be a drawing of me?" Cat's thoughts seethed. And how could Boyd have enough men to go door to door? Had he been to Toronto already and threatened her family? She knew her mother had a drawing of her, kept on the piano in the sitting room of the big house she used to call home.

Tate Murphy had sent a man to Toronto too, but Cat hadn't yet heard back from him.

Of course, Sebastian Boyd had more money than

Tate—much more—and she was learning money could accomplish nearly anything.

"Where's Roselyn?" she asked.

"Gone to the market. She'll be back soon. The thing is," Dottie leaned in further, "this man's showing the drawing to everybody, our boarders as well as the neighbors. And you did run out in the street two days ago, during the incident."

So she had, and with no cap covering her strawberry-blonde hair. And she'd clutched at Jamie's hands the way a woman might. Another chill touched her, deadly cold.

Did Boyd know where she was? Had he found her? Or did he just suspect?

She glanced at the back door, which stood open to the sunny yard. Anyone could walk in here and snatch her.

She might never see Jamie again. Never touch him, never kiss him.

"Where did this man go?" she asked and hurried to close the door and throw the bolt.

"Last I saw him he was showing the picture to a group of children two doors down. Albert, who's after you?"

"You don't want to know."

"A husband? Did you run away from him?"

"I'm not married, but it's something like that."

"Does Miss Murphy know?"

Cat nodded.

"The thing is," Dottie hesitated, "this fellow's offering a reward for word of you. Twenty dollars." Dottie's eyes widened. "Now, that's a handsome amount of money. A fortune. Me, I'd never betray you for that, but thousands would."

Cat looked at the little maid and a feeling settled over her that tasted of doom. Twenty dollars represented a fortune to this small, cheerful girl. Why shouldn't she jump at it?

"You barely know me, Dottie," she admitted. "And you don't owe me anything."

"We're friends, right? Even if you are some high lady, from the look of that picture."

"Thank you, Dottie. Does it look very much like me? Do you think other folks will be able to identify me when I'm dressed as a boy?"

Dottie shrugged. "Best to keep that hair covered. And stop kissing men."

****

When Roselyn came home, Dottie told the story all over again. Roselyn's broad, homely face flushed as she listened.

"The saints protect us! Only imagine having the brass to go through the city like that." She eyed Cat unhappily. "This man wants you back, and no mistake."

"Do you think I was seen when the police, the ambulance, and all that crowd were out in the street?"

"Maybe. Anyway, someone's clearly fishing in this neighborhood. Dottie, love, where's Ben? I need to send a message to Mr. Murphy."

"I'll go find him."

Dottie ran off, and Cat stood wringing her hands. "Will Mr. Murphy want to move me?" She hoped not; she liked it here. The work might be hard, but Roselyn ran an honest house that had started to feel like home.

"Lord only knows."

"Ben wouldn't betray me, would he? Twenty

dollars..."

"Aye, a tempting sum. Ben's a good sort but, lass, temptation's temptation. Who can say?"

Dottie returned soon to say she couldn't find Ben anywhere.

"He's supposed to be polishing boots in the cellar," Roselyn said and huffed off to look for herself.

Panic chewed at Cat with sharp teeth. What should she do? Wait here while Ben possibly led Boyd's henchmen to her? Run and flee? But where? Back to Mr. Murphy's, where she might take refuge with Jamie?

"I can't find him." Roselyn returned with a worried look in her eyes. "Dottie, you run and tell Mr. Murphy what's happened, that's a good lass." She turned to Cat even as Dottie hurried off. "Meanwhile, you had better hide in your room till we find out what's what."

"But if someone comes I'll be a sitting duck up there." Only one set of narrow stairs led up, with no other way down.

"No one goes through my house, lass." Calmly, Roselyn drew a butcher knife from the drawer. "But 'twould be all too easy to bust into this room." She gave Cat a sympathetic look. "I know 'tis warm and stuffy up there, but keep away from the window where you can be seen."

"What do you think Mr. Murphy will do?"

"Jesus only knows—Jesus and Tate. He's the one good at guarding people, not me."

The tiny attic room felt airless with the door shut and the window barely cracked. Cat ached to peer down on the street and see what might be happening. If she could catch a glimpse of this man going about after her, she might be able to identify him as one of Boyd's crew. Instead she lay on the narrow cot, breathing the hot air and thinking about Jamie.

Would he come for her? She hoped so; she felt safer in his company than anywhere else. She built a fantasy during which they ran away together and lived as man and wife. She wanted that, had ever since she kissed him—no, even before. She longed to feel his big hands all over her, on her naked flesh.

Convincing him wouldn't be easy. But maybe this crisis—terrifying as it was—might be the very thing to precipitate matters.

Yet where could they go? She might seek to disguise herself; Jamie never could. He would be eminently recognizable wherever they fled. And a crowd of people had seen her with him in the street. Once they put two and two together...

Being in her company could only endanger Jamie. She contemplated that unwelcome fact even while she shivered in longing for him. Once Boyd connected Jamie to her, the bastard would be unrelenting in pursuing him.

She'd already placed Jamie at risk, this man she adored.

She stared at the plaster ceiling while she regarded herself with unprecedented honesty. She adored James Kilter and everything about him, from the color of his eyes to the way he touched her. She loved the height and strength of him and the sound of his voice that made her breathless. She absolutely ached to welcome him inside her where no man had been. She wanted him hot and heavy on top of her.

She wanted him forever.

As for the rest of it—the scars, the half-ruined face, the taunts and insults—she barely cared, for she saw none of that when she looked at him. His propensity to go off kilter, as Mr. Murphy called it, worried her more. But she understood his triggers. At heart, Jamie Kilter was not a beast so much as a defender.

And who would have thought she, Catherine Delaney, would fall heart and soul for such a man? Oh, back in Toronto she'd expected one day to marry. She'd been courted by a number of highly eligible suitors and had rejected them all. Too choosey, her mother said. Too demanding. What if Cat had accepted one of those proposals? Would she have been able to better protect Becky from her stepfather?

That made her wonder where Becky might be now. Still safe, Cat hoped, and not in Boyd's hands. If Boyd did get Becky, would he then stop pursuing Cat? No, because he believed he owned her. He pursued her now out of wounded pride, and pure spite.

What would Becky, what would Cat's mother think of the man Cat had chosen? For she had chosen James Kilter, and no mistake—her heart had, and her heart always held true. An orphan, a workman barely educated; even disregarding his appearance, her mother would not consider him suitable. But, Cat's heart cried, what did her mother know? She, who'd chosen a lout like Everett Kraus.

Cat's ear caught the sound of raised voices then, drifting up from the street. She heard the outer door close and the muffled sounds of conversation two floors down.

Had Mr. Murphy come? Had Ben brought someone else?

Cat stiffened where she lay and heard the echo of footsteps climbing the hollow, wooden stairs. Someone came.

Chapter Twenty-Three

"I'd like to see Officer Kelly."

The desk sergeant, the same man who'd booked James mere days ago, gave him a narrow look.

"You, back here again? Most our guests can't keep far enough away once they're sprung."

James grimaced. "All the same, I'd like to talk to him. He works out of this station, doesn't he?"

The desk sergeant raised sandy eyebrows. "You do know he's an automaton?"

"Yes."

"Not much for conversation, them."

"Look, is he on duty or not?"

"Not."

James' heart sank.

"What do you want with him?"

"It's personal."

"Want to ask him for a date, do you? I have it on the best authority he likes women."

Now James' eyebrows flew up.

"Anyway, you're no pretty boy, are you?"

"It's nothing like that."

"Well he's off duty, but he doesn't sleep much." The sergeant snickered. "I happen to know when he's not working he hangs out at a bar called Nellie's, down on Perry Street."

"I've heard of it." Nellie's used to be one of the

toughest joints on the waterfront. Why would an automaton go there? But he said, "Thanks," and left the station, the sergeant's gaze drilling a hole between his shoulder blades.

Nellie's was probably a stiff five minutes' walk from the station and would be quiet at this hour of the afternoon. James set off briskly, the hot sun beating on his head.

Buffalo's waterfront, a veritable warren of docks, warehouses, and bars, teemed with life. Squads of men unloaded cargo; others trundled it about on handcarts. An airship had just come in, and James paused to look at it, remembering the first time he'd seen Catherine. His heart clenched.

Nellie's, no more than a shack, perched among a number of sister buildings a stone's throw from the harbor. It didn't look busy at this hour, but as James approached the door, which stood open, he heard music coming from inside. He stepped in and stood for a moment, letting his eyes adjust to the dim interior.

Tables dotted the warped planks of the wooden floor, and a bar built of packing crates stretched on the left. Perhaps six or seven patrons occupied the tables, and an old man sat next to a small stage on the right, playing a concertina.

On the stage…

A woman danced, clad in nothing except long stockings. Her dancing was poor, her body better, and because he couldn't help himself James watched her for a minute before he withdrew his gaze and scanned the room.

All men, as might be expected. Or were some of them automatons? He looked more closely, hoping to recognize Kelly, who, he remembered, had sprouted a crop of reddish-brown hair beneath his police cap.

He spotted the fellow at last, sitting dead center at a table with another patron, having a whiskey and watching the dancer. Amazement touched James. What was Kelly playing at? Automatons didn't drink.

He walked over to the table and eyed both occupants. He couldn't tell at first glance if the second man was also an automaton.

"Officer Kelly, do you remember me?"

Kelly gave him a salubrious look and tipped the glass of whiskey he held in a jaunty salute, a gesture James had seen Tate make a hundred times, and pure Irish.

"I was part of the coal-horse confrontation on Prospect Street," James clarified needlessly; automatons didn't forget much.

"I am off duty." Only the slight mechanical whine in the voice detracted from the illusion of pure humanity. As the desk sergeant had implied, Kelly had no need to sleep or, presumably, rest. Yet here he sat apparently immersed in recreation.

"I know; I'm sorry to interrupt. I was hoping for a word."

"Hope, Kevin. He *hopes*. Must be a human."

It seemed to be some kind of joke, for both Kelly and his companion emitted grinding sounds that, after a moment, James identified as laughter. The second automaton, who must be Kevin, got to its feet.

"I will leave you lads alone, then."

"Sit," Kelly invited magnanimously once the other hybrid moved off to the bar. "Watch the dancer. Do you like?"

James took Kevin's chair and shot another judicious—and unpreventable—look at the stage where the woman had begun to remove one stocking. She had nice legs and passable breasts, but she was no Catherine.

He said carefully, "I didn't come here to look at a woman."

"You wish to talk to me." Disconcertingly, Kelly's countenance displayed little expression when he spoke, and the nuances in his voice were few. Difficult to gauge what he thought.

Did he think, as such?

"Would you like a whiskey?"

"No, thank you."

"I can summon the bartender."

Again, Kelly raised his glass. He wore a soft white shirt open at the neck to display his brawny chest and the cuff fell back, revealing a large scar at the wrist, white and rigid.

"I'm fine," James assured him.

"If you wish to speak to me about the incident on Prospect Street, I am not at liberty to discuss it. If you want my opinion, you will probably get jail time. But it is my further opinion the cab driver was a piece of shite who deserved what you gave him." Kelly paused thoughtfully. "I have no respect for men who beat their horses. As I told you that day, the way animals are treated in this city is abominable."

"There is the anti-cruelty league."

"Yes. I am thinking of joining." Kelly emitted the grinding sound again. "Do you think they would make me welcome?"

"No doubt." James huffed in surprise. The

automaton had a sense of humor. Who would have thought?

"The horse in question has been taken into care," Kelly said. "And I have made sure the coal company is investigated for other abuses. It may just have been the one driver at fault. I am informed one human cannot be held responsible for the sins of others." He paused. "Is it about this you wished to talk to me?"

"No, though I'm glad to hear the horse is in care. Do you know a Dr. Roesch?"

Kelly cocked his head a bit like an intelligent setter. James realized he consulted his artificial intelligence. "Yes."

"I believe he studied you and your…fellows."

"My fellows, yes." Grind, grind. "We are an elite company. Oh, look—she has removed the second stocking and is completely nude." He banged his whiskey glass on the table in apparent approval. All around the room, the sound echoed. Kelly gestured to the woman, who hopped down from the makeshift stage and crossed to their table.

"Nice dance," Kelly told her emotionlessly. "This is my friend. Forgive me, friend—I did not record your name."

"James Kilter," James told the woman. She looked into his face, and he prepared for her reaction.

She didn't disappoint. "Jesus, what the hell are you? One of them experiments," she jerked a thumb at Kelly, "that went wrong?"

James shook his head. Close up, she appeared far less attractive, and reeked of sweat.

"You mean, you're human?" She did another quick assessment and offered grudgingly, "If you want to go in back, I suppose I can keep my eyes shut. You all there under your clothes?"

Robbed of the ability to speak, James nodded.

"It costs a dollar, and no funny stuff. I do the usual, including doggie style. You get five minutes. Well?"

"I will pay." Kelly pulled a dollar from his pocket and laid it on the filthy, scarred table. "My treat as a reward for your heroism the other day." Grind, grind.

"No, thank you, though I appreciate the offer."

"Fussy, are you? With a face like that?" Obviously offended, the dancer stalked off, her butt cheeks bouncing.

"Is that face of yours a disadvantage when trying to obtain women?" Kelly asked. He left the dollar lying on the table. "I would not think you would have an unlimited choice."

And what's it to you? James burned to know but dared not voice the question. Kelly seemed friendly enough, but how did one man ask another—even an automaton—if he were able to enjoy a woman?

"This is true. But I am interested in one particular woman, no one else."

"Ah, *love*." Kelly leaned back in his chair and gave a smile so purely Irish it astounded James all over again. "Another great human tradition."

And was that what took place here? Did Kelly and these others scattered about the room play at the traditions of being human? Kelly had not yet drunk from the whiskey glass, though he waved it about like some Celtic king.

Sadness touched James. As he knew very well, being an outsider didn't feel good.

"About Dr. Roesch," he began again. "How well

do you know him?"

Another woman had come out onto the stage, this one fully clothed. The man with the concertina began to play another wheezing tune, and Kelly took a long look at the woman before he replied.

"Not well, though he has looked into my most intimate places." Grind, grind.

This time James laughed with him. Then he laid his hand atop the dollar and deliberately slid it toward Kelly.

"Officer Kelly, I don't need this, but if you'd like to reward me, as you say, for trying to spare that horse a beating, you might do me a favor."

"Favor?" Kelly tipped his head again. "Ah, yes. Friends do favors for one another. What do you require?"

James lowered his voice. "I'm trying to convince Dr. Roesch to operate on my face." He gestured roughly. "To make me look—well, more human. But the surgery's not perfected, and he's reluctant. Thinks I wouldn't be able to handle the pain."

"How are you at handling pain, my friend?"

"As good as the next man, maybe better. Probably not so good as you."

"Why do you want the surgery so badly?" Kelly appeared to examine him. "Those are just scars."

"It's difficult to explain." To someone without a heart. "As I say, there's a woman."

"The one with whom you are in love."

"Well, yes." Might as well admit it.

"You have chosen one woman above all others."

"Yes. And I wish to look…well, the best I can for her."

"If she cares for you in return, she will not mind how you look. At least, that is the premise with which I have been presented."

"It's a fine premise, in an ideal world. But look at me. What woman wouldn't mind?"

"So how can I assist you in your effort?"

"Speak to Dr. Roesch for me. He knows you. Assure him I can withstand any pain or risk."

"Give me your hand."

"What?"

"I cannot give Dr. Roesch any assurance which has not been proven to me." Kelly snatched James' wrist in one of his mechanical, skin-covered hands and, from his pocket, brought a box of matches, one of which he struck against the table. He forced James' hand, palm down, over the match head and held it there while the small flame seared the flesh.

The automaton's strength was such that James couldn't have pulled away if he wanted. He didn't want; he knew this for a test and endured without a sound until the match burned back to Kelly's fingers and snuffed out.

"Very good. I will speak to Dr. Roesch about you. Come back here and talk with me again, sometime. I have enjoyed this."

James swore under his breath and shook his hand surreptitiously, against the sting.

"Thank you, Officer Kelly. I appreciate it."

"Anything to further the cause of love. But call me Patrick. You are my friend. And put some ice on that. I hear it cools the burn."

Chapter Twenty-Four

Cat's heart beat up in her throat as she heard the heavy footsteps pause outside her door, and she fixed her gaze on the latch, watching to see if it would turn. She wished she had a weapon, but the only thing to hand was the wooden coat rack in the corner. She snatched it up and hoisted it over her head.

"Miss Delaney? 'Tis myself, Michael Murphy."

The air left Cat's lungs in a rush. She lowered the coat rack with a bang and opened the door.

Tate Murphy stood there looking overly large in the confined space. His gaze fell on the coat rack, and one corner of his wide mouth twitched.

"Never say you were going to try and club me with that?"

"If I had to."

"A fine state of affairs. My sister meets me downstairs with a butcher knife and you with a great length of wood."

"Not you, Mr. Murphy so much as…whomever else. Boyd's sent men looking for me door to door, armed with a picture."

"So I hear."

"What am I going to do? Where's Jamie, do you know?"

"I do not. Off about some business, I'll be bound. For now, I want you to come away with me. I don't

Laura Strickland

believe 'tis safe here for you anymore."

"Oh." Cat's heart sank. She hated this tiny room, yet she would miss Roselyn's house.

"I will take you back to my place on Niagara for now. James will come back there when he's done with his business, and we'll tell him what's happened. All right? Best get your things."

"I don't have much."

Roselyn met them at the bottom of the stairs. Cat felt ridiculous tears come to her eyes.

"Miss Murphy, thank you for everything. If I can ever repay you in any way, you've only to tell me."

"No need for thanks. You pulled your weight, and no mistake. Come back and see us when you can."

Cat nodded and waved at Dottie, who hovered in the doorway of the kitchen.

"I've a steamcab waiting out front. I want you to hop inside quick, and we'll drive around the city for a while, lose any tail we might have. I'll not lead the hounds back to my own den," Tate said.

Cat cast one look back at Roselyn before ducking out and had to choke back foolish emotion. Tate Murphy planted a large hand on her head and urged her into the vehicle. The steamcab moved off with a rush and a belch of vapor.

"I am sorry to cause so much trouble," Cat told Murphy miserably.

"Not your fault, is it? Men like Boyd need to find out they don't rule the world and can't buy and sell people like cattle. I knew men enough like him back in Ireland—thought they could have anyone, ruin anyone." He stopped speaking abruptly. Cat wondered if there had been a woman in Ireland, someone he'd lost

172

and never forgotten.

Softly, she asked, "Have you had any word from Toronto? Do you know if Boyd has gone after my family?"

"My man sent a message; he's on his way back." Tate hesitated. "Says the news isn't good."

"My sister, Becky?"

"That's all I know as yet, lass."

"If Boyd takes this out on her, I'll never forgive myself. I should have stuck to my plan and stayed with him."

"And done what? Let him pass you around among his cronies? 'Tisn't decent, that."

"Better me than Becky."

"You're a brave lass. I admire that. But I'll be needing to ask you before we get back to my office— what are your feelings toward James? He's dear as a brother to me, you understand, and a good man to the heart. He's had a weight of trouble to bear ever since I've known him, and I wouldn't want to stand by and let him run headlong into still more."

"I understand. Neither would I."

"Good then, if you don't mind me saying: I saw the two of you back in my sister's kitchen, and I have to admit I was surprised. Most women are that put off by his appearance they refuse to get close to him."

Cat gave Tate a look. "I'm not most women."

"Clearly. But I wouldn't like to think you're toying with the lad, because, see, he's the type who gives his heart completely."

"Do I look like the sort to toy with anyone?"

"I don't know, do I? High society woman from wealthy Toronto, and him a working stiff."

"I assure you, Mr. Murphy, I am not toying with James Kilter."

"Aye, because I've been thinking about this pretty much nonstop since the other evening, and I'd be happy to pay your way out of the city."

"To get rid of me, you mean?"

"No, to help you. To help both of you."

"Mr. Murphy, the only way I'm leaving this city is if James Kilter comes with me."

"Well, then."

"You needn't look so gob-smacked."

"I've never heard anyone speak that way about our James before."

"It just proves," she told him, "you encounter something new every day."

****

"What's this, then? Another stray?" The man who spoke had a short stature, a large nose, and hair so brightly yellow Cat wondered if he bleached it. "You gonna put this one out back with the dogs, Tate?"

"Lad's here as part of a job, Drappot, and you know what that means—not a word to anyone. It's worth your job, understand?"

"Hiding him from somebody, are you?" Drappot's brown eyes examined Cat slowly and she wondered if he would guess her sex.

"Something like that. Why aren't you out on assignment? I thought you were playing bodyguard to Mr. Taylor."

"He had a doctor's appointment and gave me a few hours off. I'll be headed out soon." To Cat he said, "You got a name, kid?"

"Albert."

"Well, Al, try not to be too scared of the local boogey man. He'll give you nightmares if you stare at him too long. And make sure he don't take you out back and feed you to his dogs, especially that wild one. Damn bitch barks all night."

Tate shot a look at Cat and correctly assessed her rising temperature. "You'll be on assignment tonight, Drappot, and won't hear the dogs or anything else. Come on, lad. I'll show you where you can sleep."

"Why, that insolent weasel," Cat said as soon as they were out of earshot. "What's Jamie ever done to him?"

"Oil and water, those two. The quarrel's been going on as long as I can remember."

"Truly, Mr. Murphy? I should consider firing that toad, if I were you."

"Man's good enough at his job, and James has grown a pretty thick skin. Sorry, this room's worse than the one you had at Roselyn's, but you should be safe here. You can wander about the building and out into the yard, but I don't want you to leave the premises. As soon as I talk to our man from Toronto, I'll let you know. Just don't show your face, understand?"

"Yes. Where are the facilities?"

"The what?"

"Outhouse or water closet?"

"Christ, I didn't think of that. We men all use one bog, and that'll never do for you. Not fit for you to set foot in. For now, use the commode under the cot there. I'll think of something."

"And you'll tell me when Jamie arrives?"

Wild barking erupted behind the building.

"No need," Tate said. "He's just arrived; the dogs

always know he's here; don't ask me how."

Tate led Cat back down through the warehouse and out into the small, scrappy yard which contained a number of metal kennels. James stood in front of the first on the left while all the other dogs, save one, clamored for his attention.

Cat knew just how they felt. She wanted his attention too, and his big hand touching her. She shivered with the sudden onset of desire.

"Remember, now," Tate told her in an undertone, "you're a lad, and there are eyes all around."

James spun when he heard Tate's voice, and his eyes lit at the sight of Cat.

"I've brought young Albert here for safekeeping," Tate said quickly. "There've been a few developments, none for the good. Come in my office, and I'll explain everything."

****

Hours later Cat lay, sleepless, in still another sweltering room, this time under a metal roof that clanged and banged beneath a driving rainstorm. She didn't know how anyone could possibly attain slumber in such a racket.

Lightning flashed outside her window and thunder rumbled so close above the tin roof it made her cringe.

Her thoughts ran like a train, relentless and unstoppable. Jamie Kilter had walked her to her room a short time ago and said, as if to reassure her, "No need to be frightened. I'm right next door, so call me if you need me."

She needed him. Oh, she did! Her flesh quivered with need, and her imagination played fantastical scenes in her head: the two of them closed away together here or next door, anywhere. His hands touching her, his lips claiming her; the taste and scent of him filling her.

Thunder rumbled again, and she groaned softly. Then she slipped from the cot and, on bare feet, went to the door. Fumbling with the strange latch, she swung it open.

Darkness and a stifling corridor. How many of Tate Murphy's workers lived here? Lightning flashed again, and she saw a row of doors. Should one of them open unexpectedly and the inhabitant catch her standing in her underwear, it would be more than obvious she was no lad.

She'd better move quickly and get out of the hallway.

Jamie's door, like all the others, stood shut. Two steps took her to it, and she scratched cautiously.

No reply. Did he sleep? Surely not; perhaps he couldn't hear her above the rain. She tapped, and that went unanswered also, so she turned his latch and leaned in.

"Jamie?"

He moved at once, as if he'd been awake and listening for her after all. The room, dark as the pit of hell, didn't let her see, but she heard him.

"What is it? What's wrong?"

"I'm scared. Can I stay with you the rest of the night?"

Dead silence met her request. Cat ignored it, stepped in, and closed the door behind her.

Chapter Twenty-Five

Thunder rumbled again and lightning flashed, rattling the roof and window. James caught a glimpse of Catherine standing just inside his door, an image that seared his eyeballs like fire. She looked like an angel clad in scanty white, with her cap of short hair ruffled and hesitance in every limb. His heart began to pound great, shuddering beats high in his chest.

She couldn't be here just as if his thoughts had summoned her, as if the longing he'd felt lying here knowing she lay just ten feet away on the other side of the narrow wall had conjured her like some powerful magic. He'd been nursing the pain in his hand and thinking about how much more he'd be willing to endure for the chance to win her.

And now she came whispering in, no more substantial than a dream.

Neither wise nor safe for her to be here. Already he felt his body respond to the sight—or perhaps just the idea—of her. He should tell her to go.

But she feared the storm. Could he be so cruel?

"It's just thunder," he said, his voice sounding strange to his own ears.

"The thunder doesn't bother me so much as the lightning. Has the roof on this place ever been struck?"

"I don't think so." The dogs down in their kennels hated storms, too. He'd been thinking about braving the wet to comfort them. Now he had the chance to comfort Catherine instead.

Again, not a good idea.

"Please, Jamie."

How he loved it when she said his name that way, making of it an intimate caress only the two of them shared. He could deny her nothing.

"Not a good idea." He said it aloud this time, like a warding spell.

"I don't care." She moved from the door, blundering forward and into the foot of his bed. He could see nothing between lightning flashes; that meant she couldn't see him either.

Might he, then, pretend? Could he stretch his fantasy to include the idea that Roesch had performed some miraculous surgery upon him, and she might want him as a woman wanted a man?

She tumbled forward across the bed and fell on him. Lightning flashed again, and he saw her startled face mere inches from his. She shivered, the tremor traveling all through her body.

"It's all right," he breathed meaningless words, patently untrue. It most certainly wasn't all right. Need surged through him like racing fire.

"Just hold me, please, Jamie, till the storm passes."

He could do that. He could summon self-discipline from somewhere to cradle her in his arms, and nothing else. Sure, he could.

"The bed is very small." And he lay barely clad against the warmth, wearing nothing but a pair of trews. He'd left his window open, hoping for a breeze, and could smell both the river and the rain.

Now, though, Catherine's delectable scent flooded

upon him, making him hard as iron.

"I don't mind." She shifted around, collecting her limbs that had landed atop him, barely missing his balls with her knee. She arranged herself alongside him on less than six inches of mattress and tucked her head into his shoulder.

"You said I should call if I needed you." Her voice, more whisper than substance, tickled his ear. He went hot and cold in quick succession.

"Yes." What did a man do about a raging erection when the woman he desired more than life clung to him in the dark? He could think of only one thing. But he dared not touch her; he lay with his hands out from her body, motionless.

"This is better, Jamie. I feel safe here with you."

There, she'd said it again. *Jamie*. Something inside him abruptly melted. He drew a great breath.

Thunder cracked low over the roof, and she splayed her hand against his naked chest. Intense pleasure met and tangled with the urgency he felt lower down.

"Catherine," he began.

"Cat. Why don't you call me Cat?"

"Catherine is such a beautiful name." Perhaps he could distract himself with inane conversation.

"You think so?"

"I do. Beautiful like you."

No, that wasn't good. For one thing, it made her cuddle closer and ask, "You think me beautiful?"

"You know you are." That made more than half the problem, didn't it? And him so ugly people threw stones, and with barely a penny to his name, to boot.

"So long as you think so."

Were those her lips he felt on his neck? No, no, no. Did she forget, lying here in the dark, what he was?

Only let the lightning flash again and she'd find herself in the arms of the monster. Until then, though, he could close his eyes and pretend.

"I do believe," she whispered, "you are one of the kindest men I've ever met, and the strongest." The hand splayed on his chest began to move, scribed a soft circle on his skin. "I don't mean just these great muscles but the strength that's inside you."

He'd better dredge up strength from somewhere in order to endure this exquisite agony.

Another crash; she flinched, and his arms moved without his volition to cradle her tenderly.

"No need to be afraid," he crooned.

"I'm not, now." Her lips moved the inch or two needed to meet his. Light seared in the darkness and exploded behind James' eyes, spreading straight to his toes with a couple of interesting detours in between.

"Catherine. God, Catherine," he breathed into her.

As she had in the kitchen, she opened her mouth beneath his. At the same time her hand moved downward across the taut muscles of his stomach and, determinedly, south.

He broke the kiss and managed to gasp, "No."

"Why?"

"I wouldn't like you to regret—anything."

"I just want to touch you. Please, Jamie. I've been lying next door imagining touching you."

Oh, God, she begged him. What man could resist?

He said nothing and lay tense as iron as her fingers continued their agonizing movement. They encountered the waistband of his trews and hesitated.

"How do these come undone?"

"I don't think—" A crash of thunder drowned out the rest of his reply. His heart now pounded so loud in his ears he could hear nothing else anyway. This couldn't be happening. He must be asleep and dreaming.

"Damn." She struggled with his laces, got them open at last, and thrust her hand inside.

James nearly came off the bed. Undeterred, she wrapped her fingers around him and caught her breath.

"Oh. Oh! Nice."

She thought so, did she? Nothing to what he thought! He nearly disgraced himself on the spot, nearly erupted over her gentle fingers. Desperate, he fought for control.

"It's so warm. Strength covered over with softness—just like you."

"God, Catherine, have some pity."

"I had no idea it would feel like this. A big, great thing, isn't it? Is that supposed to fit inside me?"

Sweet Jesus, yes. He'd been created to fit inside her, nothing more.

He laughed unsteadily, and she laughed too; with the laughter still spilling she claimed his mouth again. He'd never imagined laughing with a woman in bed.

She thrust her tongue inside his mouth; he accepted it gladly. She released his member and seized his hand.

"Touch me too, Jamie, please."

"Where?"

"Anywhere. No, here." Unerringly she drew his hand—his maimed hand, no less—to her breast. She wore only a lad's undershirt and trews similar to his own. But what lay beneath never belonged to any lad.

He explored tentatively, feeling through the cloth the swell of a small breast tipped with a tight bud. Not satisfied, she made a sound of protest in her throat and guided his fingers up under the fabric.

He froze in delight, the soft weight of her filling his palm.

"Touch me," she begged again.

Ah, well—she couldn't see the scars on his fingers in the dark. He brushed his thumb across her nipple, and she moaned. What a miracle she was, her flesh soft and taut all at once, an invitation to his lips. But how could he think such a thing?

Almost as if she read his mind, she said, "I can think of a better use for your mouth."

"Can you?"

"Please."

Was that the only word she knew? Her undershirt now bunched around her neck, she slid up his body and offered herself to his lips there in the dark.

Gently, not sure of her reaction or his, he latched on to her, trying not to think about the ruined side of his mouth. She must not be thinking about it either, for her hand came up and caressed his scarred cheek, urging him closer, and then she arched into him so her whole breast filled his mouth.

Ah, but he was dying. And it was worth it.

"Oh Jamie, Jamie, Jamie." She kissed the top of his head, his hair, and the side where there was no hair, as well. He could smell the sweet scent of her and feel her heart pounding beneath her breast.

"Here. Please." There was that word again, the one he felt sure could make him do damn near anything. She guided his hand again, downward this time, inside her trews.

He released her breast even though it was the last thing he wanted to do. "Better not."

Again she asked, "Why?"

"Not right. You're better than this." A damning thing to say. He wanted to cut his own tongue out.

"I can't imagine better than this."

Neither could he; heaven couldn't be better. Her slender body trembled beneath his hand with what felt, to him, like eagerness.

She wanted him. Could a man—even he—mistake such a truth?

"Catherine—"

"Here, lower." Somehow while mostly maintaining body contact she shimmied out of her trews. He already jutted from his, like an airship.

Dangerous, his mind screamed at him, even as she once more guided his hand down.

"I love the way you touch me."

"Do you?" His head spun.

"So warm and kind." She released his wrist when the tips of his fingers touched the hot, damp nest of curls between her legs. He brushed her gently, and she pressed herself against him, breast to his mouth.

So that was the way of it? He was going to disgrace himself, and no mistake.

Thunder crashed anew, but neither of them heard it. Catherine moaned her approval as he explored her heat, a man testing the waters, one finger and then two. She parted her legs and arched against his hand.

"I want you, Jamie. There."

He wanted it too, more than breathing. He could almost feel himself sliding into the slick heat of her, the sweet channel even now tightening around his fingers.

But he said, "No. You're still a virgin. It shouldn't be me takes that from you."

"Who else?"

Who, indeed? Any of a thousand other men in the world—men of means with fine suits and fancy steamcars, the wealth to treat her as she deserved.

"You don't just give something like that away to any man you meet." To any monster. "You're frightened and lonely and not thinking straight."

"You're right, I'm thinking only of you—you, you, *you,* Jamie Kilter, and how I want it to be you."

"So you say. Heat of the moment." It felt blindingly hot, cooking him from the inside out. He opened his eyes, which he'd shut against a combination of ecstasy and pain. Lightning flashed, and he caught a glimpse of her lying there in his bed, hair ruffled, breasts bared, trews down around her knees, and his fingers—his scarred fingers—still inside her. His cock screamed for release.

Could she see him too? Ugly mask of a face, half-bald head, sweat glistening on his chest? The lightning flashed again, and he saw that she gazed into his eyes.

"Damn your honor anyway, Jamie Kilter." She took him in both hands and he very nearly came. "You know that thing the revolting Boyd wanted me to do?"

"Yes."

"I couldn't imagine doing that with any man, but I can now. Will you let me?"

"God, Catherine! Do you know what you're saying?" *Shut up*, his cock screamed at his brain. *Just shut up for once in your damn life.*

She began to move over him, and his fingers slid

out of her. Warm and beguiling, her scent rose to enfold the both of them. She kissed his chest and then licked it. He twitched like a man on the rack, and she moved lower, paused to lave his belly button, and followed the trail of hair on down. When she touched him with her tongue, his member spasmed.

"Umm," she said appreciatively. "Nice."

Tentatively, she fitted her soft lips around him, very gently took him into the hot cavern of her mouth. The last of his sense and coherence flew from his head.

Experimenting and totally without guile, she worked her way up and down the length of him with her tongue. Lightning showed him the incredible sight of her ruffled head bent over him, and his balls contracted.

Did she know what was going to happen next?

"Catherine, no." Frantic, he pulled her from him. "You don't want—"

"I do. I want you." She took him into her mouth again just as his last shred of control broke. He fountained into her on a fabulous rush, equal parts pleasure and shame. He felt his hot seed flow over her tongue and flood her mouth, and expected her to pull away in disgust.

Instead she went very still, barely breathing. He feared the worst until he felt her scouring him with sweet, little licks of her tongue.

"Astounding," she told him. "That was astounding. Kiss me."

She clambered up his body the way a kitten might climb a tree and fused her mouth to his. He could taste himself on her tongue, tangy and wild.

"Oh, Jamie, I've never felt anything like that. Oh,

thank you."

She thanked *him*?

"I'm on fire for you," she said. "On fire."

She drew his head back down to her breast. This time she didn't have to persuade him to put his fingers inside her.

He'd never made a prostitute come. Those couplings were swift, businesslike deals with no resemblance to this. Men talked, though, and he'd heard that a woman could come just like a man. But he'd not been with a woman caught in the throes of passion.

Now, with his mouth at her breast and his fingers inside her, he felt it happen: Catherine shook and writhed beneath his touch and tightened around his fingers in a glorious rush of heat.

"There now, there now," he murmured when she stopped quivering. He gathered her against him. With the passion spent, he had to be prepared for her to realize what she'd just done, and with whom.

Instead she settled against him with a sigh. "That was—well, there are no words, are there?"

"No words."

She snuggled closer, and her hair brushed his cheek. "I think I'll just stay here the night. You don't mind, do you?"

James didn't mind.

Chapter Twenty-Six

"Sweet Mary and all the saints! What the hell do you think you're doing?"

Cat pried her eyes open and shifted herself against the glorious length of Jamie's body, much of which lay beneath her. Last night's storm had moved on, and sunlight streamed through the open window, bathing the small chamber in brightness.

Tate Murphy stood in the open doorway of the room looking like wrath incarnate.

Reluctantly, she lifted her cheek from Jamie's chest, which felt warm and slightly sweaty and smelled like heaven. Somehow last night the scent of him had got inside her—maybe when he released himself into her mouth. She didn't think she could live without it now.

"Tate," Jamie said groggily. He stirred and all sorts of interesting muscles flexed. "She was frightened of the storm last night, that's all."

"That's all?" Tate's eyes bulged. "I suppose that's why she's lying there bare-assed and you with your trews wide open." Hastily he shut the door behind him. "Sweet mercy, was the girl a virgin? Roselyn will have my hide for this."

Cat blushed and slewed around till she could pull her trews up over her buttocks. Unfortunately that displayed her mostly-naked breasts, till now pressed into Jamie's side. Fresh from the ministrations of his mouth they felt swollen and tender, but she pulled the undershirt down over them anyway.

Jamie sat up. The morning light showed his scars mercilessly and also revealed that they spilled over onto his right shoulder and down that side of his chest. She'd been unable to see any of that last night, and she didn't care now. All she could think about was taking him in her mouth again.

Big strong man.

And that made her blush harder.

She glared at Tate indignantly. "How dare you come in here without knocking?"

"I did knock *and* call. I went to your door first, Miss Delaney, and became alarmed when you failed to answer. I became further alarmed when I saw your room was empty, and I came here to ask if he knew where you were." Tate concluded scathingly, "Clearly, he did."

"Well you've found me now, so please leave while I make myself decent." Cat climbed from the bed and lifted her chin. "We are both adults, and this is none of your concern."

Tate scowled. "I came to tell you my man's returned from Toronto with news. As I feared, it isn't good."

Cat's heart sank. "We'll be right down."

Tate went out, and she turned back to look at Jamie. He sat upright in the bed, head hanging and hair covering one side of his face.

Softly she asked him, "Are you all right?" He didn't look happy. Had she done something wrong last night, made some gaffe? Had it been scandalous for her

189

to do, with him, what Boyd had wanted? Did he now think less of her for it?

Swiftly he tied up his trews, slid off the far side of the bed, and turned away from her. She saw that the scars continued down the right side of his back, as well, all the way to the shoulder blade.

But oh, what a body the man had! Wide without bulk at the shoulders, and with those sleek, slender hips. The muscles of his arms rippled when he moved.

"Jamie, are you angry with me?"

He gave her a single look out of eyes blue as a summer sky. "No. How could I be? Are you upset about…upset with me?"

She returned swiftly, "How could I be?" She ached to go to him, wrap herself around him like a vine, and kiss him till she couldn't breathe. But something in his stance warned her off, and real life—not what they'd shared here in this room last night—beckoned.

Tate had word of Becky, and not good.

"Come with me," she beseeched.

He shrugged into his shirt, back turned to her, and then into trousers. Despite her worry, she couldn't help but watch appreciatively.

"Yes, if you like."

"I do. But I must go wash and dress properly first. I probably look a fright." She fished shamelessly for a compliment. She longed for him to tell her he thought her beautiful. He didn't speak, though, just shot her another look over his shoulder. But the expression in his eyes stole her breath.

Surely he still admired her. Or did he despise her now for last night's behavior? Maybe he thought her a tramp for putting her mouth on him, and enjoying it.

She couldn't bear it if she lost his respect, couldn't bear it if she lost him.

She slipped out of the room and into her own, praying no one saw her, and stood for a moment struggling to get hold of her emotions. Everything, everything had changed.

****

Bucky LaPlatte was the man who'd been sent to Toronto; he knew Canada well. He sat in Tate's office wearing a guarded look on his dark Gallic face when James filed in behind Catherine. Tate, who'd already heard Bucky's news, looked grim.

"Sit down, please, Miss Delaney. Bucky, here, knows who you are."

James drew out the chair for Catherine and remained standing behind her, arms crossed on his chest. He felt all too aware of her now, as if some connection had forged between them in last night's darkness. Every time she moved he noticed. When he heard the sound of her voice, his groin tightened.

But she had to be regretting things by now, things done in the heat of the moment that had carried her away. That sweet rosebud of a mouth on him…she never would have done that if she'd been able to see him. *Thank God for the darkness*.

He shifted on the balls of his feet, and Tate glared at him.

"LaPlatte visited your family home, Miss Delaney, in hopes of delivering a message to your mother or sister. The bad news is your sister, Becky, was no longer there."

"Snatched just the day before I got there," LaPlatte confirmed in his heavily accented English.

"Snatched?" Catherine faltered, and the color drained from her face.

"Taken by Boyd's agents, without question. Once I identified myself I was able to speak with your stepfather as well as your mother. He—your stepfather—recognized one of the men as being in Monsieur Boyd's pay."

"Where have they taken her?"

LaPlatte shrugged. "They bundled her into a steamcab. One of them said something about an airship."

"She'll already be here in the city, then," James said.

"No doubt. They will have beat me back by at least two days."

"She's been taken across an international border against her will. That's engaging in the flesh trade, that is. I'll go at once and speak with Brendan Fagan, see what can be done."

"That will take too long. It may already be too late," Catherine protested.

"Any other ideas, Miss Delaney?"

"Yes. We go to his house and get her. You know as well as I do she's probably there."

Tate asked almost kindly, "And have you an army to take at your back? Have you legal permission to go inside? Brendan will, and those automatons backing him, as well. Let me talk to him."

Catherine twisted her fingers together. "How long will that take?"

"I'm not sure, lass."

"She'll be alone and frightened. She's little more than a child. Boyd may—he may—"

"That's why I'm leaving at once. I want you to stay here while I'm gone, mind, and under Jamie's care."

Catherine exchanged a look with James. She said nothing.

Tate, who it seemed had begun to learn about her, shook his finger in her face. "I'll have your promise."

"I won't give you a promise I can't keep, Mr. Murphy. Everything I've done, I've done for Becky. I have to help her now. It's possible he'll trade her for me."

"No," James and Tate said at the same time.

Tate added, "Do you want him to have hold of the both of you?"

"At least then she wouldn't be alone."

"Foolish lass. We might need that bargaining chip before we're done, but don't toss it away now."

James gave him a sharp look Tate ignored.

"I promise you, Miss Delaney, we'll not leave your wee sister in his hands long. Trust me?"

Catherine nodded.

"Then stay here safe while I talk to my good friend Brendan. Jamie, lad, you keep her close, hear?"

Tate would not have to tell him twice.

Murphy went out; LaPlatte grunted and followed him. James and Catherine, left alone, stole looks at one another.

"I'm sorry," he told her. "I hoped for better news."

"It's all my fault," she lamented. "I should have protected her and stayed with Boyd. But I simply couldn't have done...well, what we did, with *him*."

James' face flamed. "No."

She shot him a deliberate look. "Not with him or anyone else."

Hope stirred in his heart. There she sat, looking at him as if he weren't hideous, even though she must have seen him all too clearly this morning.

But this made no fit time to speak of it, with her worried and frantic.

"Come on, Albert," he said. "Let's get some breakfast, and then you can help me with the dogs while we wait."

They spent the next hours in the yard, cleaning up, feeding, watering, and exercising the animals, most of which accepted Cat well. One, named Ginger, even crawled into her lap. Only Greta growled and barked whenever Catherine went near James.

Greta still wouldn't allow James to touch her, though, not quite. Despite edging forward in her kennel when he approached, she ducked away from his hand. When he let her out into the walled yard, she did her business and then slunk back in, grumbling.

"You must really love animals, to take her on," Catherine observed.

Before James could answer, Drappot strode into the yard. "He training you up to look after these curs, whelp?" he asked Catherine. "Better be. I'm sick to death of their racket at night."

Catherine, who wore her cap pulled well down over her face, gave him an insolent look. "Are you still complaining about that? If you don't like the noise, why don't you move out?"

"I've as much a right to be here as he does, or these mutts or you, for that matter, even if he is Murphy's pet."

"Gee, Mr. Drappot, is it? You can't be long out of the schoolyard, whining like that."

194

"You've a smart mouth on you." Drappot's face darkened.

"And you sound like a brat." Cat pushed the cap back on her head and James stiffened. She looked so feminine to him he could scarcely believe even someone so stupid as Drappot could believe her a lad.

"You need to be taught respect for your elders," Drappot growled. "Didn't get beat enough as a sprog, is that it? Not like your friend, here. His ma hated him so much she beat him every day, so the story goes."

"You take that back." Cat stepped up to him. "You don't know anything about it."

"And I suppose you do?"

"Leave it alone, Albert," James said hastily. "He's not worth the breath."

"Don't want the little lad fighting your battles for you? Then step up and fight me yourself," Drappot challenged. "You know it'll happen someday."

"Why?" Catherine planted herself between them. "What do you have against him?"

"Plenty. It hurts my eyes to look at him."

"Why, you—"

Catherine spoke a word James couldn't believe she knew and launched herself at Drappot like a terrier at a bulldog. The suddenness of the attack knocked Drappot over backward, and she fell on top of him, kicking and flailing.

James leaped and caught her back almost before either of them hit the ground, but not before she landed a blow to Drappot's throat and laid three scratches on his face. The last thing he needed was for Drappot to feel what lay beneath her clothes. He might trust LaPlatte with that knowledge; Drappot? Never.

Drappot sat up even as Catherine, in James' grasp, windmilled her arms and legs, desperate to get back at him.

"Damn brat's mad as that dog you got there!" Drappot cried.

"Apologize to Jamie at once!"

"Jamie, is it? I don't frigging think so. You'd better get out of my sight, Albert. And watch out when your big ugly friend's not close by. Two on one aren't odds I like."

"And you'd better watch out," Catherine spat, "when you're walking down dark alleys or hallways. Someone just might plant a knife in your back."

"Is that a threat?" Drappot's dark eyes blazed.

"No." James lifted Catherine higher off her feet. "Take a walk now, Drappot, and let tempers cool."

Drappot got up and stomped off, Greta barking at him all the way.

James set Catherine on her feet and she turned on him. "Why didn't you let me at him?"

"Because the man's a snake and we have enough trouble as it is. Have you forgotten your sister?"

"No." Catherine's eyes still blazed. "But he insulted you. No one insults you in my hearing, Jamie Kilter, and gets away with it."

James' heart promptly melted in his chest. "I appreciate that," he said, his emotions nearly choking him. Fierce and loyal, she shared some characteristics with the dogs in his care.

And he'd never imagined loving anyone so well.

Chapter Twenty-Seven

"I want to go with you," Cat beseeched the two big men who stood before her, shoulder to shoulder.

"Out of the question, Miss Delaney," said the one with the beautiful blue eyes, who'd been introduced to her as Brendan Fagan.

"But she's my sister."

"And we'll do everything in our power to recover her safely. I'll be taking side arms—steam cannon—and will have the Irish squad at my back."

The Irish squad, as Cat had already learned, was Fagan's name for the automatons.

"Look, lass," Tate Murphy appealed to her, "the last thing we'll be needing to do is worry about you during the recovery."

"That makes sense, Catherine," James told her. "Let them do their work."

"But she'll need me," Cat fretted.

"And that's why we'll take you straight to the station as soon as we get her there."

"Do you mean to arrest Boyd?"

"We may have no cause to arrest him," Fagan said.

"Trading in flesh, Mr. Murphy said."

"You came here with him of your own free will, and your sister was brought by an agent, not Boyd. We may be able to cite him as an accessory, but I'm sure his lawyers are very good."

"He needs to be put away. What if he does this to other women?"

"One thing at a time, Miss Delaney. You wait here with Mr. Kilter, and we'll send a message as soon as the operation's completed."

"Yes, of course. Thank you."

The two big Irishmen went out. James caught Cat's wrist. "Come on. It won't be easy, waiting, but we'll play cards or something."

"Play cards?" Instead she came and pressed herself into his arms. Here in the privacy of Tate's office no one could see them. "Just hold me, Jamie, please."

The sound of his name on her lips persuaded him. He slid his hands down her narrow back and cradled her gently.

"When do you think they'll go?"

"Straight away, I should think. They'll collect the automaton squad and their weapons, and go over."

"I hope someone hits Boyd with a cannon bolt. I wish I could see."

"You want to see the man torn up by a cannon bolt? You know what one of those can do on full blast? Stop his heart."

"Good," Cat said. "That's just what he deserves."

****

It wasn't till they'd played three hands of rummy that James excused himself for the bog and came back to find Catherine missing. At first he thought her restlessness had driven her out into the yard, but it stood empty save for the kennels. He went next to her room and then his own. His heart began to pound with panic when he found both empty.

He encountered Bill Latham outside Tate's office

and asked, "You seen Albert, by any chance?"

"You mean the squirt? He ran off."

"Ran off where?"

"Looked like he was on an errand. I thought you sent him."

"No."

"Headed north up Niagara. You can probably catch him if you hurry."

James probably could; his legs were twice as long. He had absolutely no doubt where Cat had gone, the little fool; Boyd's house lay in that direction.

He broke into a cold sweat when he reached the street and failed to see her anywhere. It didn't help that the neighborhood teemed with boys, most clad in clothing similar to hers. He cursed under his breath and pelted off at a determined run.

Up Niagara and then right onto the west end of Virginia Street, his eyes searching all the while. Charlie Crowter and his gang stood on the corner of Virginia and Prospect, but he barely heard their catcalls as he dashed past.

He should have known better than to leave Catherine alone even for a minute. He'd seen how determined she could be, that she wanted her way—even in the bedroom. He thought of how precious she'd felt in his arms, the way the tight prison of his heart opened to accept her. He'd never known anyone like Catherine Delaney. If he—a protector by trade—failed to safeguard her now, he'd never forgive himself.

Reaching into his breast pocket, he rubbed the red-gold curl he kept there, as if for luck. Then he pelted up Prospect and into the intersection at Hudson, just beginning to strain for breath. Down Hudson, and from the end he could see the circle beyond which stood Boyd's rented mansion. As he neared, gasping now, he saw that The Avenue beyond the circle was thronged with onlookers. It had plainly become the site of some terrible encounter or standoff.

As he neared, he searched for sight of Catherine's head. It didn't help that she stood shorter than many in the crowd or that her cap, a dull gray color, failed to catch the eye. Breathless and frantic, he reached the crowd and began to shoulder his way through, earning glares and curses, his eyes searching all the while.

The door of Boyd's house stood open, and two paddy wagons were parked at angles in the street. Members of the Irish squad spilled down the steps, standing as still as the machines they mostly were. Narrowing his eyes, James could see that Brendan Fagan stood in the doorway addressing the house in a roar.

"Give yourself up and send out the young woman, Rebecca Delaney, or we will be forced to come in!"

"Want us to come out, do you?" James recognized Boyd's voice, though he couldn't tell if it came from the doorway or further in. "Take this!"

Steam cannons appeared in the second-story windows of the house, thrusting out like obscene gestures. The crowd stirred, and James blinked in disbelief. Who turned steam cannon on a crowd of police and civilians? The man must be mad entirely.

Brendan Fagan stiffened and turned back an instant before the steam cannons fired. Hot jets of superheated vapor raked the crowd and hit one of the automatons, which toppled like a tenpin. People screamed, and the onlookers shifted like one big animal.

Brendan Fagan hollered again, but James couldn't hear what he said over the noise. Great puffs of steam rose from the front windows of the house. How long did it take for steam cannon that size to recharge? Now might be the time to send the Irish squad in.

Fagan must have had the same thought. He called to his men and waved an arm. But no sooner had they begun to move than the windows of the third story opened. More cannon appeared, these pointed straight down.

"Get back, get back!" Reinforcements had arrived in the form of regular police. They began trying to force the crowd back, presumably out of range, though the range of cannon that size had to be enormous. James looked for Catherine again as the onlookers shifted, but he still couldn't see her.

What if she'd gone inside before he arrived? What if Boyd held her hostage? James' guts twisted and his heart pounded like a hollow drum. He couldn't lose her, not before he'd remade himself into the man she deserved him to be.

The automaton hit by the steam cannon lay on its back like a dead insect, arms flung wide. The others stood their ground on the steps.

"Get back," a police officer told James roughly.

"I think I know somebody in there."

"Don't care. We're clearing the street."

The third-story cannons fired then, bursts of concentrated heat that seared where they landed. Two more of the Irish squad fell, and James' throat went dry.

In one of the second-story windows the cannon withdrew and was replaced by Boyd and a young girl, her hair streaming down and her face bone white.

"Is this what you want?" Boyd hollered. "You'll not have her, copper. I'll kill her first."

"Becky!" The cry came from the crowd. Not twenty feet from where James stood, a small form clad in clothing he recognized broke from the throng and darted forward. Catherine tore the cap from her head and the sun found the red-gold of her hair.

"Becky," she called again.

No need; she had already captured everyone's attention, including that of her sister and Boyd.

Boyd sneered at her, "You!"

He turned his head and gave an order. A steam cannon reappeared in the opening beside him, shoving him and Becky aside. Time and motion both seemed to slow as the cannon's operator took aim. James heard Fagan holler. James himself gasped a prayer as he leaped forward, fully prepared to shield Catherine's small body with his own, willing to accept any pain, even unto death.

He had taken no more than three great steps before the steam cannon fired. With a belch of power, and deadly accurate, it took Catherine in the chest. She was lifted by the impact and hung for an instant before she fell like a leaf in autumn; James saw her head hit the curb with a mighty thump and knew she must be senseless before she went down.

All hell broke loose then. The Irish squad—all but the three wounded or destroyed—rushed into the house, and a small army of regular officers came up behind.

James ignored all of it. He reached Catherine and threw himself down, desperately looking for signs of life. Eyes closed, she lay with the front of her shirt smoking, burned straight through to her chest. He couldn't see her breathing.

"You trying to get killed?" someone screamed at him, one of the regular police who paused at his side. The steam cannons were firing again, raking the street and sidewalk.

James barely noticed. But the officer gave him a shove and yelled, "Get under cover!" before pelting on.

James ignored the instruction; it didn't matter what happened to him, not when his whole world lay on the pavement like a bundle of spent, fragile bones. Protest arose in him, more powerful than any rage he'd ever felt when gone off kilter.

"Catherine. Catherine!"

No response. He told himself she wasn't dead, couldn't be dead, no matter how she looked. But no, she wasn't breathing, and her lips, slightly parted, didn't move.

"Out of the way!"

Still another officer barked at him. James gathered Catherine's body up in his arms and cradled her against him. Tears scorched his throat.

"Back!" And he went slipping through the crowd, all the way to the edge of the circle, with Catherine motionless but still warm, caught tight against him.

Shouting came from the direction of the besieged house; all the steam cannons had now disappeared from the windows. So had Boyd and Becky, as if they'd never been. Had Becky seen her sister fall?

James stood, his arms numb around his burden, aching, until Brendan Fagan emerged from the house, still giving orders. He checked on his fallen officers, who, much to James' surprise, stirred and got up, one by one.

Hope rose in James' heart. If they lived, Catherine might. But she was flesh and bone, not steel.

Brendan caught sight of him, checked for an instant, and ran over, dismay on his handsome face. "Is she dead?"

James stared at him, mute with pain.

Fagan repeated, "Is she dead? The blast hit her in the chest. It will have stopped her heart."

James hoisted Catherine's body in his arms, bent his ear, good cheek down to her chest, and heard no sound.

Tears flooded his eyes. He stood like a child holding a dead pet.

"Aw, hell," Fagan said. He considered James with his clear, blue eyes and then glanced over his shoulder at the house, now safely cordoned off by police both human and machine.

He called to someone, "Kelly, you're in charge. I'll be right back."

The automaton from Nellie's Bar shot James a glance and nodded slightly.

"Come on, and hurry," Fagan told James.

"Where?"

"Just follow me, quick as you can."

Chapter Twenty-Eight

James ran with Catherine in his arms until the breath burned in his lungs, seeing nothing but Fagan's broad, blue back before him. They pelted east down North Street, away from the commotion around Boyd's mansion, past several side streets, and toward the big intersection at Delaware, corners and buildings going by in a blur. Catherine's head bounced against his shoulder in time with his footsteps, but only as that of a rag doll might, and he fancied she cooled as they went.

Dead, dead, dead, dead, dead. His mind took up the rhythm of the word that matched the great, painful beats of his heart. This was it for him, then; he couldn't go on, didn't want to go on.

Yet he followed Brendan Fagan south onto Delaware and, struggling now like a spent hound at the heels of its master, past Allen. They veered onto Virginia Street and paused at last in front of a big, red brick house once fine but now gone shabby. Fagan shot him an intense look, went up the steps, and rang the bell.

James stood there not knowing where he was or why, fighting for breath, fighting for sanity, while the impossible seconds ticked by.

At last the door swung open, revealing a beautiful Negress with a small child in her arms. She barely glanced at Fagan before her wide gaze flew to James behind him.

"Officer Fagan. Oh, my, what's happened?" She hesitated before she said, "Come in."

The interior of the house smelled like furniture polish and a lot of other things James couldn't identify. The woman with the child left them standing in the hallway and hurried off down a corridor. A door half way along opened, and several children peered out at them.

James asked through his aching throat, "What is this place?"

"Mrs. McMahon's. She may be able to help us."

"How?" James tightened his arms around his burden. "Catherine's—"

"Mrs. McMahon can do miraculous things. Hush, now."

James hushed. A second woman appeared from the back of the house, led by the first, who still held the child. Small of stature, though not so tiny as the Negress, she wore an incredible costume of men's trousers, an almost-sheer white shirt, and a leather corset that defined her narrow waist. Her short hair gathered around her face like a cap of feathers.

"Brendan?" she greeted Fagan. She shot one startled look at James' face before focusing on Catherine. "What's happened?"

"Steam cannon, a big one," Fagan told her. "Took the blast in the chest."

"My God! Any other injuries?"

Fagan looked at James, who said hoarsely, "She banged her head when she fell."

The woman asked, "How long ago?"

Fagan said, "Not long since. She's still warm. Will

you help us?"

Help, how? James wondered. And did he really care? He would trade his own life to save Catherine's, if she weren't already dead, dead, *dead*.

Again the woman—Mrs. McMahon, Fagan had called her—looked into James' face.

"Do you love her?"

What kind of question was that, at a time like this? He gazed into the woman's gray-green eyes. They seemed to look through him, demanding truth.

Mutely, he nodded.

"Then I'll try. Bring her." She looked at the Negress. "Georgina, I'll need your help."

"Where's Liam?" Brendan asked.

"At work. Georgie, see if Nancy can watch Benny for you. Then fire up the boiler." She glanced over her shoulder as she led them down the dim corridor to the back of the house. "This is Mrs. Collwys, who will assist me. Your name, and hers?"

Demand filled her voice, along with kindness.

"James Kilter and—and Catherine."

"Is she your wife?"

"No."

They entered a big room loaded with strange equipment: bottles, beakers, jars, and vials, as well as a large steam plant. Mrs. McMahon indicated a wooden table standing in the center of the floor.

"Put her down."

James didn't think he could. It felt too much like surrendering hope.

Mrs. McMahon told him, "It's all right."

Mrs. Collwys hurried in and fired the generator. It started up with a throaty clamor and began to bang through the room like a mighty heartbeat.

Gingerly, James laid Catherine on the table. Her head lolled back alarmingly and, suddenly, she looked quite dead.

Fagan came to James' shoulder. "What is this place?" James asked.

"You'll be all right here. Listen, lad, I have to get back; I've an operation to tie up."

"You got Boyd?"

Fagan shook his head. "He got away out the back, and young Miss Delaney with him, which is one of the reasons I need to go." He fixed James with a stare. "Mrs. McMahon will try to help you, but you can never speak of what you see in this room, understand? Never."

What was he going to see? Doubt and hope tangled inside him, indistinguishable. He nodded.

Fagan clapped him on the shoulder and went out. Mrs. McMahon took his place.

"Let us see how badly she's hurt." She turned those wide, uncanny eyes on James. "You understand there are things I can't repair."

"Who are you?" And what? He dared not ask that.

"You can call me Clara. I have a talent, Mr. Kilter. Sometimes I can resurrect the dead."

She said it so casually, James merely blinked at her. As she did, her hands moved, laying the remnants of Catherine's shirt open very gently, exposing breasts and the great, terrible scorch mark left by the steam cannon.

She caught her breath. "Right above the heart."

"The blast will have shocked it motionless," said Mrs. Collwys from the other side of the table.

"Hopefully. You understand, Mr. Kilter, if her heart is too badly damaged I will not be able to revive her. And if she comes back there will be memory loss. She may remember very little."

James heard only the words, *if she comes back*.

"Are you saying you can—can save her?"

"No, she's already gone. But I might return her."

The woman laid her hand above Catherine's heart. Clouds of steam had begun to fill the room, obscuring most of the furnishings. With it came sticky heat—the faces of both women glistened.

Half horrified, James made as if to step back from the table. Mrs. McMahon's hand darted out and caught his wrist.

"No." Again she fixed him with those uncanny eyes. "We've learned a few things since we began this perilous practice, Mr. Kilter. You say you love her?"

"Yes."

"Does she love you as well?"

"I don't know."

"But you'd like her to." Clara smiled, and it warmed her elfin countenance. "Then your face must be the first she sees when she opens her eyes. They imprint upon their return—they orientate. You stand here. Let her see you."

James, now certain it had been he who'd died out on the street and he now inhabited some fantastical afterlife, stood where planted, alarm coursing through him. Clara stood just opposite where, both hands now touching Catherine, she raised her head and closed her eyes.

And James saw something come and fill her— some power, some force accompanied by the billowing steam, which changed and transformed her. Breathless, his throat clogged and his heart pounding, he watched in stunned amazement as she suddenly bent forward and placed her mouth over Catherine's.

A kiss, yet not a kiss. Instead, Clara breathed as if breathing for Catherine, who could not. Air—and something more—rushed into Catherine's body, a breath of impossible length and power.

James, inhibitions forgotten, leaned closer so he could see Catherine's face, watch her eyes.

Yet nothing happened. For many long moments the artificial beat of the steam plant continued. He thought Clara must raise her head and breathe again, but her fingers continued to massage Catherine's chest, and he almost saw the power leave Clara's body and fill Catherine's.

He did not know what this might be. Witchcraft? Some dire, terrible rite? And would he refuse even black magic if it brought Catherine back to him?

Almost upon the thought, Catherine's eyelashes twitched. Rosy color flooded her face, and her curled fingers scrabbled at the table.

Only then did Clara lift her head.

Catherine dragged in a great, shuddering breath on her own. The burn on her chest heaved, and her lips moved as if seeking to form words that would not come.

"There now, let her see you," Mrs. Collwys said, and pushed James toward the head of the table.

Still another breath, two, three. James placed his hand where Clara's had been, and he felt Catherine's heart beating. A sob rose to his throat.

Catherine's eyes opened and stared directly into

his. Clear they were, focused and unwavering as if she saw only him. No matter then that his face was ruined, for a smile came into her eyes. He saw gladness, he saw her soul in her eyes.

Her lips moved again and this time formed a word. "Jamie."

He slid his fingers to her hand and clenched it tight.

"Jamie, where were you? You seemed so far."

"Here now, with you." The words were all he could manage.

"Kiss me. Kiss me again."

He did, and as it had in his room at the warehouse, and in Roselyn's kitchen, her mouth opened beneath his, inviting him in. His tongue dove inside, and he tasted…what? Her essence, yes, but something else, as well: life, raw and sweet, and the remnants of power. Her tongue caressed his, her soul reached for his, she lifted her arms and wound them around his neck. Victorious madness rose to his head.

Alive. She'd returned alive, and she was his. His for all time.

Chapter Twenty-Nine

They sat in the parlor while Mrs. Collwys served tea, Catherine in James' lap. She'd started out on the settee beside him but had climbed up onto his knees and hooked one hand in his shirt before many minutes passed. Now she pressed so close into his chest he could feel her heart beating.

Precious heart.

"The intense attachment should die down gradually," Clara said, indicating their position with her teacup. "The initial rush tends to subside."

James sincerely hoped not. After almost losing her—correction, after losing her and getting her back again—he could live with Catherine as an appendage. The only difficulty he could foresee was the constant erection.

Clara smiled slightly as if she guessed his thoughts. "Or, if you're very fortunate, it won't subside."

In James' experience, good fortune rarely found him. *Except today*.

"If you do not mind me asking," Clara said gently, "how long ago did you suffer your accident?" She waved a hand at his face. "Steam burns, correct? I've seen them before but never, I think, so extensive."

"Like our Woodrow," Mrs. Collwys whispered, and set a plate of biscuits in front of James.

"Steam and boiling water both," he replied. "Over

212

ten years ago."

"There are operations, you know," Clara said tentatively, "though on injuries that old…"

Catherine released James' shirt and caressed his scarred cheek with her soft fingers. Despite himself, he flinched.

"You are perfect just as you are," Catherine said and kissed him, her fingers still busy smoothing his thickened skin.

He flushed with a combination of arousal and embarrassment.

Mrs. Collwys coughed and turned to the door. "I'll just go and check on Benny."

She went out without a sound. Very reluctantly, James ended the kiss and pressed Catherine's head back into his chest.

"You say this is a by-product of what just happened?" he asked Clara.

"Hmm. Intense attachment forms at the moment of resurrection. We've found it can be transferred from me to whomever the subject sees upon wakening. Better than it being me, which often proves inconvenient. Of course the intensity of the bonding may be augmented by preexistent emotions."

"Meaning?"

"That if she cared for you before her resurrection, she will care much more deeply now."

"Oh." James' thoughts raced over that, almost afraid to examine it. "Exactly what did happen back in that room? I mean, she was *dead*."

"She was." Clara fixed those uncanny green eyes on him. "Mr. Kilter, I have a rare ability, an inherited power. I would appreciate it if you didn't mention that to anyone. Very few people know. And I'd prefer not being the object of a witch hunt."

"Of course. I didn't thank you. How can I possibly thank you? I owe you everything."

"Do not thank me too quickly. You are likely in for a difficult ride. She may not remember much. It will be like having a child on your hands."

"I don't mind. I'm grateful. If you ever require the last drop of my blood…"

"Save it for her. I require only your silence."

The parlor door opened abruptly, and a man came in. Tall and with a crop of nearly-black hair that spilled over his forehead, he wore the clothes of a workman and moved with the confidence of a king.

His quick gaze took in the scene and he said with a lilt, very Irish, "Georgie said we have visitors. Who's this, then?"

Clara's face lit as if a beacon flared behind her eyes. She got up and went to him, laid a hand on his forearm in an act of blatant claiming.

"Liam, this is James Kilter and his friend, Catherine. Brendan Fagan brought them. Mr. Kilter, this is my husband, Liam McMahon."

McMahon's blue eyes inspected James frankly, lingering on the ruined side of his face before he nodded to Catherine and thrust out a large, work-hardened hand for James to shake. "Good to meet you."

"Same here. I'm grateful to your wife. She—" Abruptly words failed James.

"Aye, Georgie said." McMahon laid a palm against Clara's back and looked into her face tenderly. "Are you all right?"

She nodded. "But I fear Mr. Kilter is in for an

interesting time. Sit down, Liam, and have some tea."

"Tea?" McMahon grunted, crossed to a sideboard and poured two generous measures of whiskey, one of which he passed to James' hand.

"Get yourself outside of that. You're going to need it." He sprawled in a chair as if he owned the world, or at least this bit of it—for all James knew, he did—and fixed James with that bright stare. "There's a story in this, lad. Spill."

James sampled the liquor in his glass and then took a bigger, steadying gulp. He'd never tasted better Irish whiskey. What a curious household, ruled by a workman yet sporting Ireland's finest.

Catherine had subsided with her face against James' chest and her eyes closed, breathing softly like a sleeping child. Quietly, so as not to disturb her, he told her tale and his, entwined. Everyone in the city would soon know what had happened at Boyd's house anyway, and Brendan Fagan knew most of it.

McMahon and his wife exchanged several speaking glances as they listened, but did not interrupt or voice their thoughts until James concluded.

Then McMahon said, "So this bastard got clean away with the sister? How did he manage that?"

"I'd like to know," James admitted, and wetted his whistle again. "Officer Fagan had the Irish squad all round the house."

"You have one advantage," Clara mused. "This villain—and Catherine's sister, unfortunately—will have seen Catherine take that blast and fall. He'll believe her dead. That may help you protect her."

"Aye, so," her husband agreed. "For if he suspects differently, he'll not rest."

"When she wakes," James asked Clara, "will she ask about her sister? How much will she remember about what happened?"

"Not much, at least not right away." McMahon answered and tipped his glass at James. "I've been through that. Poor lass will have a great, fecking wall in her mind for some time."

Clara moved and perched on the arm of Liam's chair, where she laid a hand on his knee. "She wasn't dead as long as you, my love."

"Aye, Kilter, you'll have to wait and see."

The parlor door opened and the tiny woman called Georgina came in, once more carrying the child in her arms. The boy sported a head of black curls, but his skin was a shade or two lighter than Georgina's.

Her gaze went directly to Catherine.

"Sleeping," Clara murmured. "Just what she needs."

"And you, Clara?" Georgina looked concerned.

Clara's hand moved on McMahon's knee. "I have what I need."

McMahon said grandly, "Will you stay for supper, Kilter? The more the merrier."

James glanced at the window, startled to see the light faded into evening. Suddenly helpless, he had no idea what to do next. He could scarcely take Catherine back to Tate's.

The room full of people watched him kindly as he struggled with it.

"You'll stay here for the time," Clara decided, "until we hear from Brendan. Georgie, if you'll be so kind as to tell Ruella we have guests?"

"Yes, and then I have to get home to Timothy,"

Georgina said. She bounced the child in her arms and then touched James' arm compassionately.

"The best of luck, Mr. Kilter, to you and your lady."

His lady. If only that were true, James thought and looked into Catherine's quiet, beautiful face. He could feel her breath on the skin at the open neck of his shirt, like a caress.

His arms tightened around her protectively. From now on he lived for her benefit, nothing else.

"Thank you," he tried to tell Mrs. Collwys, but she just smiled and went out.

McMahon said, musing, "Might be best, Kilter, if you stay here the night. My love," he slanted a look at his wife, "have we room? We've a house full of bairns," he added to James with a wink.

"We'll make room."

"You've been more than kind already. I couldn't ask any more."

"You're part of the family now, lad; my wife will not be letting you go. In fact, I think we can find a series of houses for you to go to and not be discovered. What do you say, Clara?"

Clara fixed her curious gaze on James. "Indeed. Is there anything else we can do for you, Mr. Kilter?"

"Call me James, please. And if a message could be sent to my boss, Michael Murphy, I'd appreciate it. He'll be half frantic to know where we are."

"Murphy, is it?" McMahon grinned. "I think we can manage that as well. Now finish your whiskey, lad. There's always more where that came from."

Chapter Thirty

Jamie.

Cat awoke with his name hovering on her lips and filling her mind. She opened her eyes to near-perfect darkness, only a few lines of dim light outlining what must be a window on the opposite wall, and to complete disorientation. Panic arose and beat hard in her throat.

"Jamie," she whispered.

Something moved beneath her hands, beneath her cheek, warm, supple, and reassuring. Arms tightened around her, and she heard his voice.

"Hush, now. It's all right."

She knew his voice; she knew his touch. He held her in the dark. But searching her mind swiftly, she discovered she knew very little else. Who was she? She couldn't remember her own name.

Her chest hurt with a deep, burning ache just above her heart. She unclenched her fingers from Jamie's torso and rubbed at the spot, encountering bandaging.

"Jamie." It seemed to be all she could think, all she could say.

One of his big hands came up, cradled her head, and soothed her back down against him.

"Where are we?"

"Safe for now."

His lips skittered over her forehead, and just like

that she wanted him, the desire raw and bright, like raging fire. She moved, slid on top of him, her smaller body caressing his big one, and groped for his mouth in the dark. She needed him inside her, needed him filling her, the hunger rabid in her veins.

"Catherine," he said.

Was that her name? If he said it, it must be so. At that moment he was her god, her star, her reason for drawing breath.

She pressed her mouth to his. Light, searing and brilliant, exploded in the darkness. She wanted her tongue, her body, her blood to fuse with his.

Both his hands came up and captured her face. He broke the kiss. "Catherine, no."

"Please, please, please, Jamie. I need, I need, I need—" All at once she wept, sobbed over him hysterically, the tears flowing like rain.

"All right, all right." Tenderly he kissed the tears from her cheeks, worked his way to her mouth, and swallowed her sobs. She closed her eyes and absorbed the feel, the scent of him. Her panic subsided even as her arousal grew.

She moved her lips from his, not far, and whispered, "Jamie, please love me."

"Christ, Catherine! I can't."

She knew he could. She could feel him pressed hard against her, cradled beneath her thighs. "Why not?"

"I won't have it this way. You're not in a fit state of mind. No, love, don't weep again. What do you recall about what happened?"

She went very still, struggling against the fog that filled her mind. Bits and pieces of memory, images like the remnants of dreams, floated though the murk.

"There was a crowd. Weapons. What happened, Jamie?"

"You were hit by the blast from a steam cannon."

"I was? Is that why my chest hurts?"

"Yes."

"But no one survives that."

"No."

"So how is it I'm here?"

"Officer Fagan—do you remember Brendan Fagan?"

"No."

"He knew a woman, a remarkable woman. She was able to help you. We're in her house now."

"Help me, how?"

He hesitated. The breath gusted from his lungs. "This woman, Clara McMahon, has a miraculous talent. She was able to bring you back."

"Bring me back?"

"From the dead."

"What!"

"You died there, Catherine, in the street, when the steam blast hit you. I carried you here to Clara's house in my arms. We're safe for now, but Boyd got away from the police."

"Wait, you're going too fast. Who?"

"Sebastian Boyd. You don't remember him."

"No."

"Or—or your family."

"Little pieces of things. You say I was dead? Jamie, how can all this be? I'm frightened. Hold me, hold me. Tighter."

She clung to him, and he wrapped his arms around

her, drawing her still closer.

"You won't leave me? Promise you won't leave me," she whimpered.

"I promise."

"Because I need you." Arousal flared still more brightly. "And I want you, Jamie. You can't tell me differently."

"Listen, listen to me." His voice rumbled up through his chest and into her ear, grounding her, the one reassurance in the terrifying darkness. "Clara—she said there's a byproduct of this resurrection. The person who is brought back forms an attachment. It should die down soon."

"What are you saying? I don't understand."

"Those she brings back imprint on the first person they see. The first person you saw was me."

Protest rose inside Cat like madness. "She's wrong. That can't be. What kind of terrible woman is she, anyway, that raises the dead? Why would you believe anything she says?"

"Not a terrible woman at all, but kind and, I think, very wise. She took a risk helping us and bringing you back to me. That's why we can't reveal to anyone what she's done."

Cat went suddenly still, somewhat mollified. "You wanted me returned?" Did that mean he cared? Did he need her even half so much as she needed him?

"Yes, oh yes, Catherine. And I'll look after you as best I can. The police may well find Boyd soon. Meanwhile, he thinks you're dead and will have no reason to keep looking for you. So if we hide and keep you out of sight, we might weather this and come out the other side."

"And what then?" Cat tried to look ahead, but it seemed as murky as what lay behind her. She could imagine little while remembering so little. She'd never realized how much expectation of the future depended on knowledge of the past. Panic touched her again. "How can I go on, if I don't remember anything?"

"You'll remember, given time."

She shuddered. "How long was I—dead?"

"Not long, maybe twenty minutes. The time it took me to bring you here."

"But I was a corpse." She struggled to assimilate it. "Is that why you won't make love to me? Because I was a corpse?"

"No, Catherine. Christ, no." His heartbeat sped up beneath her ear. "I just want you to be sure in your mind before you give me a gift like that. Because there's no going back from it, is there? I think you just need someone right now. When you're able to choose, I want you to choose me, but I can't believe you could choose me..."

"Why not?" Who else in all the world could she choose? Every part of her craved him with a need so deep she could barely fathom it. She twined her arms and legs about him more closely.

He said, the words dragged from him, "You can't see me here in the dark, but you do remember how I look—my face?"

"You think that matters? It doesn't matter." As she had in the parlor earlier, she raised her hand and began to caress his ruined cheek, exploring the thickened skin with her fingers, smoothing the mutilated lips and ear. If only she could make him feel what she felt, convince him of her admiration. If only she could make him believe what her heart knew.

He drew an unsteady breath and went rigid beneath her touch. Ignoring his reaction, she continued to stroke him, every inch of scarring, up onto the hairless side of his head, then back down his neck and shoulder to his broad chest.

"Jesus, Catherine," he breathed.

"Jamie, I need you. Please."

She followed the motions of her fingers with her mouth, skittered her lips across his lips, dipping into his mouth with her tongue for a sweet taste and then planting tender kisses all over his cheek, his jaw, his neck and shoulder—everywhere she knew his scars lay. She had to tell him she found him beautiful. She had to convince him the light that shone from his heart transfigured everything she saw in him.

A sound that might have been a sob issued from his throat. She covered his mouth with hers and swallowed it, slid her hand down the supple muscles of his chest, over his rippled belly, and caressed him through the front of his trews. He jerked against her hand like a man in agony.

She broke the kiss to whisper, "Touch me, Jamie. Make me yours."

His hand, warm and gentle, slid down her back, cupped her buttocks, lifted her effortlessly, and settled her on top of him. Light flared in the darkness again, and her heart rose on a wave of victorious gladness. She wiggled and positioned herself against him, a willing receptacle for whatever he wanted to give.

His hand traveled back up and cupped her head. He kissed her deeply, luxuriously, his tongue exploring the inside of her mouth with strong, warm strokes until she saw stars. She felt his need then, great as her own, and she no longer doubted him. Nothing had ever been so right as this.

"Are you sure?" he asked when he stopped kissing her. His breath, when he spoke, gusted across her lips, further stoking her arousal.

"Very sure, Jamie, beautiful Jamie. I want you to touch me everywhere."

"What did you call me?"

"You are the most beautiful man I've ever known. The only man I'll ever want. Touch me."

Slowly, with delicious tenderness, he drew off her clothing, and she helped remove the barrier of his trews. Big and warm, all strength, he laid her on her back and moved over her in the darkness.

"I don't want to hurt you."

"You can't hurt me."

"Your chest…"

"Touch me there." She captured his hand and brought it to her breast. She felt on fire for him, burning up in flame. He fell upon her hungrily, his mouth a miracle of sensation, and she clung to him like a limpet, her legs, her thighs, and what lay between seeking that one strength so hard, positioning herself so he very nearly slid inside.

"Beautiful Jamie, give yourself to me."

He abandoned her breast but only to find her mouth again. She met him, open above as below, and wooed him in. He invaded her with his tongue at the same instant he slid into her, and the pain was glorious—one tearing flash of light that seared her and bound her to him before he began to move ever deeper, claiming her body, her soul, her heart.

When they became one person, when the waves of pleasure seized them both and his essence filled her, only then did her deep need ease; only then did she feel complete.

Laura Strickland

Chapter Thirty-One

James woke to the incredible sensation of lips dropping kisses on his shoulder, skittering down his chest and straight south toward his belly. Every muscle of his body tightened in response. He opened his eyes to see the top of a ruffled, red-gold head, and awareness rushed him like a train at full bore. He made an involuntary sound, and Catherine lifted her head to meet his gaze, her eyes wide, spiked by long lashes and full of wicked, avid light.

They gazed at each other for a dozen heartbeats before James, unable to endure her regard, flinched and bade her even as he had before, "Don't look at me."

The small room at the top of the house had filled with bright, merciless morning light. He turned his face away from her, pressed his ruined cheek into his pillow. Last night she had called him beautiful—something no one had ever done. This morning, though, she would once more see the pitiless truth of what he was.

His heart couldn't endure it. Better to never have her regard than to lose it now. He felt sick with the knowledge that she must inevitably reject him.

"Why? Jamie, I want to look at you. I never get tired of the pleasure in it. I'd be happy looking at you for the rest of my life, if you'd let me."

James' heart stopped in his chest. He distinctly felt it falter before struggling to beat again.

226

That's the magic talking, he thought. The effect of the resurrection. Whatever power Clara had used to drag Catherine back from oblivion had centered all of her upon him—imprinted her, as Clara had said. It didn't matter who she saw first; had it been Boyd, she'd want him now.

The pain of that tore at him, deeper than any he'd known in the past. For he'd trade his soul to the devil to have Catherine truly love him.

He knew how hideous he was. No woman who wasn't enchanted could lie here next to him, naked, and tell such a falsehood.

Not a falsehood to her, he reminded himself. *What she's been through ordained it, and she believes it to be so.*

He could take advantage of that. The idea blossomed like a flower of flame in his mind. He remembered all that had happened last night in the silken dark. He could love her again before she thought to deem him ugly, try to get his fill of her sweetness while he might.

Many a man would. Who, waking with a warm and willing woman in his bed, would hesitate?

She reached up and relentlessly turned his face toward her. Hell, he thought, this is it—she'll get a good look at me and sanity will return, putting an end to my mad dreams.

Instead she caressed his scarred cheek with her hand even as she had last night, the preamble to the wondrous claiming that followed.

Might it be the preamble again? His body certainly thought so; he was up and hard, totally shameless.

She whispered, "You have the most gorgeous eyes

227

I've ever seen, Jamie Kilter. I can glimpse your soul in them: it's beautiful."

"Oh, God, Catherine. Oh, God, oh—"

"And the most wonderful…" Very deliberately, she slid her hand down his chest, over his belly until she encountered his manhood, at full mast. She curled her fingers around him, and heat flared in her gaze. "Love me?"

He already did, utterly and completely, the way a drowning man loves air. About to admit it, he realized she asked him to make love to her in the physical sense, as he had last night. All she wanted was comfort, reassurance…not him.

Softly he touched her hair. "How will you feel in a few days or weeks when things start coming back to you and this attachment—whatever it is—fades? When you realize you've given your body to a monster?"

She gazed fully at him. "There's no monster here."

"I am trying to be responsible, Catherine. Considerate."

"Stop being so damned considerate and kiss me."

"I don't think…"

"Must I prove it to you again?"

Eyes gleaming, she slid herself up and straddled him. James caught his breath as the soft mounds of her naked breasts brushed his chest, igniting flame. From her perch atop his body, she took his face between her hands.

"Look into my eyes, Jamie Kilter. Do you see any lies?"

Lies, no; he saw impossible desire and, if he looked hard enough, the hope of eternity.

She bent and rubbed her soft cheek against his

ruined one as a kitten might, then turned her face and kissed it, a soft, wet kiss followed by the heat of her tongue.

"You taste so good. I want to taste you everywhere, Jamie. But first I want you inside me."

This isn't real, he told himself. *It's a dream*. But to save his soul, he couldn't resist.

"Not safe," he gasped in a last-ditch effort. "I could give you a child. That's the last thing you'd want."

"A lovely little auburn-haired, blue-eyed child? Why wouldn't I want that?" She smiled, wise and teasing.

"It would tie you to me."

"And why wouldn't I want to be tied to you?" All the teasing fled her eyes, replaced by intention, serious as a vow. James knew at that moment he was lost, his life hers as completely as if he'd signed it away.

He kissed her, a deep burning, intimate kiss, all need and heat. He caught her hips between his hands and positioned her where he wanted her, so she slid down onto him. And then, his mouth still fused to hers, he rocked into her, giving himself with every stroke, every wild thrust, until he made answer to her need and his own.

****

"Mr. Murphy sent word that he should be here before noon." The woman Catherine had seen last night—Clara, Jamie called her—gave Cat an appraising look from wide, gray-green eyes. "How do you feel?"

"Confused." Still ravenous for the man beside her. "My chest hurts." But the rest of her felt marvelous, as if lit from within. Beneath the dining table, where they sat, her fingers remained linked with Jamie's. Every time he so much as breathed she could feel it, as if his heart beat for both of them.

Carefully, she told the woman, "Jamie says you have some remarkable power and used it to save my life."

Clara smiled wryly. "This must be so difficult for you to accept."

"How can you do such a thing?"

"It's an hereditary ability passed down through the women of my line. I use it seldom, and I certainly don't flaunt it." Again Clara fixed Catherine with that curious stare. "It could prove very inconvenient—even dangerous to me—should it get out."

"We won't tell. Jamie says I must stay hidden anyway." There was a man called Boyd after her. She squeezed Jamie's fingers harder, and he returned the pressure. "When will I start remembering things?"

Clara's expression turned sympathetic. "It's impossible to say. It seems to vary from subject to subject, and we're learning as we go. Things may begin to come back slowly a bit at a time. Or it may come in a flood."

Cat fretted, "It's just so disconcerting to have a big blank when I try to look back. I can remember part of the scene in the street when I—when—"

"Most of those I've resurrected remember the actual death. When other things come back, they don't seem like memories so much as—well, preferences. You should talk to my husband about it. He's working now at the coffin shop."

"You—you raised your husband? That great, strong man?"

Ruefully, Clara said, "It's how we met. And

bonded, incidentally."

James' fingers spasmed in hers. Cat shot him a questioning look, but his expression remained closed. Cat's mind struggled with it. Ah, yes—he feared the bond that now existed between the two of them, and Cat's feelings for him, were just a byproduct of the resurrection.

To Clara she said, "Do you mind if I ask you a question?"

"Not at all."

"How could you be sure your husband loved you, and wasn't just in thrall to you because you raised him?"

Clara glanced into James' face and then fixed her gaze on Catherine again. "A valid question, under the circumstances. I came to believe the raising intensified an attraction that would have existed anyway. As for the veracity of his feelings, I just knew. Women do, I believe. Men are often a bit thicker when it comes to such matters."

The dining room door opened, and a woman came in. Fair-haired and lovely, she had a sweet, rosy face and blue eyes clear as a summer sky.

"Clara, Mr. Murphy is here."

A man came into the room, burly and red-haired, with a plain, broad face. Cat felt she must know him, yet when she searched for an identity, the fog in her head merely intensified.

"Tate," Jamie said and got to his feet, pulling Cat up with him.

"By God, James lad, you've done it this time." Ireland flavored the man's voice. He turned kind eyes on Cat. "Miss Delaney, are you all right?"

"I scarcely know, sir. I don't remember. I…"

"That's all right. Brendan filled me in on a few things. You must be Mrs. McMahon." He extended his hand to Clara and then turned to look at the blonde woman who had showed him in. "And—?

"Her sister-in-law, Nancy McMahon," the woman said, and held out her hand to Murphy. Even Cat, in her distracted state, heard the sizzle of attraction when their palms met.

"So where do we go from here?" Jamie asked. "Mr. and Mrs. McMahon have been most generous, but we can't stay here long. Is there any word? Boyd hasn't been caught?"

"Eh?" Tate Murphy dragged his gaze from Nancy's and tried visibly to concentrate. "Not yet. Police are following some leads, one being that he and his captive were picked up by an airship from the roof of a neighboring building."

"His captive?" Cat looked at Jamie just in time to catch him shaking his head slightly at Murphy.

"He's an unsavory character, is Mr. Boyd," Murphy said quickly. "Brandon's been after investigating him since all this began and has uncovered some things that will be of interest to the authorities in Toronto as well as here in Buffalo. All that money of his? It's dirty. Our guesses about the flesh trade weren't far off."

"Not those girls who have been disappearing around the city?" Jamie asked in horror. "Was that him?"

"Aye, or his agents."

"No respect for life," Jamie said bitterly. "He needs answering."

"Not by you, lad. Understand? You stay underground with your lady and let the police handle this. I'm here to take you to a safe house. You'll stay put there till I come for you."

Your lady. Cat thrilled to those words and moved closer to Jamie, tucking herself into his shoulder.

"Oh, and I've a message for you from Officer Kelly," Murphy went on. "Said to tell you he'll speak with the good doctor as soon as possible."

Chapter Thirty-Two

"Who is the 'good doctor'?" Catherine asked
James. She rested on the bed beside him, waving her
legs idly in the air; he found it impossible not to be
distracted. The room, small, warm, and the third they'd
inhabited in the last two days, lay at the top of still
another house. Catherine wore only her new
undergarments, donated by Mrs. McMahon, far lacier
and more fetching than those that had belonged to
Albert.

Mrs. Pidgeon, the affable Negress who owned the
house, told them this room had once been a hiding
place for escaping slaves who were then ferried across
the river to Canada. The knowledge failed to make
James feel more secure.

So far almost nothing had gone right. The police
had failed to locate Sebastian Boyd, though they'd
rounded up some of his associates, including his
henchman Carter. Catherine had failed to remember
much of her past, and James had failed to come up with
a way to tell her about her sister. He feared the worst
for Becky; his imagination ran so rampant he almost
envied Catherine her ignorance.

"What good doctor?" he asked now, and fought the
desire to run his hand up Catherine's leg, all the way
up.

"Mr. Murphy mentioned him. Said someone called

Officer Kelly meant to speak with him on your behalf."

Nothing wrong with her immediate recall, James thought ruefully. He looked at her from the corner of his eye. He knew he could distract her, and he knew exactly how.

He turned onto his side and placed his hand on her stomach, just below her delectable breasts. Outside, the city went about its business in a noisy fashion. Evening drew on. But here they seemed to inhabit a world of their own.

"Nothing for you to worry about."

"Why don't I believe you?" She gazed into his eyes, and it felt like she pulled at his heart with invisible strings, the way it always felt now when she looked at him. Almost, he wanted this to last forever. Almost, he didn't want her to remember.

No denying a powerful connection now existed between them. What concerned him was what might happen when reality began to drift back into her mind, and with it discrimination.

No matter, he told himself; he'd experienced more pleasure and happiness these last two days than he'd ever hoped to attain.

"Believe me," he said and leaned forward to kiss her. She parted her lips beneath his and purred softly in satisfaction.

She broke the kiss before he was ready and said, "Why should you want to see a doctor, though? You're not ill, are you?"

"I'm not ill."

"Then, why?"

His Catherine, as he'd learned, could be persistent. It didn't make him want her any less. "No reason. I probably won't see him after all."

She covered his hand with hers and continued to gaze into his eyes. "You know, Jamie Kilter, if anything should happen to you I couldn't go on. I can't live without you now."

"So you may think."

"Why do you always say things like that? Why do you try to blame what I feel for you on what happened when I was brought back?" She frowned. "I think—I know I cared for you even before that."

"It doesn't matter now."

"It does matter!" Anger flashed in her eyes. "It's bad enough me not remembering much, without you denying what I do know."

"I'm sorry." He bent his head and laid his forehead against her neck. "It's just hard for me to believe."

"What? That I could love you, Jamie Kilter? Well, I do." She lifted his face and engaged his eyes. "I do."

James' heart seized in his chest and then started up again with great, shuddering beats. She didn't. She only thought she did and, God help him, he had to savor it while the delusion lasted.

She laid her hand against his scarred cheek. "This means far more to you than it ever will to me. How can I convince you of that?"

Helplessly, he shook his head. She gave him a chiding look. "And have you nothing to say to me in return, James Kilter?"

"I adore you, Catherine. God knows I do. You must feel that every time I touch you."

"Then touch me. Touch me again." She lifted his hand to her breast. The soft warmth of her flesh met his fingers through the thin fabric of her chemise. He trembled as he cupped her and found her nipple with his thumb.

"I want to feel you, Jamie," she said. "All of you. Then I'll know you love me."

"Never doubt it," he said, and gave her all she could desire.

****

"The news isn't good."

Tate Murphy stood at the back door of Mrs. Pidgeon's house. Rain pelted down from a lowering, gray sky, and Cat could smell the river. Murphy looked as grim as the day.

Cat glanced at Jamie, seeking as she so often did to take her reaction from his. They stood in Mrs. Pidgeon's kitchen with their fingers linked. She felt dismay race through him and tensed in response.

"Best come in," he said and looked at Mrs. Pidgeon, who nodded before she departed the kitchen, leaving the three of them alone. Murphy shut the door against the wet and shot Cat a look.

"How are you, Miss Delaney?"

Cat shook her head. The last three days had been a swirling fog of lovemaking, uncertainty, and bits of returning memory that made little sense. She scarcely knew how she was.

"I've come about your sister, lass."

Cat froze, shock spearing through her as it always did when she heard something unexpected. She looked at Jamie, who promptly let go of her hand and raked his fingers through the hair on the left side of his head.

"I have a sister?" she asked.

Jamie grimaced and looked at Murphy. "I have not had time to tell her."

"No time?" Murphy repeated. "You've been together for three days. What have you been doing?" His eyes swept Cat. "Scratch that question. Surely you could have fitted in some conversation?"

"No doubt he was reluctant to upset me," Cat supplied. "He thinks I'll become distressed if I remember things." In truth, she found the opposite true. More and more the lack of memories drove her wild.

Yet some things had come back to her, more than she'd admitted to Jamie. Flashes of pictures, scenes like the remnants of dreams: dogs in a kennel, and a strapping woman with red-brown hair; a horse collapsed in the street, and Jamie, her Jamie, beating a man with his fists; another man with a cruel, arrogant face. Could that be Boyd? But she remembered nothing of a sister.

"Best tell her now, lad," Murphy urged. "For the situation could scarcely be more desperate."

Cat reached for Jamie's hand again. She found she could think more clearly when she touched him. His eyes, full of misery and regret, met hers.

"Here's the way of it: you have a family, Catherine—not here in this city but in Toronto, Canada."

Toronto? The name meant nothing to her. Helpless, she shook her head.

"This man you've heard us talking about—Sebastian Boyd—he knew your stepfather in Toronto and had a hold on him, financial, you said. Boyd likes young girls, and he wanted your little sister, Becky. You bargained to keep her safe and came away with him instead."

Becky. That name did mean something and roused

all Cat's protective instincts, even though she could summon no image in her mind. Fear squeezed her heart. "My sister."

"Do you remember, lass?" Murphy asked kindly.

"I'm not sure."

"You met James, here, when Boyd hired my company to keep you from bolting. James helped you escape instead. And so Boyd's been after hunting you, but now he's got his hands on your wee sister."

"Becky."

"Aye, he's holding her hostage, and making demands."

"I thought he made off in an airship." Jamie sounded as horrified as Cat felt.

Murphy grimaced.

"That was just a story that henchman of his, Carter, put about. Boyd's been hiding under our noses, and the wee lass with him. But he's taken a stand now and is making demands in earnest. One of them is for his airship, which he wants flown in to lift him off the roof of the building where he's held up. He's threatened to kill the lass if he doesn't get what he wants."

Cat felt like someone had punched her in the stomach. "You have to save her!"

"Fagan's trying, Miss Delaney. We're all trying, but to be frank, negotiations have broken down. We decided you had a right to know what was after happening, in case the worst occurs."

"The worst? You mean, if he kills her?" Cat's thoughts flailed in her mind and beat against the dark fog that enveloped it.

Murphy said, "He's threatening to do just that, if the police do not meet his demands. We debated it,

Brendan and I. Were I in your place, I believe I would want to know. I would not welcome someone coming to me afterward with such news."

"Take me to them," Cat demanded.

James' fingers clenched Cat's so hard it hurt. "No, Catherine. You stay out of it."

She turned to him and engaged his gaze with wide eyes. "How can I, Jamie? She's a young girl, yes? Alone and frightened."

A bit wildly, James shook his head. "Right now Boyd still thinks you dead, and out of it. Why expose yourself? Better to stay clear."

"But there might be something I can do. Mr. Murphy, you say negotiations have broken down?"

"Aye; it sticks in the police's craw to meet this villain's demands, and if we allow his airship to move in, there's no assurance he won't take the lass with him anyway."

"You need to get her away from him."

"You think Brendan hasn't tried?"

Cat lifted her chin a notch. "But I'm the one he's been chasing, right? I'm the one with whom he's angry. That's why Jamie's been keeping me hidden all this time. So maybe he'd trade her for me."

"No." The word burst from James' lips. He seized Cat between suddenly hard hands and turned her toward him. She felt violent protest stream from him, just as she now felt all his emotions. "I won't let you, Catherine, I won't! Anyway, what good will it do to exchange one hostage for another?"

Regretfully, she gazed into his eyes. "It will do her good, won't it? Better me, in his hands, than a child."

"No." Jamie cast a desperate look at Murphy, who

returned it apologetically.

"Sorry, lad. I never thought—"

James ignored him and shook Cat slightly. "You have no idea what Boyd is like, the depravity to which he might subject you in the cause of revenge."

"I have a pretty good idea; I've remembered more over these few days than I let on." Fearlessly she told him, "That's why I can't leave my sister in his hands. At least I know what to expect. And I'll spare her if I can."

Before Jamie could protest further, she turned to Tate Murphy. "Please take me there, Mr. Murphy. At least I can try to negotiate with him. You say he thinks me dead; maybe he'll be so shocked to see me it will make a difference."

She turned to Jamie, engaged his eyes once more, and saw the raw terror there. For her; all for her. Her heart thudded; the depth of his love both thrilled and shook her. "If you love me, Jamie, you'll let me go. Because how will I ever live with myself, if he harms her? You speak a lot about monsters, Jamie Kilter; it's time, now, I went and faced a real one."

Chapter Thirty-Three

The area surrounding the building on Franklin Street had been cordoned off, the block closed. Police were everywhere, both regular officers and what James recognized as members of the Irish Squad. Rain crashed down like iron spikes, and the bricks of the street shone slick.

At every window of the house James saw steam cannons. Narrowing his eyes against the rain, he caught glints from the metallic bodies of steamies behind them—mechanicals, not men.

He edged toward Brendan Fagan, who stood amid a group of other officers, holding a bullhorn. Fagan gave him a look that held a full measure of hard despair before sweeping Catherine, beside him, with a glance.

"I do not want her here. We've enough trouble already."

Catherine pushed by James and toed up to Fagan. "Mr. Murphy says this horrible man has my sister hostage. I want to talk to him."

James had rarely seen Brendan Fagan lose composure, but now he tossed back his head and his eyes rolled like those of a startled horse. "Out of the question. Kilter, muzzle her and get her away from here."

James swallowed hard. He suspected the only way he'd get Catherine away from this scene would be to drag her bodily, kicking and screaming.

He had no opportunity to speak, however, for Catherine bristled. "You can't give him orders, nor me! Where is my sister?"

Fagan gestured with the bullhorn. "There, on the roof. We've been attempting to negotiate, but Boyd's threatening to throw the girl off the building if we don't meet his demands."

James looked, and his throat went dry. Sure enough he saw Boyd, wet as a drowned rat and barely recognizable, standing behind the parapet of the brick building with a tiny figure in his clutches.

"What does he want?" Catherine asked.

"He's after asking for all kinds of things, and barely rational, Miss Delaney," Fagan said to Catherine, his eyes still raised to the roof. "We want this man in custody, but not at the cost of your sister's life. One moment he says he'll trade her for safe transport, the next that he'll kill her if we don't do exactly what he asks."

"If he kills her, he'll have nothing with which to bargain." Catherine's voice sounded remarkably steady, but James could feel her terror, just as he could feel everything else inside her.

"He's been raving for hours and is in a perilous position now. Unpredictable," Fagan admitted, "which is one of the reasons I sent Tate Murphy to inform you your sister's life is in danger. I can't tell what he'll do at this point, but if 'twere my wee sister, I'd want to know."

"Yes," Catherine breathed. She tipped back her head the better to peer at the figures on the roof. "Do you think he'd trade her for me?"

"No," James said immediately, just as he had in Mrs. Pidgeon's kitchen.

Catherine did not so much as flick an eyelash toward him, though her fingers clenched hard on his hand.

"I would not advise you to attempt that," Fagan said. "'Twill do us little good to exchange one hostage for another. What we want is for Boyd to take our deal on offer and release her."

"Your deal?"

"We let him go via airship to Toronto. Our associates in the Toronto constabulary will be waiting for him when he gets there. I'd rather he had no hostages at that point. For he will be trading desperate, his back to the wall, and I would not like to say what he might do then."

"He can't hope to get clean away after all this," James breathed.

"He thinks once he's on his airship he'll be home and dry," Fagan said. "If we do send it in, though, he'll have a small surprise. It may not be so firmly under his control as he imagines. But first we must get him to take the deal."

"What kind of surprise?" Catherine asked.

Fagan flashed her a look. "One of our men will be on board disguised as crew. 'Tis not much, but it may be enough to tip the scales in our favor."

"Then," Catherine said, "there should be no risk if I persuade him to trade her for me."

"There is great risk. This madman intends to take steam cannon on a dirigible. And he's unstable as a ferret in a sack. The only thing we wish to do is persuade him to trade your sister for escape, nothing more, do you understand?"

James squeezed Catherine's fingers and willed her, *Nothing more*.

The figures on the parapet moved closer to the edge, and Brendan Fagan raised the bullhorn to call, "Boyd! Have you decided to accept our deal? Your airship is fully fueled and ready to fly!"

"About time!" Boyd returned. Even after so many days James recognized his voice, full of arrogance but with an edge that betrayed his instability.

A shudder passed through Catherine; how much did she remember?

"I have told you, Officer Bog-Jumper, the airship picks me up here. My pilot can hover and drop a line."

"Aye." Brendan ignored the insult. "But first you release the girl."

"Ha! You think me a fool? As stupid as you, perhaps? If I let her go, then with what will I negotiate?"

"You won't need to negotiate," Fagan called. "We've already sent word to the landing strip. By now the airship will be on its way."

"I don't believe you. I refuse to release my hostage until I land in Canada, a free man." He drew the drenched figure of Becky closer to his side.

Catherine stepped forward, drawing her fingers from James' at last. "Will you agree to take me, instead?"

James' heart fell to his feet. Sluiced down and diminished by the rain, Catherine looked such a small, desperate figure to stand on her own.

Boyd pressed himself to the parapet and peered down. He pushed the girl he held with him; James saw her hands fly up wildly.

"Cat?" she cried.

Boyd echoed, "Miss Delaney! They told me you died from that cannon blast."

"I was hit," Catherine agreed, "but as you can see, I'm not dead."

"You led me a hellish chase," Boyd cried bitterly, "and cost me a great deal of money. You also forced me to go back to the well for what I wanted in the first place." He twisted Becky's arm, and she cried out.

"Becky!" Catherine shrieked.

"Cat, please!"

" 'Cat, please!' " Boyd repeated in a mocking snarl. "You betrayed me, bitch, and went back on the bargain we made. You attacked me! No one gets away with that."

"Then," Catherine called, "you'll want revenge on me, not my sister. You'll want to take everything out on me, not her." She glared up at Boyd, the rain running down her face like tears. "Let her go and take me in her place."

"No," James said again, a gut reaction.

"No," objected Fagan at the same moment. "Miss Delaney, I tell you it will do no good to exchange one hostage for another."

"It will do *her* good!" Catherine turned on Fagan, unleashing a sudden storm of emotion. "Can't you see how frightened she is?"

"Catherine," James began desperately.

She ignored him as if he weren't there, but Boyd leaned further over the parapet. "And who's that there with you, Miss Delaney? The ugly, lying dog I hired to guard you, who bit my hand instead?"

"Leave him out of it. Will you or won't you trade my sister for me?"

Boyd pondered, while the rain crashed down and the police line wavered and James weighed his heart's ability to go on beating. For he knew, even before Boyd spoke, what his answer must be.

"I will!"

"But it must be a fair exchange," Catherine pressed immediately, even as Fagan began to object. "Do you hear me?"

James reached for her arm. "He doesn't know how to be fair! You can't do this—"

She shook him off, not so much as glancing at him, her attention all on the girl Boyd now held pressed against the edge of the parapet.

"Don't do this, Miss Delaney," Fagan warned. "If you do, you are acting against our official recommendations. There's no telling what he'll do to you."

"Am I supposed to leave her in his hands, and no telling what he'll do to her, either?"

"He has no axe to grind with her, though, does he? I know it's difficult to think clearly when your emotions are involved, but if worse comes to worst, we'll trust our colleagues in Toronto to rescue her."

"I can't." Catherine raised both hands in a gesture of sheer helplessness, still refusing to look at James. "She's nothing but a child. Better he takes out his anger on me."

Fagan looked grim. "I won't allow it, Miss Delaney. 'Tis far too dangerous."

James let out a breath. Perhaps Fagan would halt the madness in its tracks.

Over the sound of the rain and the crowd behind them, he suddenly heard the drone of engines; the airship approached, trailing steam against the lowering sky.

Fagan called up to Boyd, "Release the girl and the airship can pick you up. That's the deal on offer, the only deal."

"I want Miss Delaney, or she dies." Boyd hoisted Becky up onto the edge of the brick ledge with unholy strength. For the first time her face, white with terror, came into view and James saw her clearly. As wet as the rest of them, eyes stretched wide in horror, she balanced like some large bird with clipped wings, arms held tight behind her back.

The crowd caught its collective breath as rage twisted Boyd's face. James felt sure they would all see Becky fall to the street below.

Desperate, still ignoring James, Catherine turned to Brendan Fagan. "Officer, you have to let me do this. I am the only one who can get her away from him. I can't fail her."

Without waiting for Fagan's approval, she called up to the roof, "Send Becky down and open the door. I'll exchange myself for her there."

Becky teetered on the parapet while Boyd thought about it. "Very well. But my steam cannon will decimate the first person who makes a wrong move. Do you understand?"

Catherine nodded. The breath whooshed in her lungs as Boyd pulled Becky from the ledge. With the drone of engines now loud in the air, she turned at last to James.

Eyes wide, face pinched from the rain and terror,

her gaze met his, full to overflowing. "I'm sorry, Jamie. I wanted a future with you. But I remember him, something inside of me does, and I don't think he will let me go."

He caught her hands in a desperate caress. "That's why you can't turn yourself over to him."

Sorrowfully, she shook her head. "It's exactly why I must. There are only two choices—either he takes his anger out on Becky or he takes it out on me. It can't be her, Jamie. I hope you understand."

He did, and it broke his heart.

"I just want to tell you," she hurried on, "I love you, and—well, you're perfect as you are. Understand me? Perfect."

Fagan pushed Tate and his fellow officers back as the door swung wide, revealing a mechanical with a steam cannon in one arm and Becky Delaney caught fast in the other. The steamie aimed its weapon not at the girl, but straight at Catherine.

Desperation rose to James' throat in a wave that nearly choked him. Catherine pulled her hands from his and stepped forward, reaching for her sister. The steam cannons stationed in all the windows shifted, trained on her; in that instant James saw her dying all over again.

"You come," the mechanical clicked. It shoved Becky out into the street with force enough to send her to her knees and reached for Catherine all in one movement. Becky cried out; Fagan bellowed, and one of the cannons on the right fired with a belch of scorching steam. Fagan hit the bricks and covered Becky's body with his own.

At the same moment James leaped forward in a desperate attempt to snatch Catherine back. He ducked through the doorway, just dodging a blast from the steamie's cannon. In the narrow confines of the portal, the heat of it seared his legs. His fingers closed on Catherine's arm, and the armored steam unit pulled with inhuman force. All three of them tumbled inside together, and the door crashed shut with a resounding slam.

Chapter Thirty-Four

"Is this not amusing?" Boyd taunted in his smooth, arrogant voice. "Not only the prize I sought so long but her faithful hound, as well. I miscalculated there, didn't I, Catherine? I chose the wrong guard dog for you. But he'll pay for it now. You both will."

"Leave him out of it," Cat said, fear washing over her in an icy wave. "Any score to settle is between you and me."

She cast a single glance at James, who now knelt at her side. As soon as they reached the roof of the building one of the steamies had knocked him down, delivering a brutal blow that took him to his knees. Blood trickled from the corner of his mouth and terror possessed Cat's heart. Steamies, most armed with cannon and no doubt the same that had been stationed at the windows, circled them; she had a sudden conviction she was about to see Jamie die.

Anything would be better than that, including being forced to board the airship, now hovering above the roof, with this man she began to remember all too well. The sound of his voice had triggered memories that came tumbling in a horrific horde to her mind.

She fastened her gaze on Boyd's, willing herself to stand strong. Showing him weakness would gain her—or Jamie—nothing. "I know what you want: what you didn't have from me before. I'm willing to give it. Just leave him behind when we board the airship."

Jamie groaned in protest, and Cat willed him to silence. What happened to her paled in comparison to what could happen to him.

"So it's that way, is it?" Boyd's lips twisted. He looked much the worse for wear; the slick, well-tended man Cat had begun to remember replaced by one as battered by the rain as she. But the cruelty remained. "Who would have thought? One of the loveliest women I've ever seen and this blighted monstrosity."

He aimed a vicious kick at James where he knelt under cover of the steam cannon. Cat moved quickly and imposed her own body between them.

Boyd laughed. His gaze scoured Cat's face. "Not so pretty anymore, though, are you? Hardly what I purchased back in Toronto. All your lovely hair gone, and dressed like a ragged boy. No matter, I suppose. Your mouth can still provide sinful pleasure."

Jamie growled again even as Cat shuddered. Somehow she held Boyd's gaze. "Whatever you want. Just so you leave him behind when we go."

"Oh, Miss Delaney, I think not. You've provided me with far too powerful a weapon, more effective, I suspect, than even these steam cannons. It looks to prove a most edifying journey."

"Why? Where are we going?" Fagan had said the constabulary awaited them in Toronto. Cat needed only to survive, and keep Jamie in one piece, till then.

But Boyd's face creased with unholy mirth. "That, my dear Catherine, you will discover in due time." He glanced up at the airship, which now hovered directly over the place where they stood. The engines throbbed deafeningly, and even as Cat watched, the pilot dropped a line.

"Bring him," Boyd ordered the steamies. "And shoot anyone on the ground who moves."

****

James lay with his good cheek pressed to the steel decking of the gondola and fought to keep hold of his senses. The throb of the engines came up through the floor and beat into him; it seemed his heartbeat pounded the same rhythm, every beat a twinge of pain.

He knew Catherine must be somewhere close by; he could feel her as well as catch the cadence of her voice from time to time, along with Boyd's harsh tones. He homed in upon his connection to her and tried to gather his strength.

Boyd must now feel himself on top of the world—his escape made successfully, the prize he'd sought in his hands, and revenge his for the taking. James regretted having placed further scope for hurt in Boyd's grasp, but he could no more have let Catherine go through that doorway without him than put out his own eyes.

He wondered what use he might be to her now. Here on the deck of the gondola, they were surrounded by crew both human and mechanical—he'd had a good look at them while being hauled aboard. Most seemed to be mechanicals; three of those now stood around him holding the inevitable steam cannons. He shuddered at the thought of one of those going off here even by accident.

Struggling mightily, he drew himself up and raised his head. He hadn't even seen the weapon one of the steamies had used to fell him, but it had taken him in the maimed side of his face and dropped him like a slaughtered cow.

Blood now trickled down his face and filled the inside of his mouth. Ignoring it, he swept a look round at his guards and concentrated on staying upright.

He'd always wanted to voyage aboard an airship, longed for the thrill and adventure of it. Now, over the rail of the open deck, the view met his wondering eyes. He saw the waters of the Niagara flowing away to his right, the river beside which he'd lived all his life. Beneath the belly of the beast slipped the city. Lake Erie spread open ahead and to the left, arms wide and gray, half obscured by rain.

At the bidding of his heart he tore his eyes from the view and found Catherine. She stood a dozen paces away, her slender back toward him, arguing with Boyd. Abruptly, the rain slackened, and he blinked it from his lashes.

How much did she remember? Clearly, things had begun to return to her. She recalled her sister. And she'd mentioned what Boyd had wanted from her back when they first met.

But what of the connection that existed between her and James? Did she sense how deep their bond extended? Was she as aware of him as he of her? If he willed her to, could she feel him?

Fighting the pain in his head, he concentrated. Pain was just pain; he'd endure far more for her sake. He believed his love for her could endure anything.

He focused his thoughts and her shoulder twitched. She stole a look at him, her expression tactile as a touch.

Joy and regret tangled inside him: joy at the authenticity of their bond, regret that Boyd would be able to use it against her.

Boyd, armed with his sharp cruelty, did not miss that glance. "I will keep your hound alive a while, Catherine. Just so long as you do everything I say. You have a great deal of recompense to make."

"I've told you I'll do whatever you ask, just so long as you release him."

"Would you like me to release him now?" Boyd gestured over the rail to where the water slipped by. To James' surprise, he saw the airship begin to maneuver away from the beckoning arms of the lake and the standard airship route to Toronto via Fort Erie.

What the hell? Spinning like a dancer in the air, the dirigible swung its nose right to follow the river northward.

"No." Catherine did not look at James again.

"Then you had better be an obedient girl indeed." Boyd gestured at one of the mechanicals standing by. "Take her."

Looking terribly small and fragile, Catherine followed the steam unit from the open deck into the interior of the gondola.

"Where is she going?" James bellowed. His voice sounded stronger than he felt.

Boyd strolled up to him with his guard of two steamies, both armed, flanking him. His gaze raked James before he said, "Fancy yourself a hero, is that it? Well, I suppose ugly dogs can still bite. It was you who helped hide her from me, wasn't it? And I suppose you've enjoyed her as well. Difficult to imagine that exquisite jewel letting such an ogre between her legs."

It was, and James didn't care how Boyd insulted him.

"You're in for an interesting time," Boyd said. "You can watch me use her before I pass her on to my associates, whom I go to meet. And then you'll pay for helping her defy me."

Rage rose to James' head. Somehow, he fought it down.

"And," Boyd continued, "you'll pay for decreasing the value of a very costly possession. I suppose it was you who had her first? Or did her stepfather lie to me?"

James, still battling against the urge to break the man in two, tried desperately to think. If they headed for somewhere other than Toronto, that would spoil Brendan Fagan's plan. How was James going to keep Catherine from harm?

He grated, "I should throw you over the side now."

"You think you could? Look around. You'd be mad to try."

James looked. In addition to the steam units he counted at least five human crewmembers, all clad as pirates. Was that all Boyd was, then? A pirate dressed as a wealthy man, stealing and transporting human cargo aboard this vessel? To be sure, how else could he have amassed such an obscene fortune? And how could one man stand against him?

In order to protect Catherine, he would do as he must.

Upon that thought she reappeared, the armed steam unit at her back. James caught his breath; gone was the boy's clothing. Instead she wore the pure white dress of a young girl, short enough to show her ankles and a pair of tiny, jeweled slippers. The innocence of the costume was belied by its neckline, ruffled and cut low to reveal the darkened wound on her chest and nearly all the perfection of her small breasts.

James felt like someone had punched him in the stomach. The likelihood of Boyd's intentions made him want to vomit.

Catherine cast one look at him and then turned her eyes determinedly away.

Desperate, James started forward. The steamie on his left hit him in the arm with its cannon—just a warning but enough to make him reconsider his actions.

What would happen if one or more of those cannons discharged aboard an airship? The steel decking beneath his feet would withstand it, but if the blast hit any of the lines or, worse, ricocheted up and struck the envelope, they would all die. James stole another look over the rail, where he could see the broad ribbon of the river beneath the belly of the gondola. If they went down they would crash into the water. But they might all burn up as they fell.

"Ah," Boyd said when he caught sight of Catherine, and the lechery in his voice set James' teeth on edge. "Much better; I actually feel myself becoming aroused. But what's this?" He gestured roughly.

Catherine's hands rose to her chest. "The burn where the steam blast took me."

"Nonsense. If it hit you there, you certainly wouldn't be alive." Boyd directed a glare at James. "I supposed that's where your ugly pet mauled you. More damages added to his account. But no worry; he'll pay. On your knees."

Catherine trembled where she stood but did not comply.

"On your knees, I say!"

"Here?" Catherine croaked. "In front of everyone?

Please, no."

"Here. Or do you want to watch your mongrel die?"

The steam units guarding James stepped closer. Catherine met his gaze then, just one glance, but it revealed all that lay in her heart. James quivered in response.

She does love me, he thought, with absolute conviction, an instant before Boyd stalked up to her, planted his feet, and pushed her to her knees.

Time stood still for an instant. The breath froze in James' lungs, and even the drone of the engines seemed to cease as his rage built—a mighty rage, unstoppable as a full head of steam, searing in its intensity.

"No!" he shouted, and the valve on his sanity burst.

Chapter Thirty-Five

Cat shuddered as her knees contacted the rough steel decking. Memory had started to return in earnest as soon as she saw Becky and Boyd—bits and pieces of things that appeared suddenly as the doorways opened in her mind. She now had a very good idea what sort of man Sebastian Boyd was, and a terrible sense of *déjà vu* accompanied this moment. He'd attempted this before, but certainly not before so many eyes, and not in front of Jamie, her Jamie whom she adored. Even though she felt revolted to her toes at the thought of this act, and even though humiliation burned in her cheeks, she resolved she could do this sickening thing for his sake. But would he be able to watch?

Her answer came almost instantly in a mighty roar that sent a shaft of alarm through her and turned her head. Her gaze found Jamie, and another memory unleashed itself in her mind. She'd seen this before: a man in a street and a horse...and her Jamie barely recognizable.

But no, she'd not seen *this*. By God, he would get himself killed.

She surged to her feet as Boyd swung away from her, suddenly rigid with alarm. Indeed, no one on the deck looked anywhere but at Jamie, who stood transfixed, his countenance dark with rage, every muscle bulging, and with absolutely no sanity in his eyes.

Off kilter—that's what he'd called it. Off his head. But facing a cart driver in a Buffalo street differed wildly from snapping here, surrounded by steam cannon.

The capacity for reason, however, had clearly flown along with all other rational thought. Jamie struck out, swinging arms and fists, and knocked down the steam units on either side, one after the other. His rage made the act look so easy that for an instant Cat's heart dared hope. One unit crashed onto its back and lost its weapon; the other tumbled toward the rail and began leaking steam from its neck joints at an alarming rate.

Jamie fixed eyes that glowed like blue fire on Boyd and started toward him.

Boyd began barking orders. Steam units rolled up from everywhere, tightening a circle around Jamie, and Cat's heart sank again.

Like a stevedore facing a day's work, Jamie took them on. Blow after blow did he rain on the steel that came at him, terrible, smashing strikes and punches that dented metal and sent the units crashing down. One of them fired its weapon, and Cat cried out. Only the fact that Jamie leaped at another opponent kept him from being blasted; the beam took out the legs of another unit instead and left them blackened and smoking.

Still another unit fired; the superheated beam traveled along the deck to skitter off the rail and over the side.

Boyd hollered, "Stop him! He's just one man!"

Members of the human crew moved in. One fixed his gaze on Cat and galvanized her into motion. She lowered her shoulder and barreled into Boyd; they both fell to the deck, narrowly missed by another bolt that flared almost in Cat's face, split the air over her and Boyd's heads, and sent her scrabbling away from him.

She ran to the rail and looked over. The river, nothing but a broad gray ribbon glimpsed through the rain, slipped past beneath the gondola between green, forested banks. Should she jump? It might be better than the fate that lay before her: subject to all Boyd's perverted demands and then passed on to his business associates and thence to the ghastly trade in which they must engage.

She knew that despite all the carnage he now wrought, Jamie couldn't win this battle. But how could she abandon him? She spun with her back to the rail and watched in gut-wrenching dismay even as three more steam units closed in on him.

The energy of his rage had begun to subside. He'd maimed many of the steam units, but they'd done damage in return; the disfigured side of his face once more streamed blood and the flesh of his left forearm, caught by the flick of a blast, smoked. Her heart twisted in her breast with helpless, hopeless love for him.

"Seize him!" cried Boyd, who had also struggled to his feet. "Finish him!"

"No!" Cat shrieked and flew at Boyd again, feet and fingernails flailing. She managed to gouge his cheek, tearing four bright furrows that welled blood, before a human pulled her off, and just in time to see one of the steam units that corralled Jamie swing the butt of its weapon and connect with the side of his head. Jamie went down like a dead man, and her heart faltered.

All Boyd's attention, though, rested on Cat. "Bitch!" he yelled. "You marked me!" He swiped at his cheek, and his fingers came away stained with blood. "That's the second time." His infuriated gaze pinned her where she stood. "You cannot imagine, wench, how you'll suffer for this."

He snarled at Cat's captor, "Lock her up while I think of a suitable punishment." He followed Cat's telltale gaze to Jamie, who now lay white and unconscious in the pelting rain. A smile twisted his lips. "And put her ugly pet with her. Let them have a few final minutes together."

****

"Jamie? Oh, my love."

The words trickled into James' ear and roused him to a morass of pain. The right side of his face—the disfigured side—flamed in agony much as it had back when he'd originally sustained his injuries. His body throbbed in time with his heartbeat, as if he'd been pummeled and dragged behind a steamcab. None of that, though, matched the pain in his hands, raw and intense.

What had happened to him? Had he fallen into a rage, gone off kilter? Damned if he could remember, but Catherine must be with him if he could hear her voice, feel her touch at his shoulder and on his chest.

He opened his eyes and looked up into her face, which hung above him like a pale flower. A streak of blood marked her cheek, and he wondered if it were his, or hers.

Where were they? On the airship still, for he could hear the steady drone of the engines, but on the deck no longer and instead out of the rain. A small space, dimly lit, it felt like a prison. Catherine sat on the floor, and he lay on his back like a felled tree, his head in her lap.

"Jamie, thank God. My love, look at me."

My love. That he did remember—the way she had looked at him there on the deck, as if he possessed her heart. No product of any resurrection, that look; he believed in the truth of it at last. But what good would it do them now?

"Did I kill him?"

"Boyd? No, my love. No."

"What happened?"

"You went off your head and damaged a large number of his steam units. I damaged him—but not seriously enough to save us."

Cat looked at her hand with its dirty nails, Boyd's vile blood trapped beneath. She shuddered. "Jamie, he's going to want his revenge. I don't know what form that will take, but you must promise me you'll let me take the brunt of it."

"Damned if I will." James struggled up, the movement tearing a groan from his throat.

"You can't possibly fight on." Catherine swallowed convulsively. "Your hands…"

James looked at them and felt a rush of sick alarm. Less hands now than two battered clubs, they oozed blood and showed the gleam of white bone in several places. What had he done with them? He had no clear memory of it, but their condition told its own story.

Broken bones? He gritted his teeth and forced himself to flex the fingers. Maybe, maybe not, for he could still move them slightly.

He looked at Catherine. Her face, dead pale except for that splash of crimson blood, appeared pinched, her beautiful eyes haunted.

"You can't expect me to stand by and let him do whatever he will to you," he grated.

"You can if it spares your life." Suddenly she pressed into his arms. He closed them about her, heedless of his pain, and felt the strength come. It returned to him softly, like faith, like certainty. She loved him. Whatever came, he had the one desire of his heart.

He kissed her forehead, and she tipped her face up so her lips met his. The kiss tasted of many things: resolve, terror, desperate courage, and enough devotion to steady James' heartbeat.

"I love you, Catherine Delaney," he breathed when it ended with a last lingering contact of tongue on tongue.

"I love you, Jamie Kilter. Whatever happens, don't doubt that."

"I won't. Where are we?"

"I'm not sure. Some small room all made of steel. I tried the door; we won't get out that way."

"At least we're together." And he could hold her one last time, glory in the feel of her heart beating beneath his.

"He's only shut us in here till he can devise a revenge that's horrible enough. Jamie, whatever it is, he'll make you watch." Her voice quivered despite her determined courage. "He's just that cruel. You must promise me you'll endure it and not fly off kilter again. Because he only needs an excuse to kill you, and I think I can survive anything but that."

"Watch him use you, debase you? Maybe give you to his crew after?"

"It doesn't matter what happens to me." She lifted a hand and fluttered her fingers over his ruined cheek. "How badly are you hurt?"

Bad, but he wouldn't admit that to her. "Listen, there must be some hope. I know what's in your mind, but please don't sacrifice yourself."

"What hope? We're completely in his power."

James' thoughts raced. Brendan Fagan would be on his game, but Fagan had a welcoming committee waiting in Toronto. The airship might not even be headed there. How quickly could Fagan scramble his forces?

"Catherine," he said, "If you see a chance for yourself, you have to take it. Don't hold back for me. Promise."

Her only response came when she kissed him again, soft kisses that rained on his lips, his chin, whispered across his wounded cheek, skittered down to bless his split and bloodied fingers.

"Catherine." He seized her face between his hands and gazed into her eyes. "I mean it. Promise."

Her eyes flooded with tears. "I can't," she said helplessly. "For you I can only battle."

"Then we'll go down battling together. Till then, tell me again that you love me."

And she did.

Chapter Thirty-Six

"So you want to fight, do you? Like a mad dog?" Boyd aimed a kick at Jamie's legs. "You did a lot of damage out there, destroyed six steam units and banged up many more. But I'm going to give you a chance to redeem yourself now and possibly save your dirty wench."

"How?" Jamie raised his chin and glared at Boyd. Cat could feel so much about him, and so easily. She felt his weakness and how desperately he sought to disguise it. She knew Boyd planned to hurt him in the worst way he could, had in fact taken the intervening time while she and Jamie whispered together of love and past sorrows to devise something awful enough to satisfy his cruelty.

She scrambled up in her now-stained and filthy dress to face Boyd. "You'll leave him alone and bargain with me."

"I think not." Boyd glanced at the dented steam unit behind him as if for protection.

Coward, Cat thought, and her lip curled.

"He owes me a heavy debt." Boyd aimed still another kick at Jamie, who pulled his legs out of reach. "He stole and sullied you, costing me more than half your value. He went on that rampage up on deck. I've thought about it, wench, and there's one deal on the table—only one."

"Tell me." Jamie, too, arose, and Cat felt him stifle his agony. Even injured, he towered over the other man.

Boyd backed a step, and Cat realized he feared Jamie precisely as he might the mad dog with which he equated him. It made a slight advantage, when they had so few.

But something avid also shone in Boyd's eyes, a desire to cause pain that outweighed the fear. Pain, and the terror of others, entertained this man. A weakness? Cat couldn't tell.

Boyd ran his gaze over Jamie thoughtfully before he said, "I will let you fight for her like the ugly hound you are."

Cat's stomach plummeted, but Jamie straightened himself. "Fight?"

"It will alleviate the boredom till we reach our destination. Have you ever attended a dog fight?"

Jamie grimaced and what little color he retained siphoned from his face. "I have, though not by choice. I've also seen the results of such 'entertainment,' and I despise the bastards who organize those pits."

"Well this time you'll take the place of the vicious dog. There's still some piss in you, I'll wager. And I've learned it's often the injured curs that are the most savage."

"Who?" Cat forced the word from her throat. "Who will you pit against him? Not more of your steam units. You know that's not fair."

"Fair? You dirty trollop, haven't you figured out life isn't fair? It belongs to the strong, to men like me. Everyone else dances to the tune I play. And he will dance now, if he knows what's good for him."

"You haven't named his opponent," Cat insisted.

With all her being she longed to reach out and tangle her fingers with Jamie's, but she would not give Boyd that satisfaction.

"One opponent, only one—not a steam unit, but a new addition to my crew. The fellow says he's a champion brawler, and I believe him. And I've sweetened the pot for him; if he wins I will pay him one thousand dollars."

A thousand dollars? Cat's mind reeled. She could barely imagine such a prize.

Boyd's lips twisted. "If he kills you, cur, I will pay him two thousand."

"No, Jamie," Cat said under her breath, not able to hold back the words.

Jamie didn't so much as glance at her, his gaze fixed on Boyd. "And if I win? What's my prize?"

"Well, I debated that. I could give you your life."

"Not mine—hers."

"I thought you'd say that, since you're such a great hero. Her life, then."

"I want her life and her freedom. You let her go safely, understand? And you don't use her first or give her to your crew."

"Jamie," Cat breathed again.

Boyd grinned. Cat had never seen him smile that way, and it chilled her to the bone.

"Very well, I agree. She's of little value to me now anyway. But you realize if you lose—if your opponent kills you—she'll be entirely at my mercy."

Jamie did look at Cat then, a single glance that seared her like a caress. He fisted his ruined hands. "Don't worry; I won't lose."

****

Out on deck, a ring had been formed of bashed and dented steamies. Some of them, James saw, were no longer operable—killed when he went off kilter. Several of those that still worked leaked steam at an alarming rate. The clouds of hot vapor rose and mingled with the heavy, wet air. The rain had now turned into mist, and, stealing a look over the rail, he saw why.

The river still slipped beneath them, but as a wide, gray band no longer. Instead it seethed, dark green studded with white where it foamed past rocks and outcroppings, hell bent to tumble downstream. Just ahead of them more mist rose and the green water dropped over a cliff. He knew, then, where they were— just above Niagara Falls, approaching the cauldron of the lower Niagara River.

He turned his head to look behind; his stomach clenched and his heart twisted on a desperate surge of hope. A second airship tailed them. Not nearly so big as Boyd's craft, and not yet within hailing distance, it had a small gondola and an envelope of dark blue.

Who chased them? He nudged Catherine who stood beside him and said, "Look."

Boyd, too, followed their gazes and scowled. "The good police tail us, Miss Delaney, but don't get too hopeful. I can outrun them any time I choose. And they won't close soon enough to stop this dog fight."

James squared his shoulders and hardened his resolve. Could he trust Boyd to keep his word and free Catherine? Only a fool would think so. But the sight of the police airship lifted his spirits. He just had to stall long enough for rescue to arrive. It didn't matter so much what happened to him meanwhile.

Could he pull it off, though? With his body

battered and his strength waning, he couldn't be sure. But he'd use everything that remained in him, for Catherine's sake.

She loved him. He closed his eyes, savoring the truth of it. He could ask no more.

When he opened his eyes again, he felt new resolve. He gazed around and looked for his opponent; all he saw in the immediate vicinity was steel in various states of damage. Had he really done all that? The condition of his hands argued so.

He fixed Boyd with a hard stare. "Where is he, this champion brawler?"

Boyd called out past the circle of metal, "Where's the pirate?"

Pirate, was it? That lent little edification; most members of the human crew wore that costume. Many of them now hung from the cables and lines, trying to get a view above the wall of steamies. At Boyd's bellow, one of them detached himself and swung down over the heads of the mechanicals to land on his feet inside the ring.

James lifted his brows. An impressive move, and one that boded ill for him. He measured the fellow swiftly, and his heart sank: at well over six feet and strapping, the man at least matched James in size. He had a kerchief bound over his hair and another tied up from his neck, half obscuring his face.

What the hell? The fellow looked like an assassin—likely he was one, too, yet another weapon Boyd kept on reserve in his arsenal. Typical of the man to make a bargain only when he was sure he'd win.

"Here are the rules," Boyd stated clearly over the throb of the engines. "There are no rules, no holds barred, and no such thing as a low blow. My man," he clapped the shoulder of James' opponent, "you do what you must to kill him, understand? And you'll have first turn with the little lady—after me, of course—as well as the two thousand dollars."

James' opponent grunted. He had bright green eyes, about all James could see of him, and the blank stare of a natural killer.

How best to take out such a man? James had no weapons but his fists, and those sorely battered.

As if to emphasize that thought, his opponent set his shoulders and raised his hands, balled tight.

Boyd stepped out of the ring and seized hold of Catherine's arm. James didn't like that much but had no chance to protest. His opponent suddenly came at him, swinging fists like hammers.

James ducked and sidestepped, calling on tired muscle and sinew, ignoring everything but the danger at hand. He knew he had to overcome his opponent quickly before he burned away what little of his strength remained. But the man appeared to possess an abundance of brute strength and had experience as a brawler, so Boyd said. James only brawled when he couldn't avoid it, caught by Crowter and his crew or set upon by the occasional abusive drunk. And this felt nothing like being off kilter, when he had no rational control of his actions.

He leaped and got in a fierce uppercut to the fellow's jaw. His right hand screamed in agony, but the man barely bobbed with the force of the blow. His jaw felt like iron.

With a roar, the man came at James, arms reaching out like those of a bear, more a wrestling move than anything else. Shocked, James absorbed the impact and struggled to get an arm free to land a blow. His opponent had massive strength, like that of an automaton.

Christ, how would he ever prevail against such a foe? How spare Catherine the ordeal Boyd planned for her before the police ship closed in?

Face to face, virtually nose to nose, he and his opponent growled at one another, straining in a dance for domination. Glaring straight into James' eyes, the man tightened his hold until it became unbearable.

And winked at him.

James faltered, staring in disbelief. Against all likelihood, the man released him, gave him a slight shove and set him on his heels. As if the kerchief he wore over his mouth distracted him, he tore it off and cast it aside.

And James knew him. He blinked in stupid disbelief even as he remembered Fagan saying, "We have one of our men on the airship…"

Man, he'd said. Not automaton. Yet facing James, fists raised and with something that, were it not entirely impossible, looked like glee in his face, stood Patrick Kelly.

An automaton, after all.

A new surge of hope—far more real this time—rose in his heart, lifted him, and lent new strength. He wanted to call out to Catherine who stood with her face white, agonized, but could not.

Instead, he raised a brow at Kelly, who promptly rushed him again. They grappled together, landing blows that did little real damage, and Kelly spoke in James' ear. "He doesn't know what I am, friend. None of them does. Let's make this look good."

Friend? Breath bellowed from James' lungs as Kelly landed a punch to his chest. He could make it look good, but they couldn't spar forever. What then?

With a blow to the jaw, Kelly knocked James to the deck and fell on him. Under the guise of pummeling him, he growled, "Be ready to follow my lead. My fellow officers are back there. We'll get you out of this."

"Both of us?" Did Kelly understand James cared little about himself as compared to Catherine? Could an automaton comprehend love?

Obviously he comprehended friendship…

James grunted, rolled over, and pummeled Kelly in turn. Even though he pulled the punches, his hands protested.

"Here now." In a dirty move, Kelly elbowed James in the gut, effectively breaking his hold, and surged to his feet, bringing James up with him.

"Bastard!" the automaton hollered in glee. "Die, bastard!"

He aimed a blow at James' throat that barely skittered off his windpipe, doing little damage. Catherine screamed, letting James know the brawl must look authentic. Kelly seized him with iron hands and threw him toward Boyd and Catherine, who stood in the ring of steamies. Kelly followed with fists swinging.

At the same moment, Kelly said, "Now."

Now? Now, what? James felt himself fly backwards into Boyd and through the ring of steamies toward the rail, crashing past Catherine and the operative steam unit on one side of her.

He found himself suddenly intensely grateful to

have Kelly on his side. The automaton's enormous strength argued James never could have bested him.

But now he came barreling, wild-eyed, looking very much as if bent on mayhem. Had a cog slipped in his mechanical mind? Did he remember the plan?

Catherine screamed again and laid hold of James with both hands. She stepped in front of him as if to block Kelly's rush, a terrier facing a mastiff, and James felt her love enwrap him.

Whatever came next, he knew himself upheld by her feelings for him, made whole and complete.

Invincible.

Chapter Thirty-Seven

Trembling badly, Cat stood with her head high, heart pounding like a piston, in the face of the onrushing brawler. She could feel Jamie struggling for breath behind her, as if he breathed for her and she for him. Jamie Kilter was part of her, perhaps the better part.

But he now stood with his back hard against the rail of the open deck, and she feared what could happen if his opponent got those hands, like great weapons, on him. She'd stolen one horrified look, as she was flung aside, at what now lay beneath the belly of the airship. A rushing avalanche of water foamed, surged, and plunged down an impossible distance to a deep, green-gray pool. They hovered directly over the mighty falls of the Niagara, and the airship began to come about as if to face the ship that pursued them. Buffeted by the mist and turbulence off the water, did Boyd mean to stop here and fight?

Just like Cat, Boyd and his guards had been flung aside like ninepins by Jamie's velocity. The howling brute that was James' opponent barreled in like a steam train…and at the last instant veered aside to seize Boyd in those large, merciless hands.

For an instant time froze, letting Cat observe the scene. The shock on Boyd's face told the whole story. He had not seen this coming, had not expected to be the target of his tame cur. Her heart struggled to rise on hope that wouldn't quite come. How could this be? Why would Boyd's champion turn against him?

James moved Cat aside with gentle, bloodied hands. "Get down."

"But—"

"Get down, Catherine, love. They're still armed."

By *they* he meant all the steam units that now stood by, seeming to await orders. The order came as Boyd, breaking his paralysis, barked out, "Shoot, you fools! Shoot them!"

The first blast raked the deck almost at Jamie's feet. He leaped aside and the beam seared the steel between him and Cat. She felt the breath of superheated air before the steam dissipated in the mist.

If either of them took a blast here, she knew it would mean death, with no time to reach the home of the kindly Mrs. McMahon.

"Down!" James barked again, and shoved her flat against the rail before he went wading back into the confrontation. His former opponent now had Boyd by the throat, one large hand nearly encircling Boyd's neck. But the remaining steam units, to say nothing of the human crewmembers, had their orders. As a single man they readied their weapons.

Cat rose to her hands and knees from where she'd fallen. She saw Jamie's opponent swing Boyd around, one forearm across his throat, and heard him bellow, "Put your weapons aside or he dies!"

The breath gusted from her lungs, and she struggled to her feet, swaying against the rail. An ugly sneer twisted Boyd's features; despite his position he didn't look like a man defeated.

"Kill her!" he croaked. "First man to slaughter her earns a fortune."

Cat went rigid where she stood, pinned against the rail. Jamie spun, his face a mask of blood that obscured his expression. But she felt his love, knew his spirit leaped for hers an instant before his body followed.

From whence came the blast? Cat never knew, but it struck the deck directly in front of her and seared her toes. She leaped onto the rail, half stunned by the heat and acting on pure instinct. She saw the agony in Jamie's eyes a split second before yet another blast hit him, took him in the shoulder, and spun him half around. His body struck hers, her hands caught at him, and they tumbled over the rail together.

For an instant Cat knew only the sensation of free falling, weightless, as her stomach tumbled inside her. Then came a bone-jarring impact as momentum abruptly halted. She cried out and tightened her grip on Jamie, the only thing keeping her from plunging into the rushing waters below.

But what kept him from falling? She looked up through her own locks of hair to see his face just above hers, rigid with tension. Up, up and up she looked— better than down—and saw that he'd caught a dangling line in both his bloody hands.

She tried to draw a breath and failed. Those hands—they appeared to be little more than torn pulp; she didn't see how he could use them to hold both their weight, not for long. Even as she peered upward the cable slid through them a scant inch, slick with blood.

"Hang on," he gasped. "Don't you dare let go of me. Do you hear?"

She heard, but already her own fingers cramped

with pain. What was happening up on deck? She heard shouting, and another weapon discharged. Before that fracas ended they would surely both fall.

"Jamie," she breathed.

"Hang on." He groaned and his right arm—that which had been struck by the blast—began to quiver. Having taken that blast to the chest, she knew the pain that gripped him. Would he be able to hold them by only one ruined, bloodied hand?

And what chance of rescue? She turned her eyes to search for the police vessel and got a sweeping view of what stretched beneath them instead. Her stomach fell to her feet.

Boyd's airship had swooped as it swung about and they now hung low over the rushing water, just above the lip of the falls. Mist and thunderous reverberation both rose to engulf them, a maelstrom of sensation. The motion of the falling water seemed to draw Cat irresistibly, and she thought about letting herself tumble with it.

Precisely as if he could read her mind, Jamie grunted, "No! Hang on to me. Don't you let go, Catherine, hear?"

"I hear you." She closed her eyes against the terrible seductive lure of what lay below and clung to him like a monkey, using both hands and legs. She had given him her heart. Could she do anything but give him all her trust?

But his whole body now shook with strain. Abruptly they dropped another inch and a sob broke from his throat.

If she had to die, at least it would be with him.

She heard a loud drone and realized the police ship

had come alongside Boyd's vessel. Someone aboard shouted at them, but Cat couldn't distinguish the words above the roar of the falls.

She opened her eyes and stole a look. The police vessel struggled to maneuver closer; she could see people leaning over its rail, engulfed in spray.

Jamie and she slipped again, and she turned her gaze up to see the very end of the cable clutched in Jamie's fist.

From above there came a cannon blast. Superheated air streamed above Cat's head; Boyd's crew, she realized, fired on the police vessel. Boyd's airship rocked as the police returned fire; someone bellowed from the police ship: a warning.

"Jamie," she gasped.

He didn't reply; his body, rigid beneath hers, told the story of his agony and determination.

The airship rocked again. Jamie gasped out what sounded like a curse—or a prayer—and said, "Forgive me, Catherine. I can't—"

"Friend! Here, take my hand!"

The voice came from above their heads. Almost afraid to move, Cat craned up and saw Jamie's former opponent leaning over the rail, reaching down.

"Kelly," Jamie said, "pull her up!"

"Grab my hand. I'll haul both of you up."

A blast seared the air just above Kelly's head; he ignored it.

"Can't." Jamie bit the word hard. "We'll fall."

Kelly leaned down further, his hips on the top rail. Cat, her cheek pressed to Jamie's chest, had a sudden conviction he would go over and take both of them with him. The battle still raged above and beside them. The airship careened in the currents kicked up by the wild water below, and Kelly lunged.

It took Cat an instant to see he'd seized Jamie's wrist.

"I've got you, lad! Give me your other hand."

"Can't. Shoulder's blasted."

"Never mind, I'll pull you up."

He couldn't possibly, Cat thought—no one could haul so much weight by one hand. But she saw him close his other fist on Jamie's forearm and pull with deceptive ease.

They began to rise slowly, inexorably, swinging like fish on a line. The bottom rail came even with the top of Jamie's head. A blast struck nearby, and Kelly wavered for an instant, their progress arrested.

"Kelly!" Jamie shouted. "Are you hit?"

The top of Kelly's head smoked, but his eyes remained open and he stayed upright. Cat's breath stilled in her throat as he set his feet against the bottom rail and began hauling them upward again. How could he endure a direct hit? How could anyone?

Jamie grunted again as Cat came level with the rail. "Grab hold!" he bade her. "Do it!"

Did he, too, fear Kelly would suddenly collapse? Cat unwound one hand from Jamie's shirt and wrapped her fingers around the iron rail, now slick with wetness from the mist. With a gasp of agony, Jamie forced his damaged shoulder to move and followed suit.

"Over the rail with you, man," Kelly shouted.

"Over the rail," Jamie grated in Cat's ear.

Now that she could see the wholesale battle on the deck of the airship, she wondered if it would be any safer than dangling over the rushing waters. But Kelly grabbed her by the shoulder, his grip painful as iron pincers, and lifted her over the top rail. She landed on the deck and immediately ducked a blast that kissed the air over her head and bounced over the railing.

Jamie! But he came over the rail, bloody, grimacing with pain, yet all in one piece.

He collapsed and drew Cat's body beneath his in an attempt to protect her from the blasts that arced about the deck and issued from the police vessel as well.

Where was Boyd? Cat peeked out from beneath Jamie's torn sleeve in an effort to locate him but couldn't. Too much mist and steam filled the air.

"Stand and desist!" Someone on the police vessel had a bullhorn. "Stop firing!"

The battle continued. Cat, her head tucked beneath Jamie's chest, couldn't believe the envelope of either ship had not yet been struck.

"Throw down your weapons, or we'll shoot you out of the sky!"

Cat shut her eyes on a rush of terror. Surely Kelly hadn't hauled them up just so they could all crash onto the rocks and streaming water below...

Above her, Jamie lifted his head. Cat caught a glimpse of the police airship close alongside Boyd's and then one of Boyd himself—still alive, damn it, perhaps twenty paces away and still shouting orders.

"Turncoat!" he shouted at Kelly. "You'll pay for that. Shoot him. Shoot him!"

Kelly, who stood guard over Cat and Jamie where they huddled against the rail, did not reply; he didn't move either, but stood like a man in a trance with his arms dangling at his sides. The back of his head still smoked and, straining to look up, Cat saw an incredible sight where his hair and flesh had been burned away: not the bone of a human skull but steel plating.

Before she could make sense of the sight, one of Boyd's minions followed his orders and fired. The blast took Kelly square in the chest and lifted him from his feet. With the grace of a dancer, he tumbled backward and disappeared over the rail.

"No!" Jamie roared and surged to his feet. He spun to the rail, which caught him in the chest as he leaned over it. For an instant Cat feared he would fall, as well.

She scrambled up in his wake, feeling his agony precisely as if it were her own. She turned, and her gaze encountered Boyd's across the smoldering deck with the impact of two swords clashing.

Rage arose and filled her, bringing victorious strength. At that instant she ceased to be Catherine Delaney and became nothing so much as a force for vengeance. She flew across the deck like a small, fiery missile, her one goal Boyd's smirking countenance, and struck him in the chest and took him down.

Colors danced in her vision as she glared into his face, both knees planted on his chest—the red of rage predominant, augmented by flashing orange and black dots that erupted and swam. Her hands came up of their own volition and seized his throat. The smug expression fled his face, replaced by a grimace of fear.

"Get her off me! Get—" His words became a strangled wheeze. His head had hit the deck hard when Cat bowled him over; now, using strength she'd not suspected she possessed, she tightened her fingers on his flesh and rammed his skull against the steel deck again and again until his eyes rolled back in his head and he went limp beneath her.

That's for Becky, she thought as a few stray shreds of sanity returned, *and for all the other young girls you've harmed, and for Kelly—but most of all for Jamie.*

Upon that thought she spun and looked for him. He'd moved away from the rail, devastation in his eyes. Their gazes met even as the police began to boil over the rails onto the smoking deck. She lifted her hands and reached for him; as if the two of them were alone, he crossed the deck and took her in his arms.

Chapter Thirty-Eight

"Tell me everything that happened," Cat beseeched the man beside her. She remembered too little and far too much; jumbled images, most of them garish, filled her mind like pieces of a nightmare, surely too lurid to be true.

But now all the noise, the cannon blasts, and the steam had died away into quiet. The only thing of which she could be sure was that she lay wrapped in Jamie's arms.

His voice rumbled above her, the very sound of reassurance. "You passed out."

"Fainted, you mean? Impossible. I never faint."

She fought her way up from her prone position and looked at him. They lay together on a bed in a room lit by a single lamp—night or evening, then—a room she did not immediately recognize.

She ran her gaze swiftly over Jamie—her Jamie—and blinked in dismay. He lay shirtless in the warm room, all swathed in bandaging. A bulky pad covered his right shoulder and continued part way down his arm. Both hands had been wrapped like the appendages of a mummy, and the entire right side of his face lay hidden beneath a white mask.

He looked so very different with the mangled side of his face covered. His auburn hair tumbled down the other side, emphasizing the strong lines of his cheekbone and nose. She realized she saw him as close as ever she would to how he should have looked, had he never been burned.

And he was handsome.

Her eyes filled with tears, and he started up, looking alarmed. "What is it?"

"I—" But she couldn't say the words, couldn't tell him how she wished he could have the face with which he'd been born. He'd take it the wrong way, wouldn't understand she wished it for his sake and not her own. Because she loved him as he was. She did, eternally.

"Here, stop crying." He tried to reach for her with his bandaged hands, and she raised her fingers to her own cheeks, surprised to find tears falling.

"Reaction," he said softly and drew her clumsily against his bare shoulder, where she inhaled the marvelous and beloved scent of him. "You aren't hurt, you know, save for some scrapes and a lot of bruises. Exactly what do you remember?"

"I'm not sure." She selected one question from the dozens clamoring for her attention. "Is Boyd dead?"

"No, but you did a job on him, didn't you, there on the deck? He's in police custody and will stand trial on a list of counts. They're still preparing the charge sheet."

And Becky?"

"In hospital, getting patched up. Her injuries aren't serious, and she'll be brought here just as soon as she's released."

"Where's 'here'?"

"We're back at Mrs. McMahon's. Don't you know the place?"

Cat blinked again, and things shifted in her mind so

285

Laura Strickland

she did. "Jamie, I seem to have lost a bit of my hold on reality. Have you ever wondered if the world and everything in it is only here because we all hold fiercely to a picture we've made of it?"

"Yes," he said gravely. "I've thought that."

"Because if you let go of that picture, you can see it's all a kind of image held up to a mirror." She shivered. "Makes you wonder what's actually real, doesn't it?"

"I'm not sure there is a 'real' the way you mean it."

"Am I losing my mind?"

"Catherine, look at me."

From two inches away, she did. His eyes, deep blue, looked rational and sane. "Go easy on yourself, love. You took a couple big hits, what with the resurrection and what happened on the airship."

"What did happen on the airship?"

"You went a little bit out of your head."

"I went off kilter," she corrected him softly. "I understand now, Jamie."

"Do you?"

"It felt so powerful, and so terrible. We're linked, aren't we? You and me."

"It seems so."

"And that means we should be together always. Tell me, after all that's happened, we will be."

He hesitated, the thoughts visible in his eyes. Cat knew what she wanted him to say: she wanted him to offer her his life, marriage, eternity. Nothing else would do for her.

But he didn't speak the words, and so she kissed him.

Warm, dizzying sweetness rushed upon her from

the place their lips met. Her heart rose, and her emotions threatened to overwhelm her.

If he wouldn't say the words, she would. She drew her mouth from his and breathed, "Marry me, Jamie Kilter."

"Ah, God!" His eyes grew dark, and he caught her between his bandaged hands. "You don't want me. You can't want me; not that way."

"You're all I want. And if you insist what I feel is a product of my resurrection, I will bop you on that rock-hard head of yours. You know better. You felt what I felt on the airship."

"I felt it."

"Then what else is there but that we join our lives?"

"Catherine, you've seen the man I am."

"Yes, I've seen." Her heart beat faster, for she adored that man.

"I have little to offer a woman like you. I'm a pariah in this city; I've a job only by the grace of Tate Murphy. No real prospects—"

"I don't want prospects; I want you. Besides, who exactly is 'a woman like' me? I was sold by my stepfather. My own mother didn't fight to protect me."

"Better than being accused of killing your mother." Agony flooded his eyes. "You know that's what they say of me."

"And I know it's not true."

"How can you be sure? You have no proof, only what I've told you."

"And I believe what you've told me, because I've learned all about the man you are. I've watched you with those dogs—yes, Jamie, most of it has come back

Laura Strickland

to me now, so you can't say I don't remember what I've seen. You only fight on behalf of those who can't fight for themselves. And you'd die before you hurt those you love."

"I did love my ma, you know." His face contorted. "I hated her too, sometimes, and I hate what she's left me—this awful ability to go off kilter."

Cat's heart swelled with sympathy. "I'm aware of that also—you don't even have to say."

"I do, Catherine, because you declare you want to marry me. *Marry me*. And you need to know what kind of bargain you'd be getting. I sometimes wonder if my ma didn't go off kilter when she beat us. And I wouldn't see you tied to a man who carries that tendency. I've already tainted you by sending you off your head against Boyd."

"Boyd invited that. And give me some credit. I attacked him because of what he was—a true monster. And because of how he hurt Becky, and you. If we don't stand up and fight for those we love, who will? Answer me that."

"I can't."

"You can't because there is no answer."

"Well, what about this?" He gestured to the bandaged side of his face. "It looked bad enough before. The doc Mrs. McMahon called in said he couldn't guarantee good results with any healing."

"You're not hearing me, James Kilter. I want you, understand? The warm, courageous, and loving man you are inside, regardless of the shell you may wear. And you are going to marry me as soon as possible, understand?"

"Yes, ma'am," Jamie said, light flaring in his eyes.

"Now kiss me, and I don't want to hear any more nonsense."

****

"I have news." Brendan Fagan stood in Mrs. McMahon's parlor with his uniform hat in his hands and Tate Murphy at his side. Fagan wore a scattering of bandages as well as assorted abrasions. At one temple, his hair had been scorched away.

Been through the wars, haven't we? James thought. Yet Fagan's blue gaze remained honest and unswerving.

"Tell us," James bade. He glanced at Tate, but his friend appeared completely distracted from business by the presence of Nancy McMahon, who had shown them in. A look passed between the two of them, so hot the air virtually sizzled.

Well, well, James thought. About time Tate found a woman—just like me.

He tightened his fingers on Catherine's and focused on Fagan again. "Good news, or bad?"

"I'd say a bit of both. Sebastian Boyd was brought up this morning on a long list of charges. He'll get prison, and no mistake. When he's done with us he'll face the Toronto constabulary, who have their own list."

"Good," Catherine said and took a step closer to James so her side pressed against his. "And my sister?"

Fagan smiled. "A spunky lass, I have to say. She will probably be released from the hospital within the hour. If you do not mind me saying, Miss Delaney, that's where you should be—in hospital, I mean."

"I'll not leave Jamie."

"Fine, that; he should be there also. But leave it for

now. Your sister says she does not wish to return to Toronto. Would you be willing to assume responsibility for her?"

"Of course." Catherine lifted her head. "We'll be getting married as soon as possible, and can offer her a home."

James clenched her fingers in his. A home? Where? She knew he lived above Tate's office and barely scraped by.

Brendan Fagan raised his eyebrows and gave James a searching look. "My felicitations. You're a lucky man."

"Don't I know it," James agreed. "What about my charges?"

"Well, about that—in all the confusion you missed your last court date. I've rescheduled that, and I think we can get you off with a warning or two. Right, Murphy?"

Tate came to himself with a start and dragged his gaze from Nancy McMahon's radiant face.

"Aye, lad. There'll be a fine, of course. You'll owe me."

James slumped where he stood.

"Sure," Tate twinkled at him, "and I could consider it a wedding present."

"And then there's the other news," Fagan said, and cleared his throat. "Bit of a stunner, actually."

He gestured to Nancy, who smiled and opened the parlor door.

In stepped Patrick Kelly.

James nearly fell down. Like the rest of them, Kelly looked the worse for wear; here and there patches of his skin had burned away, revealing the underlying metal frame. In other places great seams and tears had been sewed up with visible stitches. As he advanced into the room, he came with a limp on his left side and an audible click when he moved that leg. But his green eyes looked bright and, against all odds, serene.

"Kelly!" James exclaimed in gladness. "I thought you dead for sure. We saw you go over the side and into the falls!"

"Hello, friend." Kelly stretched his lips in a somewhat lopsided smile. He leaned forward with a slight whirring sound and shook James' hand. "That turned out to be a wild ride. I went over the cataract, made contact with several large boulders on the way, and plunged into the gorge below. It put out the fire in my boiler, but as you can see it didn't kill me."

"I'm very glad." Abruptly, James' throat closed. With some difficulty, he said, "You sacrificed yourself for us."

"That is what friends do, lad."

"If there's ever anything I can do for you in return, it's yours."

Kelly's grin widened. "I have very good auditory perception," he announced. "And while waiting outside that door, I couldn't help but overhear you say there's going to be a wedding." He gave Catherine a wink. "Any chance I might serve as best man?"

James smiled. "I wouldn't have it any other way."

Epilog

From where she stood in the bedroom, Cat could hear church bells ringing, the sound tumbling through the open windows from further down the street.

She looked at herself in the glass critically.

"I still think I look like a boy, or a little girl." She'd borrowed the dress she now wore, since she seemed to possess nothing of her own save Jamie Kilter, and she didn't plan on giving him back. But during the three intervening weeks her hair had not grown very much, and she looked far too pale and scrawny. The fashionable young woman with whom Jamie had fallen in love had disappeared for good.

"You look beautiful. Here, put this on." Her sister, Becky, clasped a locket around her neck.

Cat started. "This is Mother's."

"I know. She sent it as soon as she heard you were to wed." Becky's eyes met Cat's in the glass. "She said she'd rather come herself but was indisposed."

"Indisposed," Cat repeated. Their mother had frequently employed that word when she found herself overwhelmed and unable to stand up for her daughters. Some things, it seemed, never changed.

No matter. Cat didn't really want to see her mother anyway. Many hurdles, including several postponed court appearances, still remained, but she wanted to turn her gaze forward to a new life with the man she loved.

"I'm just glad you're here," she told Becky. "But I thought it would be a small, private ceremony. This whole event has gotten out of hand."

Becky smiled. With the resilience she and Cat seemed to share, she had come through her ordeal at Boyd's hands somewhat wounded in spirit, but stronger. At least, as Becky had confided to Cat when they were alone together, Boyd had not demanded the ultimate of her, so the memory of terror was the worst she had to bear. Cat experienced a stab of pride. What a fine woman her little sister would be.

"The best man took over the planning—and he outdid himself," Becky said. "A church full of guests and, I hear, a fine reception afterwards."

Kelly had, indeed, proved a fine and fierce friend.

"I also hear," Becky went on, "there are a few surprises planned for afterwards."

"Such as?"

"I'm not at liberty to say, but prepare yourself for a ride around the city and a full police squad salute."

"Well"—Cat gusted out a breath—"that's not so bad."

A knock sounded at the door. Becky hurried to answer it while Cat stood gazing at herself, her heart beating much too hard.

"No," Cat heard her sister say. "You can't see her before the ceremony. It's bad luck."

"Just for a moment." Jamie's voice. Cat's pulse leaped, and she bade her sister, "Let him in."

"But Cat!"

"It doesn't matter, Becky. I'm hoping we've had all our bad luck."

Becky opened the door, and Jamie stepped in. Becky slipped out behind him, leaving them alone.

Cat turned from the glass; she and Jamie gazed at one another. How tall and broad he looked, all got up in a fine suit of black broadcloth with tails. She wondered if Patrick Kelly had procured it for him. The automaton seemed to have very definite ideas about how a wedding should be.

She raised her eyes to Jamie's, and her breath caught. "Not having second thoughts, are you?"

"I wondered if you were."

"Not a chance. I'm marrying you today, Jamie Kilter."

He took a step toward her, halted, and cleared his throat. "I've been talking to Kelly," he said.

"He talks a lot, for an automaton."

"That's because, above and beyond an automaton, he's an Irishman. You know, I always thought Tate a great friend to me, and he is."

"Yes, a rock."

"But Patrick Kelly looks to prove even better. Catherine, he's procured a property for us."

"He has! What kind of property?"

"On Niagara Street, just down from Tate's. It's been repossessed by the city for some reason, and Kelly put his own money down on it." Jamie looked perplexed. "Says he doesn't know what to do with his money anyway."

"A house?"

"Not exactly. Seems at one time it was a trading office. There's a big space out back where a warehouse used to be. Kelly thinks it would be perfect for a new kennel. He says I—we—should set up a refuge there for abused animals, like what's at Tate's only much bigger. That is, if you like the idea."

Cat smiled and her heart rose. "I think that's a wonderful proposition."

"I'm not sure how he expects us to fund it. He said something about donations."

"I can work, can't I? And you can probably still work for Tate part time." Cat seized his hands and squeezed them gently, heedful of healing skin. "You have to do it, Jamie. No one understands those poor creatures better than you."

"There's another thing." He drew a breath so deep it expanded his chest, and for the first time his gaze wavered from hers. "We're about to get married, Catherine, and as far as I'm concerned that's for good. I can't offer you much, and God knows I'm no prize. But Kelly also told me he spoke with Dr. Roesch on my behalf."

"Who's Doctor Roesch, exactly?"

"He's the man I mentioned back at Mrs. Pidgeon's, who's worked extensively with the automatons. In fact he's growing Kelly's skin back now and helping make the rest of his repairs. Dr. Roesch does a lot of reconstruction work." Determinedly, Jamie's eyes met Cat's again. "And Kelly's persuaded him to operate on me."

"What!" Cat dropped his hands.

"Work on the scarred side of my face, I mean. So you see, there's hope. If you do marry me, I might not always look like this—"

"What will you look like?"

"Eh?"

"This doctor, how does he accomplish the

'reconstruction'?"

"He takes a face from someone else, usually a cadaver—"

"So that side of your face wouldn't look like you. It would look like somebody else—somebody who died!"

"It will look human, Catherine." Impulsively he caught her hands again. "Not like a hideous monster. People wouldn't stare at me on the street. Our children" —abruptly he faltered—"if we have them, wouldn't have to be afraid to look at their father's face."

Cat's eyes flooded with tears. "Oh, Jamie, Jamie," she cried. "I thought you knew better than that! I hoped you knew better than that."

Baffled, he shook his head. "I don't understand."

"My love," she stepped up to him, so close her wedding dress rustled against his knees, "why do you want this thing? If it's for you, because you mind the way you look so much, then I'll stand behind you even though it will grieve my heart."

"Grieve you?"

She laid her hands on both sides of his face. "It's just that I love you so very much the way you are. This is the face with which I fell in love. Don't change it on my account, Jamie, or for our children who will love you for your gentle strength, your great kindness, and all the beauty you carry inside."

"My God, Catherine." He bent his head and kissed her hands, one after the other. "Do you mean that?"

"Look at me, Jamie Kilter. Do you see any lies?"

He gazed deep into her eyes, and she hid nothing from him. She saw the joy rise from his heart and flow to engulf her, lighting him like flame.

"No lies," he whispered, "not ever, between us."

"Then put away all this nonsense. We've a wedding to attend and a very special best man waiting."

"He'll just have to wait another minute while I kiss the bride," Jamie said, and to Cat's great satisfaction Kelly waited a considerable length of time.

A word about the author...

Born in Buffalo and raised on the Niagara Frontier, Laura Strickland has been an avid reader and writer since childhood. To her the spunky, tenacious, undefeatable ethnic mix that is Buffalo spells the perfect setting for a little Steampunk, so she created her own Victorian world there. She knows the people of Buffalo are stronger, tougher, and smarter than those who haven't survived the muggy summers and blizzard blasts found on the shores of the mighty Niagara. Tough enough to survive a squad of automatons? Well, just maybe.

Thank you for purchasing
this publication of The Wild Rose Press, Inc.

If you enjoyed the story, we would appreciate your
letting others know by leaving a review.

For other wonderful stories,
please visit our on-line bookstore at
www.thewildrosepress.com.

For questions or more information
contact us at
info@thewildrosepress.com.

The Wild Rose Press, Inc.
www.thewildrosepress.com

Stay current with The Wild Rose Press, Inc.

Like us on Facebook

https://www.facebook.com/TheWildRosePress

And Follow us on Twitter
https://twitter.com/WildRosePress

www.ingramcontent.com/pod-product-compliance
Lightning Source LLC
Chambersburg PA
CBHW051520260626
47170CB00003B/716